The Boy Who Swam with Alligators

ISBN 979-8-218-09850-6
Imprint: Independently published

Edited by Kelli S. Baxter
Contributions by Kelli S. Baxter
Cover by Rod L. Baxter
Illustrations by Rod L. Baxter
Photographs by Rod L. Baxter

Dedication

This novel is dedicated to those who advocate
to protect the water, land, and animals of South Florida.
And to those who are passionate about preserving our paradise.

Contents

Part One: Southwest Florida.. 1

    Chapter One 2

Part Two: Sarah and Cayman 27

    Chapter Two.. 28

    Chapter Three.. 43

    Chapter Four 60

    Chapter Five.. 87

    Chapter Six.. 102

    Chapter Seven 146

    Chapter Eight 156

Part Three: Emma... 171

    Chapter Nine 172

    Chapter Ten... 197

    Chapter Eleven.. 258

Reference Guide 260

    Map of Key Locations.. 260
    Glossary of Names, Words, and Meanings....................... 261
    Sketch and Photo Reference 262
    Timeline of Significant Events 264
    Book Club Discussion Guide 268

Acknowledgements 269

About the Author... 270

Part One:

Southwest Florida

Chapter One

It was a warm morning, just before sunrise, during the summer of 1981 in Cypress Cove. The storyteller and her 12-year-old daughter, just months from thirteen were heading out for a walk on the beach when her daughter pleaded, "Mom, tell me the story again. The story about the boy who swam with alligators." Her mom took a sip from her coffee mug and replied, "Honey, I've told you that story so many times."

"Mom, I know. But I really want to hear it again. Please tell me the story, and don't leave anything out."

"Okay, honey. This time we're going to start the story about 40 years ago, when two families, the Taylors and Coopers, were drawn to a tiny little tropical town in the farthest reaches of beautiful Southwest Florida. The story goes like this."

Mary and Robert Taylor were a wealthy industrialist couple, who had founded Taylor Tire and Rubber Company. They lived in Dimerling, Ohio, and they had a son named Grayson. Vicki and Henry Cooper lived in Westwood, Illinois, just outside of Chicago; they had a daughter named Sarah. Henry was a writer and Vicki was a photographer. They lived a simple and modest life.

The story is about Grayson surviving tragedy, Sarah not giving up, and having faith that love always finds a way.

The storyteller told her daughter, "Before we explore the lives of the Taylors and the Coopers, you need to know a little bit about where their journey took place in Southwest Florida. There were two towns: one was called Cypress Cove and the other was the Native American Poaceaehatchee Village. We'll start with Cypress Cove, then I'll tell you about the Poaceaehatchee Village."

The first families arrived to this area of Southwest Florida by boat in the 1880s. They were enamored with the long, white, sandy beaches along the Gulf of Mexico. As they made their way south along the coast, they came to the mouth of a large river. When they traveled up the river to the bay, they knew they arrived in paradise. As they neared the edge of the bay, they could see large cypress trees in every direction. Thus, they named the area Cypress Cove.

The settlers of Cypress Cove later adopted the name of the river from the Native American Tutelar - Pavati, meaning clear water. The name was given to the river nearly 100 years earlier by the Tutelar tribe who lived in the Poaceaehatchee Village. The Tutelar's village was located southeast of the river. The natural beauty in and around Cypress Cove was unspoiled and picturesque. It was bordered by mangroves, a cypress forest, the Gulf of Mexico coastline, and everglades. There were innumerable varieties of trees in the area, including large cypress trees, banyans, oaks, and several types of palms. The settlers didn't need to search far to see dozens of varieties of birds, including eagles, ospreys, egrets, ibises, herons, wood storks, Roseate spoonbills, and flamingos, to name a few. It was also common to spot panthers, bears, alligators, dolphins, manatees, river otters, and sea turtles.

Cypress Cove was founded by the Beckett family in 1886. It was a sleepy little town with a population of 80. Cypress Cove enjoyed a mild, warm climate that averaged seventy degrees in the dry months of October through April, and a hot, humid climate that averaged ninety degrees in the rainy months of May through September. At the center of town was a three-acre lake named for Harriet Fuhrman, who passed away in 1928. Harriet fought to save the lake, when some townsfolk suggested draining the lake and using the area for additional farm land.

By 1938, Cypress Cove had grown to a population of 1,253 full-time residents. The climate was similar to that of the Florida Keys. During the dry months, the population nearly doubled with a draw of approximately 900 seasonal visitors and tourists. Visitors flocked to Cypress Cove to get away from cold winters and the bustle of city life. They took advantage of the pleasant weather, beautiful scenery, and abundant fishing. Cypress Cove's economy was steady during the rainy off-season and boomed during the warm, dry months when visitors came to town for week-long vacations and seasonal living.

Everyone who was available during the busy, dry season was called upon to help. Nearly every Cypress Cove resident was needed to accommodate the out-of-town tourists and seasonal residents in some manner. The people of Cypress Cove were busy preparing and serving food, supporting overnight accommodations, and taking tourists fishing or sightseeing. Seasonal residents and tourists enjoyed dining at local eateries for southern dishes, seafood, and a variety of cocktails. It was quickly becoming a tropical paradise for out-of-towners.

Visitors had several options for making the journey to Cypress Cove. By December 1926, the Fort Myers Southern Railroad extended its rail line to the Cypress Cove Depot on the northeast edge of town. The rail service offered morning and afternoon stops in Cypress Cove, with return service to Fort Myers. By late 1928, the

SoFlo Trail highway was officially opened. It passed by the east edge of Cypress Cove, and was aptly named SoFlo Trail, as it was South Florida's connection highway. Travelers from downtown Fort Myers could also take the ferry from the dock on the Caloosahatchee River south to the 750-foot-long Kendrick Pier in Cypress Cove.

The Kendrick Pier was named for the family who donated funds to build the original pier in 1914. At 13 knots - or 15 miles - per hour, the 45-mile ferry ride from Fort Myers to Cypress Cove was three hours. From the rail depot or the pier, visitors could take a taxi or ask a local for a ride to their final destination in Cypress Cove. Those looking for a social visit took the short ride to the majestic (and only) hotel at the center of town. Adventuresome and budget-minded visitors found transportation to their accommodations from local residents to one of the many small, open-air, one-story cabins.

Many of the cabins were built on the edge of town or just outside of the town limits. Some cabins provided beach access, where visitors could enjoy sunning themselves and swimming and fishing in the warm Gulf of Mexico. Other cabins were mixed in with the cypress forest, which provided a wild, natural getaway, offering opportunities to spot lots of wildlife. Yet other cabins were among the mangroves and along inland waterways; these cabins were rented primarily by visitors who enjoyed fishing from canoes and small boats.

Some local residents offered visitors a room in their home to rent while staying in Cypress Cove. Local resident accommodations were to be found in the center of town, on the edge of town, and outside of town in the forest or everglades for the really adventurous traveler. For out-of-towners who wished to enjoy a stay-at-home feel, renting a room from a local resident was a perfect option. The owners typically provided meals as part of overnight stays and often provided other services, such as fishing, hiking, or touring sites in and around forests and parks.

The Beckett Hotel, built by the founding family of Cypress Cove in 1890, was the choice of visitors looking for social activities – parties, dancing, and fine dining. The hotel was the centerpiece of town, located on the edge of the Harriet Fuhrman Lake. The Beckett family had believed that people would come from up north to enjoy the warm, sunny weather during the dry months. The hotel was originally built with four guest rooms, then renovated in 1912 – due to fire – to provide six additional guest rooms. It was expanded in 1925 to include sixteen rooms, a larger dining room, a swimming pool, and an entertainment parlor. The hotel was known for lavish parties and was the place to see and be seen, as notables and celebrities from across the country often visited.

The storyteller continued, "Now let's explore the Poaceaehatchee Village."

Often seasonal residents and vacationing tourists made a trip to the Poaceaehatchee Village, home of the Tutelar tribe. The Tutelar were a Native American people, who migrated to Southwest Florida in early 1700s. Tutelar meant spirit protector of the land; the village Poaceaehatchee meant grass river, named for the great everglades (also known as the river of grass).

While tourists and visitors from Cypress Cove traveled to the Poaceaehatchee Village, seldom did the Tutelar visit Cypress Cove. The village was situated southeast of Cypress Cove near the southern tip of Florida; it was surrounded by mangroves, everglades, and cypress forest. The Aquene River cut through the eastern edge of the village, and was often used by the Tutelar for fishing from boats and canoes.

Visitors had a few options to get to the Poaceaehatchee Village. They could travel three hours by boat, south along the Gulf of Mexico coastline and then east through the Ten Thousand Islands to the village docks. Or they could travel by car, taking the hard-packed limestone-surfaced SoFlo Trail. They could park in a limestone lot along the road about two miles north of the village. From the parking lot, they hiked two miles into the village.

The Tutelar quickly realized that tourists and visitors were good for their economy and trade. By 1938, the Tutelar built the Igasho Trail, a single-lane trail wide enough for cars to travel two miles from the main road to their village. Visitors could also get there by riding horseback along the trail and through the cypress forest. Once visitors arrived to Poaceaehatchee Village, they were treated to stories of the Tutelar culture, traditional song and dance, and the opportunity to purchase handmade jewelry, clothing, and art.

Most of the homes in Poaceaehatchee Village were constructed with wood-framed walls and either metal or thatched roofs. The building construction helped to maintain comfortable temperatures during the hot, rainy season, as well as during the dry, cooler season. Roads were built with crushed sea shells and limestone, and the sidewalks were made of packed sand. The village reflected nature, with native plants and trees growing throughout.

Chapter One

The Tutelar people lived a simple life, and they believed family and community were most important. Often, families lived together in the same home their entire lives. If anyone in the village needed help, they were all there to help any way they could. They also lived as one with nature and animals. From the land and the sea, they took only what they could use. The Tutelar believed they were there to serve the earth and to regard the lives of the birds, animals, and sea creatures as important as their own. They understood that without the land and animals, they would not survive.

In 1938, the Poaceaehatchee Village's population was 240 Tutelar: 183 adults and 57 children. Children ranged in age from newborn to those who completed the rite of passage to adulthood, typically during the older teen years. The rite-of-passage mission was decided by the tribal elders; it was different for boys and girls. The Tutelar got their food primarily by fishing and growing crops. They also made traditional Tutelar jewelry, clothing, and art. The Tutelar lived together in harmony with each other, the plants, animals, sea, and residents of Cypress Cove. The peoples of Poaceaehatchee and Cypress Cove traded goods and services needed or wanted by each community.

The storyteller's daughter asked, "Mom, what about the two families and their son and daughter?" The storyteller replied, "Ok honey, let's get back to the Taylors and the Coopers and their journeys in this story. First, we'll talk about the Taylors, and then we'll bring the Coopers up to date."

Mary Dennis and Robert Taylor attended the University of Dimerling together. Mary graduated in the spring of 1938 with a Juris Doctor, and Robert graduated that same year with an engineering degree in rubber technology. Mary and Robert were married in September 1938, and spent their honeymoon in Cypress Cove. On a whim, they purchased a seventy-five-acre tract of land on the south edge of town. The land they purchased was bordered by a half mile of beach front on the western edge, along the Gulf of Mexico. It was also bordered by the Pavati River and mangroves on the south edge. An eight-acre lake was surrounded by cypress trees on the northeast section of the property.

Upon returning home from their honeymoon, the Taylors moved into a small, one-bedroom apartment in Dimerling, Ohio. Mary and Robert founded Taylor Tire and Rubber Company in early 1939. And they launched the company with a total of five employees. Mary served in several office and administrative roles, including sales, marketing, and legal. Robert was everything operations and engineering. He hired two engineers and a logistics position to help with day-to-day operations.

Over the next four years, Taylor Tire grew at a rapid rate. By 1942, their company had grown to 194 full-time employees, with plans to triple in revenue and size over the next few years. With the growth of staff and employees, the Taylors' roles changed. Mary served as head of legal counsel and Robert held the position of president and CEO. Taylor-made tires were being used as original equipment by the four major automobile manufacturers and sold as replacement tires across the country.

The Taylors returned to Cypress Cove for vacation each year since their honeymoon. They hoped that one day they would build a winter retreat home on the land for their family and friends. The seventy-five-acre lot was a beautiful slice of paradise; it had everything they could want. Their love for the land and this area grew stronger with each visit.

Chapter One

Mary Taylor's parents, the Dennis family, were wealthy industrialists during the early 1900s. Her father passed away shortly after Mary and Robert were wed. Mary's mother died in the spring of 1942, shortly after they learned that they would be adding a new member to their family. Her parents lived in a large home outside of Dimerling, Ohio. It was a grand, three-story home, situated on 12 acres of wooded land, built at the turn of the century. The quarter-mile long driveway entrance was lined with large shade trees on both sides. Located on the property were beautiful rose gardens and wildflower fields. Near to the gardens was a large reflection pond with two fountains.

During the summer of 1942, the Taylors moved out of their small apartment and into the Dennis family home. They began to make plans for the arrival of their baby. The Taylors set up a fully outfitted nursery down the hall from their bedroom in their new home. They were both very busy growing Taylor Tire and Rubber Company, sometimes working 12 hours a day. They decided to hire live-in staff to help with the home and to care for their new baby. They interviewed and hired a nanny to care for the baby, and housekeeper to take care of the house, and a maintenance person to maintain the equipment and property.

Mary's and Robert's son Grayson was born in Dimerling, Ohio, and welcomed into the family on January 4, 1943. Over the next five years, his personality evolved as he grew and played at their country home in Dimerling. Even at his young age, he enjoyed playing outdoors and had learned to swim in the lake. When Grayson turned three years old, his parents gave him an all-black puppy. He named the puppy Luna. He chose to name the dog Luna because he loved looking at the moon on clear nights. He played with her every day, running through the woods, and swimming in the lake. He was as curious as they come. He loved playing outdoors with Luna, and he wanted to learn about everything outdoors. He was curious about the different birds, animals, plants, and trees. At five years old, Grayson knew as much about the animals and plants in that region of Ohio as most adults.

Grayson's parents were strict and provided structure. They expected him to eat with the family, keep his room clean, and brush his teeth every day. They were also patient and loving, and encouraged him to be curious, make new friends, and explore his surroundings. Mary and Robert decided early that they would encourage Grayson to follow his dreams, even if that meant he would not pursue a career in the family business. With Grayson's interest in and exploration of the outdoors, they realized that he may not be happy working in a plant or office job. Grayson was finding his place in the world, and his parents were guiding him, while giving him freedom to make his own decisions.

It had been 10 years since 1938, when the Taylors honeymooned and purchased land in Cypress Cove. Since that time, Cypress Cove's population grew from 1,253 to 1,465. For the past ten years, the Taylors had been dreaming and talking about building a vacation home in Cypress Cove. Their company, Taylor Tire, continued to grow rapidly, producing a strong, diversified customer base and solid profits. They had expanded their workforce to 2,500 employees. The Taylors felt they were financially and personally set to build their winter retreat in Cypress Cove.

Chapter One

While planning their summer vacation in 1948, they decided to spend much of the time in Cypress Cove, getting ready to build on their 75 acres of land. As usual, they planned to stay at the Beckett Hotel, and they were going to focus their energy on surveying the land and sketching a layout to build a winter retreat. The Taylors' plan was to fly down in their new single-engine Cessna 170, which they had purchased earlier in the year. They named their new Cessna "Osprey," for the powerful and efficient flight of their favorite bird in Florida.

The Taylors intended to cover the 1,200-mile trip to Cypress Cove as a two-day flying journey. They planned to fly six hours each day, with fuel stops every three hours. Their combined flying experience, since their second year of college, was mostly in Ohio, Michigan, and Pennsylvania. With nearly one hundred and fifty hours of combined flight time, Mary and Robert felt they were well prepared to fly to Southwest Florida. The two of them mapped out the flight plan, identified fuel stop locations for each day, and arranged an overnight stay with friends in Charlotte, North Carolina.

On a warm early-July day in 1948, Mary and Robert Taylor filed their flight plan, and took off in their single-engine Cessna 170. Grayson and Luna were onboard as they lifted off from a small airport in Dimerling, Ohio. During the first day of flying, the Taylors made their scheduled fuel stops and radioed in their status and location regularly. They landed the Cessna 170 at a small airfield near Charlotte, North Carolina. Their friends were waiting at the airfield to take them to their home for dinner and to spend the night. The first leg of the flight went smoothly; they had enjoyed the sights, and flying over the mountain ranges between Ohio and North Carolina. The Taylors relished the evening they spent with their friends, who were delighted to meet five-year-old Grayson and his dog Luna. After breakfast the next morning, the Taylors' friends drove them back to the airstrip and waved goodbye as they took off for Southwest Florida.

On the second day of their journey, as planned, they stopped for fuel in Atlanta, Georgia, then quickly resumed their journey south. They were in constant radio contact as they flew to Page Field in Fort Myers, Florida, for their second scheduled refueling. While in Fort Myers, the Taylors took extra time to visit the Edison Botanic Research Corporation (EBRC) on McGregor Boulevard. The EBRC laboratory sat on 20 acres of land next to the Caloosahatchee River, where there were 400 species of plants and trees from six continents. It was operational until 1936, five years after Thomas Edison died, at which time the U.S. Department of Agriculture took over the effort.

As founders of Taylor Tire and Rubber, Mary and Robert were especially interested in Edison's research, to learn more of the origins of rubber compounds. Thomas Edison, Henry Ford, and Harvey Firestone formed the EBRC in 1927, over concerns of the United States' dependence on foreign rubber sources. Edison led the effort by testing 17,000 plant samples in his research laboratory. He ultimately selected goldenrod as the optimum plant for producing natural rubber. Once the Taylors' tour was complete, they made their way back to Page Field to continue their short flight to Cypress Cove.

The extra stop delayed their planned arrival to Cypress Cove. While there was no official airport in Cypress Cove in 1948, there was a stretch of land northeast of town that had been cleared and layered with sand and limestone for unofficial air traffic. The Penton family had cleared a 1,500-foot strip of land in 1933; it had been used occasionally for landing small, single-engine planes. Mary and Robert expected to land at the Penton strip before sunset on July 4, 1948. They planned to spend two weeks enjoying the weather, relaxing on the beach, and surveying their land, before making the flight back home to Ohio.

The Taylors never landed at the Penton strip in Cypress Cove. They weren't expected to return home to Dimerling for at least two weeks, so no one was aware that they hadn't made it to Cypress Cove. When the Taylors didn't return home after two weeks, as planned, officials at Taylor Tire got worried. Bonnie, in human resources, contacted the Beckett Hotel in Cypress Cove. She soon learned that the Taylors never checked into the hotel and no one in the town had seen or heard from them.

Even though it had been just two weeks since the Taylors had gone missing, Taylor Tire and Rubber immediately hired South Florida Investigation Services based in Miami, Florida. Taylor Tire hired the investigation services firm to determine what happened to the Taylors. A team of investigators from the company searched for the Taylors and their plane for three weeks with no results. South Florida Investigation Services determined that the Taylors' plane had flown off course and had been lost due to inland storms. As a result, their Cessna 170 most likely crashed somewhere in the 1.5-million acres of The Everglades on July 4, 1948.

The plight of the Taylor family made national news. Newspapers across the country printed heartbreaking articles about the Taylor family lost in The Everglades. Articles were titled "Tragedy in The Everglades," "Rubber Barons Crash in The Everglades," "Ohio Family Lost in The Everglades," "Wealthy Family Lost in The Everglades." Even Henry Cooper wrote a column for the Chicago Tribune titled, "The Tragic Loss of the Taylor Family."

South Florida Investigation Services and the world would not learn the truth for more than a decade. They would eventually learn that, due to severe storms, the Taylors' Cessna veered off course by approximately thirty miles. They were unable to find a safe place to land and crashed their single-engine Cessna among the mangroves on the edge of The Everglades. Their crash site was a few miles east of the Poaceaehatchee Village, home of the Tutelar tribe.

A few Tutelar villagers were out in the backwaters fishing when they saw the plane go down. By the time the fishermen arrived to the plane, it was mostly submerged into the swamp. The Tutelar fishermen were able to get the Taylor family out of the plane and took them and their dog Luna back to the Poaceaehatchee Village. Five-year-old Grayson was shaken up and covered in scrapes and bruises, but was otherwise in good shape. Luna, Grayson's dog, was ok, and was there to help comfort Grayson. Grayson's mom, Mary, was in critical condition and in need of immediate attention. She was put in the care of the Tutelar medicine woman, who was the healer and spiritual leader.

Tragically, Grayson's father, Robert, was killed upon impact of the crash. He was given a traditional Tutelar funeral the day following the crash. The Tutelar funeral began with Robert's body being wrapped in burlap and placed on a wooden pyre platform above a fire for cremation. The Tutelar spent the day chanting prayers and preparing Robert for the spirit world.

At sunset, several of the Tutelar villagers played traditional funeral music of drums and flutes, while other tribe members danced in customary dress and body paint. By tradition, the closest relative lit the fire for cremation of the body. One of the tribal elders helped shaken Grayson with the lighting of the fire. This part of the ceremony lasted until the next morning's sunrise, when the ashes were collected and spread in a place of the relative's choosing. Grayson chose to have his father's ashes spread at the crash site. Even in the few days since the crash, with the rainy season, vegetation had grown rapidly. The plane and crash site were already difficult to locate. Once they found the site, Grayson and the elders spread Robert Taylor's ashes.

The Tutelar medicine woman and elders attempted to nurture Mary back to health, yet she died four days after the crash. Knowing she was not going to survive the injuries from the plane crash, Mary asked for Grayson. She told Grayson, "Honey, follow your heart and your dreams. You can be whatever you want to be and whatever you chose to be." Grayson was only five years old, yet he never forgot her words. Upon saying goodbye to Grayson, Mary made one final request of the Tutelar elders. "Please take care of my son Grayson," she said.

Less than a week after Robert's funeral, the Tutelar held a second customary funeral for Grayson's mom. Grayson chose to have his mom's ashes also spread at the crash site – next to his dad's.

The Tutelar were unaware that merely a few weeks after the crash, there was a search crew looking for the Taylors. The Tutelar were not attempting to hide Grayson; they were simply honoring his mother's last wishes – to take him into their tribe and care for him as one of their own. Grayson lost both of his parents that summer – something no child should have to experience and endure.

The entire Poaceaehatchee Village welcomed and accepted Grayson as one of their family members and a member of the village. Following his parents' death in the summer of 1948, the Tutelar Deere family took Grayson into their home. Grayson shared a room with their son Etu in their small Poaceaehatchee Village home. Etu was the same age as Grayson and was happy to have a new brother. Sakari was Grayson's Tutelar adopted mom – her name meant sweet. Alo was Grayson's Tutelar adopted dad – his name meant spiritual guide. Etu was Grayson's new brother – his name meant sun. His new family's surname, Deere, meant precious. Having the Deeres as his new family helped Grayson cope with the horrible loss of his family.

The Deeres' home was built of limestone and mud walls, and with a thatched roof to keep them cool during the hot summer months. Their 900-square-foot home was located near the edge of the village and a short walk to the Aquene River that led to the Ten Thousand Islands. The Deeres' home consisted of four rooms – Etu's parents' bedroom, a shared bedroom by Etu and Grayson, a room for personal care, and a larger room with a kitchen and living area. From their home, they had easy access to canoe up river for freshwater fishing or down river to the Gulf of Mexico for saltwater fishing.

Grayson remembered his home back in Dimerling with the many rooms, the lake for swimming, and the woods for playing with Luna. In some ways, living with the Deeres on the river and having a cypress forest nearby, helped him feel a little closer to the home he remembered. The Deeres were good to Grayson. They showed him around the village and introduced him to all of their neighbors. He soon made friends with other kids in the village. Etu and Grayson quickly grew to become brothers. They played together and attended school together with 35 other children in the village.

School in the Poaceaehatchee Village was held in three separate buildings, setup for three levels of learning groups. The first learning group was for the youngest of the school children, typically four years to eight years old. This group learned through observations, discussions, reading, and writing. They watched adults in the village and learned from their stories. The students observed, identified, and discussed plants, trees, animals, birds, and fish in the village. Each school day they practiced writing and talked about different topics assigned by their teacher. First-level students participated in ceremony, while learning about their heritage and culture. Through these learnings, the youngest students began to understand the importance of their relationship with the land and animals. Even at their young age, they were taught about Tutelar history and living with nature in Southwest Florida.

When they were ready, children advanced to the second-level learning group. In this learning group, they advanced their skills of reading and writing. The children learned about applying math and science to the expectations from the first-level learning. This group was taught to live with the plants, birds, animals, and sea creatures in Southwest Florida. They learned to live safely in the Florida environment and to respect the natural world around them. Their school lessons were conducted both in the classroom and in the outdoors among nature. They learned how to be contributing members of the Tutelar tribe and culture.

The third group was for the older, more advanced children. They continued their learning, along with learning to be proficient at fishing, planting crops, and caring for the land on which they lived. This group was groomed and prepared for the rite-of-passage assignment. Those who completed the rite-of-passage ceremony were considered young adults, but of course, they did not stop learning. Each new young adult was then matched with a tribal elder who served as a mentor until she/he was prepared to serve as an elder her/himself. Poaceaehatchee schools and learning approaches were not like traditional American schools where the children earned grades. In the Poaceaehatchee schools, the children were given assignments, missions, and quests. Often, they must work in teams to complete their assignments. Their approach placed more emphasis on practical application, rather than theoretical learning.

While it was difficult for Grayson, having lost his parents and living with a new family in a new land, he loved the animals and the outdoors. Over the next few years, the bond between Grayson and Etu grew stronger every day. Together, the boys learned basics about fishing and planting crops. They helped each other with their assignments, missions, and quests for school. Both boys benefited from their new brotherhood. Etu's parents, the Deeres, couldn't be happier with how Etu and Grayson had bonded and helped each other grow.

It was 1951 when Grayson and Etu turned eight years old and received their first team assignment. Tutelar students were taught to respect all things living – the land, animals, birds, and sea life. Their team assignment was to build a raft and paddle it to and back from a small, sandy island one-half mile off shore. They were permitted to use dead wood, palm fronds, and vines to build the raft and make the paddles. Grayson and Etu were successful building the raft, and paddling it to the island and back in the required time limit. As part of the assignment, they were required to present to the class how they built the raft and what lessons they had learned. They shared their story with the class, describing that they learned to work together, solve problems, and to not give up.

While on the small, sandy island, Grayson found a large white feather with a black tip. He did not know from what bird it had come, but he was thrilled about finding it. He showed it to his teacher, who told him it was a young golden eagle tail feather – a rarity in southern Florida. In fact, it was unlawful for a non-native person to possess such as feather. Yet, because Grayson was adopted into the Tutelar tribe, he was permitted to keep the feather. He proudly displayed the feather by placing it in the band of his large-brimmed hat. It soon became Grayson's signature; wherever he went, he wore his hat with the eagle feather.

Over the next five years, Grayson and Etu grew and learned together – both at home and in school. They observed the village adults, learning the Tutelar ways and how to be a respectful and contributing member of the village. They attended ceremonies and learned about their heritage and customs. They succeeded in every assignment given them by their teachers. Their parents showed them how to survive off the land and how to take care of their home. The two of them learned to prepare and cook the crops they had planted and gathered, the fish they caught, and the bounties from their hunts. They loved fishing and working the land together.

Sadly, Grayson's lifelong dog friend Luna died in early January 1956. Luna had been with him since he was a young boy in Dimerling, Ohio. She survived with him, when their plane crashed on July Fourth, 1948. Luna helped Grayson through his toughest times. Knowing the cycles of life and understanding that Luna's time had come, Grayson was still devastated by the loss of his friend. He wanted Luna's spirit resting place to be with his parents at the site of the plane crash.

Grayson asked his brother Etu if he would help him give Luna a proper Tutelar funeral. Luna had become a good friend to Etu over the years, and Etu shared Grayson's sorrow. Together they performed a shortened version of the Tutelar funeral ritual for Luna. The two of them collected Luna's ashes to take to the site of the plane crash. They drove their boat to the location of the Taylors' plane crash eight years earlier. Grayson and Etu said goodbye to Luna as they spread her ashes next to the plane in the mangroves.

Nearly three months later, on an early morning in mid-March, Grayson and Etu were fishing from their canoe on the Aquene River. Grayson noticed a young pup on the river bank – in danger of being attacked by several alligators. While Grayson had great respect for the alligators, he was not afraid to be around them. Without taking a moment to think about his own danger, he jumped from his canoe, and swam toward the pup. Miraculously, Grayson swam past the group of alligators, retrieved the little black and brown pup, and returned safely to his canoe.

It was an instant bond for Grayson and his new puppy friend. He decided to name the puppy Boone – a word that simply meant a blessing or a miracle. Etu and the others who were fishing with him that morning went back to the village and told the elders of Grayson's incredible feat. When the Tutelar elders heard how Grayson saved the small pup, they gave him a new name – a tribal name of "Cayman," meaning alligator. At age 13, Grayson became known as the boy who swam with alligators. After that day, his story of saving the pup was told to Cypress Cove visitors who came to the village to learn about the Tutelar. In the story, the boy was known as Cayman.

Shortly after Cayman saved Boone from the alligators, he began sketching. His first sketch was of his lifelong friend Luna, who had died a few months earlier. He signed the sketch with his tribal name and a small feather just below. Incidentally, when finding the eagle feather five years earlier, Grayson had begun including a sketch of the feather each time he wrote his name on something.

The storyteller told her daughter, "Ok honey, now let's talk about the Coopers, and what they've been doing for the past fourteen years."

Vicki Dawson and Henry Cooper grew up together in Westwood, Illinois, where they were neighbors and childhood friends. They attended the same grade school, middle school, high school, and university. They graduated in May 1942 from the University of Chicago, where Vicki received a degree in photo journalism, and Henry in journalism. They were married in October 1942 – the same year they graduated college. They decided to save money by delaying their dream honeymoon. They spent much less money by escaping for two nights to the Sea Gull Inn on North Avenue Beach in Chicago, Illinois.

After their honeymoon, the Coopers moved into an apartment in Westwood, near Chicago, where Vicki did freelance photography for the Chicago Nite Life magazine, Chicago Times magazine, and the Chicago Tribune newspaper. Henry was hired as a writer for the Chicago Tribune. They welcomed their daughter Sarah to the family on September 3, 1943; she was born in Chicago, Illinois.

In 1945, Vicki started a photography business, called Special Moments Photography. She focused her business on weddings, families, children, and professional portraits. Vicki still did the occasional freelance photography work for local magazines and newspapers. Her daughter attended Westwood kindergarten during the fall of 1948. She was a curious, inquisitive five-year-old girl, who was excited to begin school, to learn, and to meet new friends. After two years of writing, Henry published his first novel – a romantic, mystery story.

Sarah turned seven years old in 1950, and she enjoyed helping her mom with photography sessions. She helped carry and maintain Vicki's camera equipment, prepare sets for children and professional portraits, and any other chores in her mom's studio. Sarah loved watching her mom take photographs, and she wanted to help and learn all about being a photographer. When Sarah turned nine, her mom taught her how to prepare and develop film. In 1954, when Sarah turned 11, her mom bought her a basic 35mm camera as a gift. For the next two years, Sarah practiced and honed her photography skills, even taking some of the children's portraits for her mom. She loved photography and knew she wanted to be a photographer like her mom, when she grew up.

During the fall of 1956, the Coopers scheduled a month-long vacation. They had heard about a little slice of paradise in Southwest Florida, called Cypress Cove. The town was growing quickly from 1,465 in 1948 to 4,656 residents in 1956. Seasonal residents and tourists were flocking to the town by car, train, and boat. The Coopers wanted to see what Cypress Cove was all about, and decided to vacation there with their daughter Sarah.

To make the month-long vacation more affordable, Henry and Vicki planned to do some freelance work for the Chicago Tribune while in Cypress Cove. Vicki believed she would be able to snap a few good photographs for Henry's columns and she was hoping to take some photos she could sell through her business, Special Moments Photography. She also planned to advertise her photography services to families vacationing in Cypress Cove, capturing their special moments in Southwest Florida.

Chapter One

Sarah had just turned 13 and was excited about her first trip to Florida. She had always told her parents that she wanted to follow her mom into the photography business. Sarah thought that by using the camera she got as a gift a few years earlier, she could prove to her mom that she could be a good photographer. While on the month-long vacation at Cypress Cove, Sarah planned to attend eighth grade at the local school to stay current with her studies.

The Coopers wanted to make their first family vacation a budget-conscious adventure by enjoying scenery in states they had never visited. As a family, they decided not to fly to Cypress Cove. They took a bus 1,200 miles from the station in downtown Chicago, to Tampa, Florida. From Tampa, the Coopers took the train to the Fort Myers, where they made their way to the ferry dock on the Caloosahatchee River. From Fort Myers, they took the three-hour ferry ride up the Caloosahatchee to the Gulf Coast, and south to the Kendrick Pier in Cypress Cove. From the pier, a local resident gave them a ride to the beach cabin they had rented for the month. For Sarah, it was a scenery-packed, three-day adventure from Illinois through Indiana, Kentucky, Tennessee, Georgia, to Florida.

Having heard about the local Tutelar tribe, Sarah and her mom made a Saturday trip to the Poaceaehatchee Village. During their visit, Sarah took several photographs of the village, the Tutelar people, and the surrounding scenery. Her mom, Vicki, had taught Sarah how to develop film several years earlier, so Sarah developed the photos she had taken while at the village. As she was developing the photographs, Sarah noticed she had captured a single picture of a boy, about her age, standing in the background of the Tutelar villagers. He had long, sandy-brown hair, and was wearing a wide-brimmed hat with a large feather sticking out of the band. She was proud of her photographs and excited to show them to her mom. No one knew just yet that Sarah had captured a photo of young Grayson Taylor, who had gone missing eight years earlier, when his parents' plane never made it to Cypress Cove.

The Coopers spent a wonderful month at Cypress Cove, enjoying the sun and beach, before returning to Westwood, Illinois. The three of them were certain that they wanted to spend more vacations in Cypress Cove. By the time the next school year rolled around, they did just that.

Sarah was thrilled to learn that her mom and dad were planning a return trip to Cypress Cove for the fall of 1957. She was even more excited that they decided to transfer her to Cypress Cove for her freshman year of high school. Sarah's mom, Vicki, helped her send a portfolio of her photographs to the teacher overseeing the Cypress Cove school newspaper. The teacher was so impressed with Sarah's work that she invited Sarah to join the school newspaper at the start of her freshman year. The newspaper team included two freshmen journalists, Mila and Avery, and they needed a photographer. Sarah couldn't wait to meet Mila and Avery and to be a member of the Cypress Cove High School newspaper team.

Vicki advertised her Special Moments Photography business in Cypress Cove – to provide photography services of weddings, vacationing and local families, newborn children, and professional photographs of local businesspeople. Henry took a job with the Cypress Cove Chronicle and began writing his second novel. He also wrote a weekly travel column for the Chicago Tribune about vacationing in Southwest Florida. The Coopers sublet their apartment in Westwood, Illinois, to a young family, and they rented the same Cypress Cove beach cabin as the previous year.

Cypress Cove was growing rapidly and the Coopers saw several changes since their last visit only one year earlier. The new

Chapter One

Clearwater Inn was built on the bay of the Pavati River a few miles from where the river opened into the Gulf of Mexico. The Cypress Cove Airport opened an extended runway to commercial flights. A new movie theater and four new restaurants opened in downtown. The Kendrick Pier was reinforced and lengthened to 1,000 feet after being severely damaged by a storm during the summer. The longer pier extended into water twenty-two feet deep and could handle larger boats.

There was also talk around town that a year earlier, a thirteen-year-old boy jumped into the water and swam past alligators to save a puppy. Even the kids in school talked about the boy who swam with the alligators. Nobody knew who the boy was or where he lived, but he soon became the legend of Cypress Cove. It was a story told to tourists and visitors for many years to come.

Part Two:

Sarah and Cayman

Chapter Two

The young girl asks the storyteller, "Mom, have Sarah and Cayman met yet?" Her mom replies, "Honey, not yet, but they will soon."

Sarah's freshman school year was off to a great start. She made new friends, and she loved working on the school newspaper. Early in their freshman school year, Sarah, Mila, and Avery were given a newspaper assignment to visit the Poaceaehatchee Village, to write an article, complete with photographs, about the Tutelar culture. Sarah was the photographer; Mila and Avery were the reporters.

They left early in the morning with their teacher by bus to meet with the Tutelar elders. Sarah was to take photographs of the elders and scenes of the village, while Mila and Avery interviewed the elders. While taking photographs of the village, Sarah saw two boys with hair down below their shoulders. One boy had black hair, and the other boy had sandy-brown hair. They were talking while standing with an adorable black and brown dog. She tried to snap a photograph of them, but they had stepped out of view of the camera.

Sarah approached the two boys to see if she could take their photograph, along with their dog, for the school paper. The sandy-brown haired boy was immediately kind to Sarah, but shy and did not want his photograph taken. He introduced himself as Cayman, and introduced the black-haired boy as his brother Etu, and the dog as his friend Boone.

Sarah knew they weren't actually brothers, but she did not question him about his introduction. Cayman was polite to Sarah. He showed her around the village and helped her get several photos that were perfect for the article in the school paper. One of her favorite photos was of an entrance to the Poaceaehatchee Village. The spirit of the community and the simple life it represented made it feel like home to her. Sarah and Cayman became instant friends, talking for several hours until her bus

left for Cypress Cove. The three students released one of the best-written stories the paper had seen in a long time. They each received an "A" for the assignment. Sarah was happy with her grade, but she was more occupied with the memory of Cayman, whom she couldn't get off her mind. She was trying to figure out how and when she could go back to the Poaceaehatchee Village to see Cayman.

It wasn't long before Sarah hoped to have another chance to see Cayman. Her biology teacher scheduled a field trip to Marsh Trail in The Everglades. To get to the entrance of the trail, there was a small parking area, just off the SoFlo Trail, east of the Poaceaehatchee Village. Marsh Trail was one mile long with a three-story observation tower at the mid-point. During the rainy season, the land on both sides of the trail was a swamp; during the dry season, it was dry as a desert. The students were instructed to bring drinking water and to dress for hiking, heat, and sun. Sarah was excited and ready with her camera in tow, secretly hoping she may see Cayman. The assignment during the hike was to work together with lab partners to identify as many birds as possible. All of the teams identified nine different birds, including, pelicans, ibises, snowy egrets, ospreys, moorhens, great egrets, great blue herons, anhingas, and spoonbills.

Chapter Two

The teacher asked each student to name and describe one of the nine birds they had seen while hiking on the trail. Sarah raised her hand first and she described the pelican as large, brownish-grey bird with a wide wingspan. It had a long neck and huge bill with a stretchy pouch underneath, a large body with a stubby tail, and sat on two short, squatty legs. Her lab partner described the ibis as a white bird with black wing tips. It had an oval-shaped body with long red legs and a long, curved red bill. The next team described the Roseate spoonbill as a large pink bird with a white neck and a long flat bill. Her lab partner described the snowy egret as a white bird with a four-inch-long, pointy beak.

The next team described the great egret, by calling it a large version of the snowy egret. It had long legs, with a curved neck and a larger version of the pointed bill. His lab partner chose the moorhen, and described it as a mostly black or dark-grey bird, with a short yellow beak surrounded by a red-colored bald spot and yellowish, green legs. The final team chose the great blue heron, describing it as a huge, grayish-blue, prehistoric-looking bird, with a large, sharp bill, a long neck, and long legs. Her lab partner described the anhinga as a large, gray-black bird that could fly and dive underwater, had a pointed bill and long tail. Everyone had had a turn, so Sarah chose to describe the osprey, the other bird the teams had seen. She said it was a majestic bird that looked like a giant, brown, white, and gray hawk.

All of the students saw the alligators along the trail, but none had noticed the pair of wood storks that had flown overhead. The teacher declared the day a success. Sarah thoroughly enjoyed the day, but it wasn't a complete success; she didn't get to see Cayman.

The next time Sarah met Cayman, she told him about her class trip to Marsh Trail. She was dissapointed that she wasn't able to see him during the trip, but she described several of the photographs she had taken of different birds. Cayman remembered her describing a photo of a pelican standing in shallow water and the reflection on the surface ripples. Since he wasn't able to see her at the trail that day, he wanted to give her a sketch to remember the day. Cayman sketched the pelican from his memory of her description and gave it to her a few months later.

The storyteller's daughter asked, "Mom, are Sarah and Cayman in love?" Her mom smiled and said, "You'll have to wait and see."

The school year was more than half over and flying by for Sarah. She was doing great in her studies, and she was having fun working with Mila and Avery on the school newspaper. People around Cypress Cove recognized and liked Sarah, the newcomer.

Sarah had created a new plan to see Cayman. She convinced her parents to let her spend Saturday afternoon at the Poaceaehatchee Village, taking pictures and learning more about the Tutelar. She hadn't told them about Cayman, so they had no suspicions that she wanted to spend the afternoon with a boy. Saturday arrived; Sarah had lunch before her mom drove her to Poaceaehatchee. She had money for a snack, if necessary, and was ready to spend the afternoon with Cayman.

Sarah's visit to the Poaceaehatchee Village didn't go exactly as planned. After asking around the village, Sarah learned that Cayman was fishing with his brother Etu and wouldn't be home until dinner. While Sarah was disappointed, it wasn't a total loss. She spent the afternoon learning as much as she could about the village and the Tutelar people. Sarah also discovered how to get in contact with

Cayman. She learned where to send him a letter and how to leave him a message on the village telephone. Later that afternoon, Sarah's mom picked her up as planned. Even though she didn't see Cayman, Sarah felt good about the day.

The end of Sarah's freshman school year was fast approaching, and soon she would be returning to Westwood for the summer. So, she wrote a letter to Cayman. She told him how much she missed talking with him and that she wanted to see him again soon. She wrote about the field trip to the Marsh Trail and her afternoon at the Poaceaehatchee Village, missing him on both trips. She told Cayman she wanted him to come to Cypress Cove to visit her. Because Poaceaehatchee and Cypress Cove were so close, mail was almost always delivered the next day.

Cayman wrote back to her the same day he received her letter. He said he missed talking with her, and thought about her every day. Cayman told her about fishing with Etu that day he missed her in the village. He had never been to Cypress Cove, but he had seen the pier from their boat when he and Etu were fishing in the gulf. He agreed to meet Sarah at Cypress Cove on Saturday. Once he got to the pier, he

could dock his boat and spend a few hours visiting with her. Cayman was becoming good at sketching, so he drew her a scene of palm trees on the beach with the moon setting over the water. He signed it with his name and a small sketch of a feather below his name. They were both excited for the weekend to come, when they would see each other again.

Saturday morning arrived and the waters were calm – perfect for Cayman to take his boat the three-hour trip to Cypress Cove. He left at sunrise and made his way through the islands and up the coast to the pier. Sarah had been waiting on the pier an hour, and began waving as soon as she saw his boat coming toward shore. She helped Cayman tie his boat to the pier. Then she grabbed his hand led him to a shady bench at the entrance to the pier. They sat and talked about everything they had been doing during the school year. The last time they saw each other was early in the school year, when Sarah visited Poaceaehatchee and the Tutelar elders for the school newspaper.

They only had a few hours to visit. Cayman needed to get home before sunset, because after sunset it was difficult to navigate around and through the Ten Thousand Islands to get to his village. They made the best of every minute of their time together. Sarah showed Cayman a few special places in Cypress Cove, each got an ice cream and shared a soda, then headed back to the pier.

Sarah cheerfully shared with Cayman that her parents recently decided to spend each school year in Cypress Cove. Cayman gave Sarah his parents' telephone number and asked her to call him when she returned to Cypress Cove for her sophomore year. Sarah smiled because she was glad to have an easy way to contact Cayman in the fall. She helped him untie and push off his boat. They waved goodbye to each other as Cayman steered the boat away from the beach and turned south to go home. A few days later, Sarah and her parents returned to Westwood for the summer.

Sarah and Cayman were only young teenagers, yet they formed a strong bond that would last them a lifetime. While Sarah and Cayman weren't going to see each other again until the next school year, they wrote all of the time. They kept each other up to date on everything going on in their lives. They asked each other for advice when things came up, and they never stopped planning for how and when they would see each other again.

Cayman added a sketch to every letter he sent Sarah, and always included the drawing of a feather with his name. His sketches were usually things he saw that made him smile, like birds, animals, fish, and scenery. One of his sketches, dated 1956, seemed to be a self-portrait, and it was extra special to Sarah. It was of a young boy sitting on a large rock. He was looking down at his puppy. In the background was a swamp with an alligator laying on a dead piece of wood on the edge of the Cypress Forest. Sarah didn't yet know the significance of the sketch, but she saved it, along with every one of his other sketches.

The storyteller tells her daughter, "You're going to like this part. The Coopers are going to move to Cypress Cove." Her daughter responds back with a smile. "Mom, that means Sarah and Cayman can see each other as much as they want!"

The Coopers weren't back in Westwood more than a few days until they realized Cypress Cove was where they belonged. It was late spring 1958. The Coopers had several family conversations about where they should spend the next phase of their lives. The three of them talked about how they had deep roots with family and friends in the Westwood and Chicago areas. They also talked about how they had loved spending the last school year in Cypress Cove. The Coopers made many new friends during their time there, and they looked forward to seeing them again. They all agreed that leaving their school and jobs in Westwood to move permanently to Cypress Cove was what they wanted to do.

Henry contacted the editor at the Cypress Cove Chronicle and convinced her to hire him as a full-time reporter. He also planned to continue writing novels and thought Cypress Cove was a perfect place for a writer to live. Vicki's Special Moments Photography business did really well the previous year in Cypress Cove. She had stayed busy photographing weddings, families, and children – for locals and visitors alike. She contacted the Cypress Cove store owner, who was happy to let Vicki continue to rent space for her small studio. Sarah loved attending school in Cypress Cove and she was especially happy about the idea of being near Cayman.

On June 1, 1958, the Coopers turned in a thirty-day notice to the landlord of their apartment in Westwood and began packing for the move. Henry turned in his letter of resignation to his boss at the Chicago Tribune, and Vicki closed her photography business in Westwood. Vicki helped Sarah enroll for fall in the Cypress Cove sophomore high school class. Vicki and Henry made arrangements to rent a two-bedroom apartment, starting in July, in downtown Cypress Cove.

Their new adventure began on July 1,1958, when they left Westwood, with a U-Haul containing all of their belongings in tow. The 1,200-mile journey to Cypress Cove, Florida, took three days; they arrived in time for the town's fireworks on the Fourth of July. Their new apartment was ready and waiting for them when they arrived.

It was in a perfect, central location for Sarah's school, Vicki's photography studio, and Henry's newspaper job. Sarah could walk or ride her bicycle to school and Vicki walked only one block to get to her photography studio. Even though Henry had a short drive to the Cypress Cove Chronicle office, he spent as much time out of the office as in the office. They spent the next two days moving their belongings from the U-Haul into the apartment and putting everything in its place. They loved their new home and were excited to start their new life and adventures in Cypress Cove.

The Coopers had been living in Cypress Cove for a week, and Sarah had not yet seen Cayman. She had missed him badly during the few months they were apart, since finishing her freshman school year, returning to Westwood, and her family moving to Cypress Cove. Their telephone had finally been installed, and Sarah's first call was to Cayman's parents' telephone number. His mom answered and told Sarah, "He hasn't returned home from night fishing with his brother Etu. Is this Sarah?"

"Yes, it is. Would you please give him my telephone number and ask him to call me when he gets in?"

"I certainly will! He's missed you, and he'll be happy to get to talk with you."

Sarah was glad to hear that Cayman had missed her, and couldn't wait to tell him that she moved to Cypress Cove. Cayman was so eager to hear her voice, he called her as soon as he returned home. Curiously Cayman asked, "Sarah, where are you? This is a Cypress Cove telephone number." She told Cayman, "You won't believe it, but we moved to Cypress Cove! We have an apartment downtown, and I'll be finishing high school here. When can we see each other?" Cayman was so surprised, he didn't say anything and Sarah asked, "Cayman, are you still there?" He replied, "Yes, I was just so surprised and happy, I didn't know what to say. Tell me everything." Sarah told Cayman about their family discussion, her parents leaving their jobs in Westwood, and moving into their new apartment. The two of them knew, now that she lived in Cypress Cove, they were going to be able to spend more time together.

While they were talking, Cayman asked Sarah if she would like to go on an airboat ride. She didn't know what an airboat was, and asked him to describe it to her. He told her, "Don't worry, it'll be fun. The boat ride will start in the mangroves on the edge of my village, and we'll ride the airboat through the shallow waters into The Everglades and back. It's only ninety minutes long." Cayman told her that his mom would bring him to Cypress Cove to pick her up, they would go on the airboat ride, then have dinner at his house before bringing her back home. Sarah asked Cayman to hang on a second while she checked with her parents. She got back on the telephone and said, "They said it's okay, so come and pick me up after lunch."

Cayman and his mom picked up Sarah in Cypress Cove about an hour later. They talked with Sarah's parents a few minutes, then headed back to the Poaceaehatchee Village. Sarah and Cayman walked to the village docks to meet with Cayman's brother and a few young tourists. Sarah saw the airboat, and it didn't look like any boat she had ever seen. She thought it looked like a big rectangular, shiny, flat metal pan. It had two wide bench seats for passengers and two raised seats for the driver and another passenger behind the bench

seats. There wasn't even a steering wheel, just a long lever that stuck up in front of the driver. Behind the driver's seat was a car engine, and a giant fan behind the engine. It was a strange-looking thing, but Sarah was ready to give it a try.

The airboat driver introduced himself. "My name is Nodin, and I'll be your airboat driver. In Tutelar, my name means wind."

Chapter Two

Some of the kids chuckled when they heard that the airboat driver's
name meant wind. Nodin helped everyone get aboard and handed
each person a pair of earplugs as he asked them to take a seat.
Cayman told Sarah to put in the earplugs, because an airboat's motor
was much louder than a normal boat motor.

Nodin started the boat and, even with the earplugs in, the
sound was roaring. The giant fan propelled the boat forward as they
made their way through the narrow river into the mangroves. Once
they entered the mangroves, Nodin sped up the boat taking the turns
as fast as he could without crashing into the mangroves. The boat felt
like it was gliding on top of the water.

All of a sudden, the airboat exited the mangroves and the
passengers saw rivers of water running through the tall everglades.
Nodin drove through the tall everglades, sometimes turning the boat
so quickly, it slide sideways on the surface of the water. Everyone on
board was laughing and screaming with excitement during the airboat
ride. Nodin gradually slowed the airboat until it came to a complete
stop; he turned off the engine. Just like that, it was quiet; there was no
roar of the engine. It was perfectly still. They took out their earplugs
and they all started talking at the same time. It was so much fun; they
couldn't stop talking and laughing.

Nodin told everyone to take a look over the left side of the
airboat. The edge of the airboat was less than two feet off of the
surface of the water, so they were startled to see a huge alligator
swimming toward them. Then they noticed two more large alligators
swimming nearby. Nodin said to the passengers, "It's not legal to feed
alligators in the wild, so please, no one jump off the airboat to go
swimming." They laughed nervously, and sat and watched the
alligators. Nodin told them he was about to start the engine, so they
needed to put in their earplugs again.

Nodin started the airboat and turned it around to head back through The Everglades. He made several quick turns, sliding the airboat sideways, before entering the narrows of the mangroves. He zipped through the winding mangroves until he came to a wider opening. Nodin slowed the airboat and turned off the engine to let it drift up next to the mangrove roots.

They all looked where he was pointing to see a family of racoons looking back at the passengers on the airboat. Sarah snapped a photograph of the family. Three of the racoons seemed to pose just in time  for the photo. The driver started the airboat and made some final runs in the windy rivers before finishing the ride back at the village docks.

They all thanked Nodin for an exhilarating airboat ride as they turned to walk back into the village. Etu, Cayman, and Sarah told the others goodbye and headed back to the Deeres' house for dinner. Boone was there to welcome them home, where the Deeres had already prepared dinner. The five of them sat at the picnic table in the backyard and ate while the three kids talked about their exciting airboat voyage. When dinner was over, they all helped clean up the dishes. Sarah said "goodbye" and "thank you" to Mr. Deere and Etu and petted Boone, before jumping in the car with Cayman and his mom to go back home to Cypress Cove. She thanked Cayman for the airboat ride and Mrs. Deere for dinner as she got out of the car to go into her parents' apartment. Cayman beeped the car's horn as his mom headed the car back toward the Poaceaehatchee Village.

It was fall 1958, and 15-year-old Sarah was starting her sophomore year of high school as a full-time resident of Cypress Cove. She was eager to start school and see her friends, and she was thrilled about living in Cypress Cove in Southwest Florida. She didn't know what the school year would bring, but she felt it would be good, and she was ready to find out.

On the first day of school, Sarah met her school newspaper friends, Mila and Avery, for lunch. They were excited and happy when Sarah shared her news about moving to Cypress Cove. The three girls talked about all of the things that happened over the summer, and the things they wanted to do during the new school year. The three of them took the same classes, they planned to study together, and they were going to work on the school newspaper together. Their friendship was a sisterhood that would last a lifetime.

The school year just started, and Cayman had been planning a surprise for Sarah for the last two months. He and Etu were surf fishing late one night in July when they were treated to a rare sighting. It was sea turtle nesting season, and a momma loggerhead crawled out of the surf past the two boys while they were fishing. She crawled up to the top edge of the beach, where the tall grasses grew, and she dug a nest. Once the momma loggerhead dug her nest, she laid more than 100 eggs.

She turned her huge, three-foot-long, 400-pound body around and covered the nest by throwing sand back over the eggs with her large, rear flippers. Once she was happy that her nest and eggs were covered safely, she made her way back down the slope of the beach. She crawled past Cayman and Etu and into the water to swim out to sea. The entire nesting process took more than 45 minutes, and Cayman and Etu watched it all quietly and in complete amazement.

The boys learned about sea turtles' nesting habits during their school studies classes, but this was the first time they actually witnessed it happening. Cayman also learned that it took 60 days before the eggs hatched and for the baby loggerhead hatchlings to make their way out to sea. Cayman could hardly wait to share this incredible experience with Sarah. He made plans with her to meet for a late-night walk on the beach during the exact evening in September that the nest was supposed to hatch. He did not tell her about the surprise, but he knew she would love seeing the nest hatch. It was a perfect night to witness the miracle of life, when under a full moon, more than 100 hatchling sea turtles would rush to the sea.

Sarah didn't know it yet, but she was about to discover something that thrilled her as much as photography. As they were walking in the surf to the place where Cayman had marked the nest, Sarah noticed the water was shimmering and sparkling. She was so amazed that she snapped several low-light photographs of the yellow, green, and blue sparkles under the water. Cayman explained that they were taught in school that the colorful sparkles were due to the bioluminescence in plankton, when a chemical reaction produced light energy from the saltwater. Sarah was amazed by the beautiful, sparkling colors.

When they arrived at the place where Cayman and Etu had marked the nest, Sarah and Cayman sat in the sand. Cayman still hadn't told her why they were there. He used their sighting of an immeasurable number of stars in the clear sky as a distraction. After only a short wait, the nest began to "boil," and more than 100 hatchlings were digging their way out of the nest. As they made it to the surface, the baby loggerheads scurried to the water. Sarah jumped up with excitement as she watched the hatchlings digging their way out of the deep, sandy nest. They had both learned that when a sea turtle nest hatched, it was called a boil. Yet this was the first time either had seen it happen.

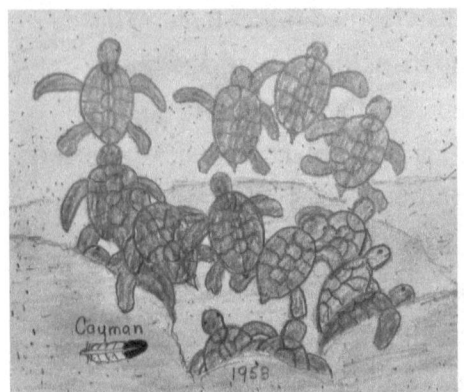

Loggerhead nests typically contain between 100 and 150 eggs buried up to three feet deep in the sand. The hatchlings must dig their way through the sand to the surface and orient themselves to crawl to the water. If the hatchlings are not snatched up by a ghost crab or night heron on their way to the surf, they then swim out to sea. Even in the first few feet swimming in the water, away from shore, they are in danger of several different predators. The hatchlings must swim until they reach floating seaweed beds where they will float near the surface during their growing years. Only one in one thousand loggerhead hatchlings survived to be an adult sea turtle.

Even in her excitement, Sarah took several low-light, long-exposure photographs of the hatchlings climbing out of the nest and making their way to the gulf waters. She was thankful that Cayman thought to share this event with her. Sarah and Cayman spent many more adventurous times together, and that night he had given her an incredible gift. The gift of seeing the world around her in a new way. She quickly learned that she could combine her passion of photography with that of being an advocate for the plants, birds, animals, sea creatures – of all living things.

Chapter Three

On January 4, 1959, Cayman's 16th birthday, he was given his rite-of-passage assignment by the Tutelar council of elders. It was a yearlong mission that was to be completed with a ceremony on his 17th birthday. The mission included several elements that would be performed successfully as determined by the tribal elders.

Cayman would be required to demonstrate and represent his knowledge of Tutelar history and culture. During the yearlong mission, Cayman served as a teacher and mentor for a class of young Tutelar students. He needed to prove that he could achieve all aspects of overseeing a Tutelar home and serving as an adult member of the village. Cayman was also required to perform a significant, selfless act for the people of Cypress Cove over the 12 months of the assignment. The elders monitored and evaluated Cayman's progress toward achievement of the mission.

A few days after Cayman received his rite-of-passage assignment, he asked Sarah if she would go fishing with him and Boone. She had never been fishing, but she was excited to learn, and to spend the day with Cayman. They were going to be on the water most of the day, so they packed a picnic lunch and plenty of water to drink. It was a beautiful winter morning in Cypress Cove. The water in the Gulf of Mexico was as smooth as glass. The sun was just about to come up in the eastern sky as Sarah, Cayman, and Boone pushed his boat away from the Cypress Cove town docks. They slowly headed down the Pavati River to the Gulf of Mexico to find a spot to fish. As they headed out into the deeper water, Cayman explained to Sarah that Tutelar respect and honor the fish for providing nourishment for their families. They didn't take more than they needed and they didn't fish purely for sport.

Chapter Three

Once they reached one of Cayman's favorite spots, he put out an anchor and helped Sarah prepare her bait for fishing. They quickly caught several fish that were too small to keep. They gently released the small fish back into the water. Their patience paid off, and soon Sarah felt a nudge on her line. Then the tip of her pole was bent nearly to the water's surface. She pulled back to set the hook, as Cayman had taught her when they were catching and releasing the smaller fish. Sarah had hooked a large fish and it took all of her strength to crank the reel.

Cayman was as excited as Sarah about her catch, and he cheered her on as she reeled in the fish to the side of the boat. They did not know yet what she had hooked, but he was ready with the net. As she reeled in the line, her catch got closer to the boat. They soon saw that it was a large red grouper, nearly thirty inches long. Once the grouper was close enough, Cayman got it into the net and then into the boat. They were all excited, even Boone, about Sarah's first big catch. Cayman quickly grabbed Sarah's camera and snapped a photo, as she smiled holding up her fish. Her grouper was a keeper, and they placed it in the ice chest to take home. Cayman said he would prepare it for dinner for Sarah and her parents.

They had been out on the water fishing for a few hours, and it was time to take a break to enjoy the picnic lunch they had packed and brought along. As they sat and replayed Sarah's big catch, they were treated to a rare sight of a large hammerhead shark swimming near their boat. Sarah had never seen a hammerhead shark. She took several photographs, as it seemed as interested in them as they were in it. Boone had seen plenty of dolphins, large fish, and sharks, so he sat attentively wagging his tail as he watched the shark swim near the boat.

After lunch, they fished for a few more hours, catching and releasing several small fish. They each caught a couple of larger red snappers, which they also put on ice. Cayman planned to take the extra fish home to his parents. Cayman pulled up the anchor to head back to the docks. It was an hour boat ride back to the dock. They held their hands out of the side of the boat causing the water to spray in their faces. Both of them were wearing big smiles, as it had been a wonderful day on the water.

Once they arrived at the dock and tied down the boat, Cayman began filleting their catch. He cleaned Sarah's large grouper that they planned to have for dinner with her parents. He also filleted the red snappers to put back on ice and take home to his parents. Sarah and Cayman walked to her parents' apartment for dinner. While Cayman grilled the fish, Sarah and her mom prepared corn and a salad to accompany the fish dinner. They all sat down for dinner and the two of them told her parents about their exciting day. They talked about the fish they caught, the shark they saw, and the water spraying in their faces. They all agreed it was one of the best meals they had ever eaten.

Spring had arrived and Sarah finished her sophomore year at Cypress Cove High School. She had done well in school, got good grades in all of her subjects, and made lots of new friends. And she once again served as the photographer for the high school newspaper with her friends Mila and Avery.

Sarah was no longer the new kid in school; she had become an actual member and resident of the Cypress Cove community. While she was sad that school was ending, she was excited about having more summer adventures with Cayman. Every time they were together, Cayman showed her new ways to see the world around her.

Chapter Three

The summer of 1959 was just getting started for Sarah and Cayman, and they were ready for new adventures. Sarah had never gone snorkeling before, and Cayman wanted to share the experience with her. They had been planning to go for a few weeks, and Cayman could hardly wait to share his favorite snorkeling spot with Sarah.

It was a beautiful summer morning when Sarah's mom drove her to the Poaceaehatchee Village. They wanted to get an early-morning start for a day of snorkeling in the crystal-clear waters around the Ten Thousand Islands. Cayman was an excellent swimmer, and he had snorkeled in the waters around the islands many times. He knew all of the best spots to see interesting sea life.

Sarah and Cayman waived goodbye to Sarah's mom as they walked with Boone toward the village docks. Sarah and her mom had packed a picnic lunch for them to enjoy while out on the water. Cayman had also packed some extra food and water for Boone. They loaded their supplies on Cayman's boat, and headed out into the open water.

It was a short, thirty-minute boat ride to get to Cayman's favorite snorkeling spot. They put out the anchor and prepared their snorkeling gear. Cayman and Boone got in the water first, then Cayman helped Sarah out of the boat and into the water. Sarah was also a good swimmer, yet this was her first-time snorkeling. She was a bit apprehensive, yet excited to see what was below the surface of the water.

It was a picture-perfect day; the water was smooth and clear for snorkeling and exploring the sea creatures beneath the surface. Cayman suggested that they would be careful not to disturb or injure any of the sea life they came in close contact with. He also suggested that he would signal her if it was ok to touch a sea creature or if there was potential danger that they must avoid.

They dove down about six feet near the coral, and they quickly found a stingray laying on the sandy bottom. Cayman approached it first and guided Sarah's hand to softly pet it on its back. The skin of stingray looked silky smooth, but felt a little rough to the touch.

They surfaced to take a breath, before diving back down to see what else they could find. Every time they surfaced, Boone would bark with excitement to see them. Once back down, Cayman picked up a sea star and motioned Sarah to go to the surface. At the surface, he asked her to hold out her hand and he laid the sea star across her palm. She was amazed at how it slowly moved around on her hand and how gentle it felt. Sarah dove back into the water and lightly laid the sea star on the bottom; she watched until it settled into the sand, nearly burying itself.

She swam back to the surface to get another breath and to express her delight to Cayman. They swam on the top of the water for a long time, breathing through their snorkel and watching all of the different and colorful fish through their goggles.

They were both getting hungry, so they took a break for lunch. Cayman pulled up the anchor and drove the boat to a small, nearby island. He beached the boat on the island, and they got out their blanket and set up a picnic lunch on the sand under some shady palm trees. They sat for over an hour eating lunch and replaying all of the remarkable things they just experienced. Boone quickly ate and drank, before running and playing on the island. Cayman told Sarah how grateful he was that he could share this special place with her.

After lunch, they got back in the boat to sightsee in the channels around the islands. At one point they were followed by a pod of dolphins that were swimming and jumping in the wake behind their boat. Sometimes the dolphins would jump completely out of the water, then land back in the water on their sides. It was if they were enjoying playing with the boat and its passengers.

The day went by so quickly. It was late afternoon, and they needed to head back to the dock before it was completely dark. As they made their way to the Poaceaehatchee Village docks, they turned

to look to the west, just as the sun was setting behind a palm tree that extended from the beach, over the water. The top of the palm tree filled the sun's glow perfectly, and Sarah snapped one photograph – the ending of a perfect day.

As the summer of 1959 continued, so did 16-year-old Sarah and Cayman's adventures. Cayman had shared with Sarah the amazing view of the stars on the dark nights in The Everglades. Sarah had been learning about the planets and the stars and she wanted to see if they could spot the Milky Way. The two of them learned that the best months to see the Milky Way in South Florida were between April to September. Just after sunset, they needed to look in the southeast sky to see the Milky Way, and it would move toward the southwest sky before sunrise.

It was mid-June 1959, and for the next several days, the moon would rise and set during the daylight hours. This meant that dark night skies would make it easier to view the Milky Way. Sarah asked her mom if she and her dad would drive her and Cayman to Marsh

Trail to see the Milky Way. Her parents were excited about being asked to take part in their daughter's explorations.

The three of them left Cypress Cove around midnight to pick up Cayman and Boone at the Poaceaehatchee Village. From the village, they drove a short distance east on the SoFlo Trail to the Marsh Trail parking lot. With flashlights in hand, they made the short, half-mile hike to the observation tower at the mid-point of the trail. It was the rainy season, so both sides of the trail had filled with a few feet of water. With Cayman and Boone along, they were comfortable hiking the trail at dark. From his time growing up in the area, Cayman had become keenly aware of any potential dangers and how to avoid them.

Upon arriving at the observation tower, they made their way to the top. They could easily and clearly see the stars and the Milky Way. The four of them stood in awe and amazement as they looked at the countless number of stars in the sky. Sarah's mom Vicki was pleased that Sarah wanted to photograph the Milky Way, and she had brought her best camera equipment along for Sarah to use. They set up the camera on a tripod stand and took several low-light, long-exposure photos of the Milky Way and the stars.

They were all so excited about what they saw, they couldn't stop talking about it the entire way back to the Poaceaehatchee Village, where they dropped off Cayman. When they returned home, Sarah and her mom developed the photographs. They were pleased to find that they got several exceptional photographs of the Milky Way.

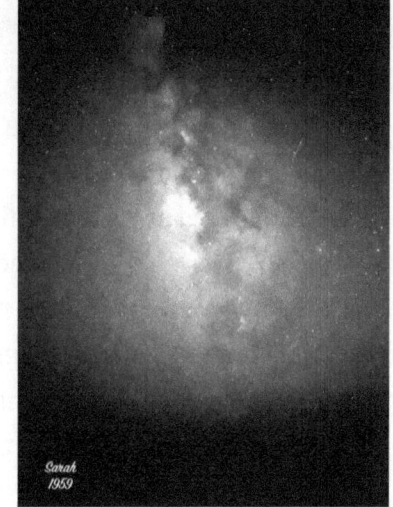

Sarah
1959

Chapter Three

Sarah got some photos with palm trees in the foreground and a couple with silhouettes of the four of them in the foreground. The best photograph was an exposure that captured only the Milky Way.

The next day, Sarah's dad Henry wrote a short story about their Milky Way adventure for the Cypress Cove Chronicle and he included a few of Sarah's best photos along with the story. Sarah asked her mom to drive her to the Poaceaehatchee Village so she could share the photos with Cayman. Cayman was so impressed that he showed Sarah's photos to his parents and the tribal elders. For the Tutelar elders, the stars and Milky Way were spiritual sightings. They were pleased that Cayman was sharing important Tutelar cultural beliefs with families of Cypress Cove.

Summers were the times to prepare for the busy tourist season in Cypress Cove. The summer of 1959 was no different, and it brought more changes to the town. The Beckett Hotel underwent several improvements, for the first time since 1925. It was expanded from 16 rooms to 24 rooms to provide for the increased tourist demand. The dining room was remodeled and expanded, and the pool was drained and resurfaced. The older, original guest rooms were updated with new wallpaper and paint. New shingles were put on the roof, and the exterior walls and trim were painted. It looked like a new hotel, and it was ready for the fall rush of guests.

There was a lot of new construction happening on the bay and along the Pavati River. To support the growth in tourism, new restaurants, hotels, and stores opened. Due to the increase in boat traffic, the town council modernized and expanded the Cypress Cove Town Docks. Improvements to the docks included a full-service fuel pump, small marine store, restrooms, thirty new boat docks, and upgrades to the existing docks.

The growth boom in Cypress Cove over the last few years meant additional tourism traffic to the Poaceaehatchee Village, as well. The Tutelar council of elders recognized the benefit of tourism to the village. They worked with local villagers to identify and provide goods and services that visitors wanted.

The village council of elders helped Nodin expand and relocate his airboat ride business to a new location one mile east of the village. The new location provided for additional parking spots for visitors, extra dock space for five new airboats, and a small visitor center, which displayed local goods.

The council of elders helped villagers open two new eateries for tourists who came for food in the village. One Tutelar family opened an eatery called the Stone Crab Café, just off of the SoFlo Trail near the entrance road to the village. The café was open air, and specialized in all things crab, yet also offered several other seafood options. The second new eatery was called the Hatchee – meaning river – Diner, located on the Aquene River near the edge of the village. It was a casual diner that offered several traditional Tutelar dishes. The dishes were offered in individual or family sizes, so visitors could try and enjoy as many different foods as they wished.

The council of elders worked with village jewelers, clothiers, and rug makers to make shopping more available to tourists. The village built two general store buildings for villagers to display and sell their goods. One was built next to the Stone Crab Café along the SoFlo Trail, and the other was built in the village center with access to the boat docks and eateries.

As a result of the rapid growth in Cypress Cove and the Poaceaehatchee Village, leaders of the two communities got together and formed a joint council. The joint council consisted of members

from the Cypress Cove town council and the Poaceaehatchee Village
council of elders. They planned to meet once each quarter at
alternating locations between Cypress Cove and the Poaceaehatchee
Village. The members of the council defined the mission of their
charter, along with its authority. *The mission of the Cypress Cove and
the Poaceaehatchee Village joint council is to define opportunities for
the betterment of Southwest Florida. Opportunities shall be limited to
those that do not endanger the local natural environment, land, and
wildlife.* The members of the joint council believed that their new
combined council would serve both communities positively for many
years to come.

Cypress Cove and the Poaceaehatchee Village were hit with a
tropical storm on July 17, 1959. The storm tore through Cypress Cove
in a matter of 45 minutes. The wind and rain of the front edge of the
storm pounded the Poaceaehatchee Village, before it had passed
through Cypress Cove. Wind damaged buildings and roofs, and rain
flooded the streets. Fortunately, no one was injured by the storm, but
the damage was extensive. Cayman was worried about Sarah; he
didn't know if she and her parents were safe from the storm.

The day after the storm, the sky was clear and the water was
calm. Cayman got up early, and drove his boat to Cypress Cove to
check on Sarah and her parents. The pier was badly damaged, so he
traveled up the Pavati River to dock at the town docks. He ran from
the docks to her apartment to check on her. Sarah and her parents
were fine, and she was happy to see Cayman. She gathered her
camera equipment and the two of them went off to get photographs of
the storm damage in Cypress Cove.

Sarah asked her parents if she could go with Cayman to the Poaceaehatchee Village to get photographs there, as well. They were reluctant at first, but they trusted Sarah and Cayman, and permitted her to go. She took several photographs that she shared with the villagers; a few were put on display in the village. Her photos of the storm's destruction were printed in the school newspaper and in the Cypress Cove Chronicle.

The next few weeks were spent cleaning up debris left in the wake of the storm. Cayman helped with cleanup and repairs in the Poaceaehatchee Village and in Cypress Cove. Along with the cleanup, people were helping with repairs to the buildings and roofs. Cayman was learning about repairing roofs, doors, and windows. Those who couldn't help with repairs, helped by preparing and serving food to the workers; everyone pitched in. The Tutelar worked alongside of the residents of Cypress Cove. They knew that together they were stronger in all ways – as a community and as an economy. Because of the storm, the school year started a few weeks late during the fall of 1959. By mid-September, little evidence of the storm remained.

Cayman began his final year of school, and he was working diligently to successfully complete all of the elements of his rite-of-passage mission. He volunteered to present history and culture of the Tutelar tribe once a month at the Cypress Cove middle school. He also took over one of the first-level classes for the younger children at the Poaceaehatchee Village school.

Cayman assumed all of the duties at home for his parents during the months of September and October. He even took care of grocery shopping, fishing, and gathering crops from the gardens. He did all of the chores at home, including budgeting, cooking, cleaning, laundry, and small repairs. Cayman was doing all of these tasks to achieve the rite-of-passage mission, and along the way learned that he enjoyed what he was doing. He proved to himself that he was a responsible and contributing member of the Poaceaehatchee Village.

Sarah was entering her junior year of high school, and was eager to do something important that made a difference for Cypress Cove. Sarah and Cayman regularly went for morning beach walks, and she was noticing a big difference between the cleanliness of the beaches at Cypress Cove and those at the Poaceaehatchee Village. The Poaceaehatchee Village beaches possessed a natural look and were clear of human debris and trash.

Often during their beach walks at Cypress Cove, the beaches showed leftover trash from beachgoers. Sarah told Cayman she wanted to start a beach cleanup campaign, and he encouraged her to go for it. The next day, Sarah met with her school newspaper teammates, Mila and Avery, and told them what she wanted to do and why it would be good for Cypress Cove. They agreed with her, and they prepared a newspaper article to release on the upcoming Thursday.

> *Calling All Volunteers*
> *Please meet us at the Kendrick Pier parking lot this Saturday morning at eight a.m. We need your help for two hours to make our beaches beautiful. All volunteers get a beach cleanup tee shirt and drinking water. We'll provide buckets and gloves for the beach cleanup. Please stay afterwards, as we plan to go for a swim in the crystal-clear, warm waters of the Gulf of Mexico. Please, please come and help us with this important campaign to clean up our beaches. See you there!*

On Saturday morning, Cayman, Sarah, and Boone arrived at the Kendrick Pier at seven-thirty a.m. Loaded in the back of a pickup truck, which Cayman had borrowed from a friend, were buckets, gloves, and drinking water. A few minutes later, Sarah's newspaper teammates, Mila and Avery, arrived with a stack of tee shirts. The tee shirts were white, with smiling sea turtles on the front. On the back, "Beach Beautification Volunteer" was printed.

By eight a.m., seven volunteers, who were also Sarah's classmates, had arrived. For two hours, they collected trash left behind by beachgoers. They laughed and talked while they worked. They had collected twelve buckets of trash in all, and were proud of their accomplishment. They sat, drank water, and talked about their morning. Suddenly they all jumped up, cheered, and ran together into the gulf to swim.

The school newspaper team, Sarah, Mila, and Avery, put together a story for the next publication. Sarah took photos, while the other two members of the newspaper team got quotes from the volunteers about how fun and rewarding it was. The word had spread quickly, and by the next cleanup date, the number of volunteers increased from seven to twelve.

The Cypress Cove Chronicle got wind of Sarah's beach cleanup campaign. They arrived at the pier to take photographs and write an article for the Cypress Cove Chronicle. The town loved the idea of a beach cleanup campaign, and by the middle of the school year, adults, young kids, and grandparents showed up to help with the beach cleanup. Some of the local businesses brought drinks and snacks for the volunteers.

Sarah realized that her cleanup campaign had taken on a life of its own. Cayman and Sarah's parents were proud of what she had started for the town. Sarah was interested in finding a way to build the beach cleanup into an ongoing community program. She met with the Cypress Cove mayor to discuss how that might work. The mayor realized that what Sarah had started had reaped positive impacts for the community, even beyond making the beach pristine and beautiful.

People and businesses had come together for a common cause, and the mayor did not want to lose that energy. At the next town council meeting, the mayor proposed a resolution to make the beach cleanup campaign a formal town policy. The resolution listed Sarah Cooper as the honorary founder of the "Beach Beautification Crusade." And it passed unanimously. The formal program was taken over and led by the Cypress Cove Parks and Recreation Department.

During her junior year, Sarah started spending more time with Cayman at the Poaceaehatchee Village. She got her driver's license when she turned 16, on September 3, 1959. Sarah was permitted by her parents to drive to the village occasionally during daylight hours.

Every visit to the village and with Cayman led to new discoveries of Southwest Florida. Sarah's photography preferences were unlike her mom's, whose photography business was centered around photographs of people, weddings, families, and children.

Sarah preferred natural scenery and animals in the wild as her photography subjects. With Cayman's help, she was able to find locations in the Cypress Forest, The Everglades, and among the islands to get photographs of things most people did not see. One of her favorite photos was a field of Florida sunflowers near the edge of the Poaceaehatchee Village.

Sarah's and Cayman's photography explorations included scenery, plants, trees, and water. She took photographs of birds in the air and on the ground, sea life in the clear waters, and animals in their natural habitats. As a team, with Cayman as the guide and Sarah as the photographer, they took numerous photographs of rare sightings, and they wanted to share them with others.

The Tutelar elders were impressed and inspired that these two young people – from different worlds – came together to capture beautiful images of the nature that surrounded them. The elders offered Sarah and Cayman a small space for a gallery in one the buildings in the village. Sarah named the gallery, "Sacred Moments."

When Sarah was back in Cypress Cove, Cayman opened the gallery to tourists and visitors. Those visiting purchased the photographs as souvenirs of their visit to the Poaceaehatchee Village in Southwest Florida. Word of the small photography gallery, full of exceptional photos, spread to Cypress Cove. It became one of the top recommended stops for visitors to Southwest Florida. The money Sarah and Cayman received from selling the photographs was used to pay rent for the gallery space and to cover Sarah's photography and camera equipment expenses.

Cayman's big day arrived on his 17th birthday, January 4, 1960, when the Tutelar held his rite-of-passage ceremony. The rite of passage was mostly ritualistic, since all of his mission assignments were conducted, monitored, and ratified by the Tutelar council of elders throughout the year. The rite-of-passage ritual was presided over by the council of elders and attended by many of Cayman's classmates, friends, and family. Cayman sought and received permission from the elders to include Sarah and her parents as attendees of the ceremony.

Very few times have outsiders attended the rite-of-passage ceremony. Sarah had gained great respect from the elders with her nature photography. The council made an exception for her and her parents to attend Cayman's ceremony. Sarah asked her mom to take photographs so she could participate in the ceremony and be in some of the photos. Her mom cheerfully agreed to take photos for her and Cayman.

During a rite-of-passage ceremony, the Tutelar people dressed in traditional and colorful ceremonial clothing. They painted their arms, necks, and faces with vibrant ritual designs. So as to be fully immersed in the ritual, Sarah dressed and painted herself as the other members of the tribe. She was humbled to be permitted to participate in the ceremony and to be accepted as an honorary Tutelar for the day.

Cayman followed tradition and cut his hair for the ceremony. While it was not a requirement, it had become a tradition that the boys cut their hair before they participated in the rite of passage to become an adult.

The ceremony began with members of the village playing drums. After several minutes of beating drums, the elders joined in with traditional prayer and chanting. Drumming and chanting lasted 30 minutes, then the chanting gave way to flutes joining the drums.

The ceremony kind of reminded Cayman of his parents' funerals. He was sad that they weren't there, but he knew they would be proud of him and his accomplishments. Shortly after the flutes began playing, a ritual dance ensued – lasting hours.

Except for the elders, drummers, and flautists, everyone that attended the ceremony participated in the dance. Even Sarah's parents joined in for some of the dance. When the dance finished, Cayman approached the elders, and the elders placed a ceremonial necklace around his neck. The necklace signified Cayman was a Tutelar adult. Everyone clapped and cheered with celebration as Cayman transitioned to a new part of his life's journey. There was a feast in the village park under the large shade trees. It was one of Cayman's happiest days, and he got to share it with his best friend Sarah.

Chapter Four

Spring in Southwest Florida was high nesting season for a variety of shorebirds, such as terns, sandpipers, and plovers. The birds flocked to the sandy coastlines to make scooped nests in the sand.

Cayman had seen the large flocks of birds many times and he wanted to share them with Sarah. He had a favorite spot on a deserted beach that few people visited. It provided beautiful views of the Gulf of Mexico, trees, and hundreds of birds. Cayman and Boone met Sarah at the Cypress Cove docks one early April morning in 1960. It was a two-hour boat ride to the secluded beach. Once they got close enough, Cayman anchored the boat a mile down the beach from the nesting site.

Sarah and Cayman waded onto shore and walked up the beach to the nesting site. Cayman described some precautions they would take while watching the birds. He shared with Sarah that she should be able to get photographs, but that they would not be getting very close to the birds while they nested. They needed to avoid any activities that could disturb the birds and potentially damage their nests. Cayman continued on, saying that some of the biggest threats that prevent the birds' nests from hatching were storm surges, algal blooms, and human intrusion.

Boone was well behaved and seemingly understood that he needed to be equally cautious and calm as they got closer to the nesting area. Even from a distance, Sarah noticed that the birds, in what appeared to be choreographed motion, took flight in a large flock. The birds flew far out over the water, only to return to their same resting spot. It was an amazing sight to see and hear.

As the two of them and Boone got closer to the large flock of nesting birds, Cayman held up his hand, indicating that they were as close as he felt they could be without causing any disturbance. They stood very still while they watched and listened to the hundreds of birds nesting on the beach, singing and chirping. Usually, when the birds took off in a large flock, they flew out to sea, away from Sarah and Cayman. But there was one time when they took off, and the entire cluster flew right in front of them, almost as if they were providing Sarah with a special photo moment.

After watching the birds and getting a few photos, they walked back down the beach to the boat to head back to Cypress Cove. Sarah liked driving the boat sometimes, and she drove back to the town docks. They tied the boat to the docks, and walked the short distance to her parents' apartment. Sarah told her mom and dad about what it was like to see and hear so many birds in one place.

Cayman needed to head back to the village to do some work for his parents. Sarah walked Cayman and Boone back to the dock. She gave them both big hugs and thanked Cayman for sharing the special place with her. She helped Cayman untie the boat and shove off for the trip back to the village. Boone gave Sarah a couple of barks goodbye, and Cayman waved, as they headed away on the boat.

Chapter Four

Sarah's junior year was coming to a close, and it was only a few days until the spring dance. She was excited that Cayman said he would pick her up at home, and escort her to the dance.

When the day arrived, Cayman, was dressed in a suit he shared with his brother, Etu. And he borrowed his friend's pickup truck. He had cleaned the pickup truck the best he could, and headed to Cypress Cove. When Cayman pulled up in front of Sarah's parents' apartment, Sarah's dad met him at the door and welcomed him in. Cayman was a little embarrassed that he was wearing a shared suit and had borrowed an old pickup from a friend in his village. Sarah's dad had a calming way about him, started talking with Cayman, and soon Cayman forgot about his uncomfortableness.

Sarah's mom had been helping Sarah get ready. She styled Sarah's hair and helped Sarah put on the dress the two of them had made for this dance. Sarah's long, dark hair flowed down the back of her dress. The dress was a long, lightweight, pink linen dress with a scooped neck and short sleeves. Sarah wore pink-heeled shoes that her mom let her borrow. When she came out of her room, she nearly took Cayman's breath away. Until now, they had not seen each other dressed in formal attire.

Cayman was handsome in his suit and Sarah looked beautiful in the dress her mom helped her make. Sarah's mom took several photographs before they left for dinner and the dance. Sarah and Cayman enjoyed dinner at an outdoor restaurant on the Pavati Bay. Following dinner, they headed to the school for the dance. Cayman confessed his embarrassment to Sarah; she smiled and said she didn't care about fancy things, and liked that he didn't either. Sarah cared much more about the fact Cayman was a good person than what he did or didn't have. She liked that he was always helping others in his village and how he respected the land that provided for them and the animals they lived with. That mattered a lot more to her than material things.

Sarah had danced with Cayman just a few months earlier at his rite-of-passage ceremony, so she knew it wouldn't be difficult to get him out on the dance floor again. And it wasn't difficult at all. They danced and laughed all evening. Sarah introduced Cayman to her friends, Mila and Avery, from the school newspaper. The girls mentioned, more than once, how the two of them were able to find such amazing sights and things to photograph.

A few of her friends had heard the stories of the Tutelar boy who swam with the alligators, and now they wanted to hear all the details. They didn't know that the story was about him, and Cayman kind of shrugged it off as just a story people made up. All of Sarah's friends were nice to Cayman and made him feel welcome and comfortable to simply be himself. These two 17-year-old adults spent a memorable, fun evening together.

The spring dance was over, and only a few weeks later, Sarah finished her junior year of high school in 1960. She was going to miss school, but she was also excited for the summer break and new experiences. Last summer was full of exciting adventures and she hoped this summer would be even better, minus the tropical storm, of course.

She soon got her wish; Cayman had been planning another fun day for the two of them. They were going horseback riding on the trails near the Poaceaehatchee Village. Cayman and Etu cared for several horses for the villagers at Poaceaehatchee, and Cayman made arrangements for himself and Sarah to have two of the horses to ride the trails for the day.

Chapter Four

In his friend's pickup truck, on a gorgeous sunny morning, Cayman and Boone drove to Cypress Cove to pick up Sarah. They sat and talked with Sarah's parents for a short while, telling them about their plans for the day. They were soon heading back to the village to go riding. They stopped by Cayman's parents' house so Sarah could see his mom and dad, and to pick up a picnic lunch Cayman had prepared earlier that morning. They talked for a few minutes, then headed out the door for a short walk to the horse stables.

Cayman rode often, but this was Sarah's first time on a horse. He helped Sarah onto a mare, named Dahteste, whose name meant warrior woman. Cayman reassured Sarah that Dahteste was a perfect horse for her first time riding. Despite her name, she was a calm horse that was protective of her rider. Cayman helped Sarah get comfortable on Dahteste. He held the reins and led her around the fenced stable area a few times.

While he was leading Sarah's horse around the stables, he described how she could guide her horse. If she wanted to go left, she would gently pull the reins across the horse's neck to the left. If she wanted to go right, she would gently pull the reins across the horse's neck to the right. To stop Dahteste, Cayman described how to draw back on the reins. And to go forward, simply shake the reins and say, "Nocona."

When Sarah felt comfortable, Cayman handed her the reins to ride Dahteste on her own. Once Sarah was comfortable with her practice ride, they were ready to head out onto the trail.

Cayman got on his horse, a young stallion named Migisi, meaning eagle. He took the lead, as they rode their horses to the edge of the village to get on the trails. Sarah was getting much more comfortable by now, and she was ready for their ride. Boone followed as Sarah, Cayman, and their horses slowly rode along the trail.

Once they were away from the village and others, Cayman called back to Sarah, saying they were going to trot the horses into a slow run. Sarah was a little nervous, but ready to give it a try. Cayman told her that Dahteste was used to running with Migisi, and there was nothing for her to do, but stay with the motion of the horse while she was trotting. Once Cayman started Migisi to run, Dahteste kept pace. Sarah was smiling and laughing with joy! This was fun! They rode the horses for several hours on the trails along The Everglades and in the Cypress Forest.

Cayman signaled that it was time to give the horses a break and to find a place they could enjoy their picnic. Sarah pointed to a shaded spot with plenty of space for the horses, their blanket, and a picnic lunch. Cayman hopped off his horse first and helped Sarah get down from Dahteste. The two of them were ready to get off the horses for a while, and the horses were happy to have a break. They made sure that Dahteste, Migisi, and Boone had plenty of water before sitting down for their picnic. Sarah and Cayman sat and enjoyed their picnic, while they talked and laughed about how much fun they were having.

They rested and picnicked for an hour, before hopping back on their horses. Sarah proudly mounted her horse without any help from Cayman. They leisurely rode back the trail toward the village, enjoying the sights along the way. Cayman still had another surprise for Sarah, something he wanted to share with her, before their ride was finished.

As they got closer to the village, they took a different trail. It was a short ride to get to a clearing that opened on the edge of the beach. Cayman called back to Sarah, "Get ready to run the horses again." Then he took off on Migisi, and Sarah soon followed on Dahteste. Cayman ran Migisi along the beach in the shallow surf of the water.

Sarah was riding next to Cayman, and Boone was running along in the shallowest part of the water. They were laughing with delight as their horses ran and splashed in the water and sprayed it high into the air. They rode the horses in the shallow water for a short time, then turned them back to the village. Once in the stables, they removed the horses' saddles, washed and brushed the horses, and gave them fresh water and food.

Sarah, Cayman, and Boone stopped by Cayman's house, and he helped his mom prepare dinner. They talked and laughed through dinner, while they told his parents about their horse-riding experience. After dinner, Cayman drove Sarah back to Cypress Cove to her parents' apartment. He went inside with her, and they told her parents about their fun-filled day riding horses. Cayman headed home thinking about how grateful he was for Sarah's friendship and for the day they had shared together.

It had been a few weeks since Sarah and Cayman spent the day horseback riding, and they were ready for another exciting excursion. Sarah told Cayman she wanted to load up the boat for a weekend exploration of the Ten Thousand Islands. Cayman was thrilled with the idea, and he knew several places in the islands that he was certain she would enjoy.

Sarah got up early on Friday morning, and hitched a ride from her friend Mila to Cayman's parents' house in the Poaceaehatchee

Village. Etu and Cayman made breakfast for their parents and for their guests Sarah and Mila. They all sat down for breakfast on the back patio, while they talked about what Sarah and Cayman had planned for the weekend. Cayman shared that they planned to go to a few of his and Etu's favorite islands for snorkeling, fishing, star gazing, and camping. Cayman and Etu had taken many overnight trips in the Ten Thousand Islands together, so nothing sounded out of the ordinary.

Mila said to Sarah, "I'll see you Sunday afternoon," as she waved goodbye to head back to Cypress Cove. Etu went with Sarah, Cayman, and Boone to the boat dock, where they loaded the boat with equipment and supplies for two nights of camping. They packed snorkeling gear, fishing equipment, camping necessities, food and water, Sarah's camera bag, and extra fuel for their excursion. Etu said to them, "I'll see you for lunch on Sunday. Have fun and be careful." Cayman backed the boat away from the dock and Boone let out a goodbye bark. The boat turned toward the open water and sped away.

Sarah wanted to drive the boat for a while, so Cayman pointed toward an island off in the distance and said, "Take us there." It was a spot where he and Etu often went swimming and snorkeling. Forty-five minutes later, they arrived at a spot near the island where they anchored the boat for a swim. Boone jumped in the water first, then Sarah and Cayman jumped in. They were anchored close enough to shore to easily swim to the beach, sun themselves, and to take breaks from swimming. Boone sometimes swam up to shore and barked at them while they swam, then he'd jump back in the water and swim with them.

They swam and snorkeled for a couple hours. Cayman had taken Sarah snorkeling before, so this time she was much more comfortable diving down to see the coral and sea life near the bottom. She carefully picked up and held a sea star to show to Cayman. Sarah placed it softly back on the bottom, as she and Cayman swam over to a stingray partially buried in the sand. They gently petted it on the back, and it seemed to enjoy the soft petting. The two of them saw a variety of fish, including sheepshead, snapper, permit, and grouper.

They were getting hungry; it was time to take a lunch break on the island beach. The two of them sat on the beach and ate the sandwiches that they had packed. Boone snacked on the food and water they brought for him. After lunch they climbed back in the boat and headed to another island where they planned to spend the night.

Sarah drove the boat while Cayman guided her between and around the islands. The next stop was the island where Etu and Cayman had fished and camped many times. It had a nice spot for pitching a tent and making a camp fire. They beached the boat, unloaded the camping equipment, and set up the tent. Once the campsite was ready, Sarah and Cayman took out the fishing gear and set out to catch dinner.

First, they needed to catch some small bait fish. Cayman wanted Sarah to get the full fishing experience, so he taught her how to use the bait net to catch small bait fish. Even though it wasn't the first time Boone had seen Cayman use a bait net, Boone seemed to think that throwing it into the water was a game he was supposed to join in on. Despite Boone's participation, they soon had enough bait in the bucket to fish for dinner. The two of them caught several smaller fish that they carefully released back into the water. Then Sarah caught a large grouper, about twenty-five inches long; it was perfect for the two of them for dinner.

Cayman filleted and cleaned the grouper, while Sarah prepared rice and vegetables on the camp fire. She sat the pan with the rice and vegetables on the edge of the fire to stay warm, while Cayman fried the fish. They enjoyed a delicious fish dinner under the starlit night in the Ten Thousand Islands. After dinner, the two of them cleaned up the dishes and pans, and packed them away in the tent for the night.

They sat and watched the stars until they couldn't stay awake any longer. They made sure the camp fire had safely burnt out, and moved into the tent for the night. Boone took a spot inside the tent, near the opening. Cayman had set up a water catch system by using one side of the tent and a large jug with a filter. When it rained at night, the water ran off the side of the tent, through the filter, and into the jug, providing water for washing and drinking.

The next morning, they got up with the sun. It was another beautiful day in paradise. They collected coconuts and bananas for breakfast. After breakfast they took down the tent and loaded the boat with their equipment and supplies. They decided to explore a part of the Ten Thousand Islands in which Cayman had not spent much time. They had motored around the islands for a while, when they came across a huge sandbar extending out from one side of an island. They agreed it looked like a great place to beach the boat and explore.

Sarah was amazed at the size of the sandbar! She jumped out of the boat first, and Boone followed her as she ran across the sandbar. She stopped near the water's edge to find a large sea star partially buried in the sand. Sarah thought it looked like a flower in the sand, and she snapped a photograph to put in the Sacred Moments Gallery in the Poaceaehatchee Village. They swam in the warm, shallow water and  played on the sand bar for several hours. The two of them even had lunch while sitting on the sand bar.

Chapter Four

After lunch they drove the boat around the island to find a good place to set up camp and beach the boat for the night. Sarah pointed out a clearing on the beach with lots of shade for the tent. Cayman beached the boat and tied its long rope to one of the palm trees. Before setting up the tent, the two of them wanted to explore the island. There were banana trees and coconut palm trees from which to collect breakfast the next morning.

When they returned to the boat, the two of them collected their camping gear and set up the tent and the rain water collection system. Cayman fished for dinner while Sarah sat on the beach and gazed at the incredible scenery that surrounded her. It didn't take Cayman long to catch a nice redfish for dinner. Sarah and Cayman sat at the camp fire, enjoyed their fish dinner, while talking about their two-night adventure. It had been another great day, and they were exhausted. Shortly after dinner they retired to the tent with Boone.

The next morning, they snacked on the coconuts and bananas before packing up their equipment and loading the boat for the trip back to the village docks. They loaded all of their supplies on the boat and pushed it off the beach. While they were floating near shore, Cayman attempted to start the boat, but the motor would not start. He couldn't find anything wrong; everything seemed to be connected properly and there was plenty of fuel to get them home.

He didn't want to let the boat float too far from shore, or it would be difficult to get it back to the beach. Sarah and Cayman quickly jumped into the water and pushed the boat back to the beach to take a closer look. They pushed and pulled the boat up on the beach as best as they could, and retied it to the palm tree.

Cayman tried everything he knew about boat motors to get it started, but with no luck. He checked the spark plugs and made sure fuel was making it to the motor. Everything appeared to be okay, but the motor wouldn't start. They soon realized that they weren't going anywhere in the boat. They were expected home for lunch, but Cayman knew that his parents and Etu wouldn't think a lot about it if they missed lunch. He realized that by the time Etu figured that there might be a problem, it would be getting dark and too late to look for them. Cayman thought the soonest Etu would start looking would be the next day, so they needed to make plans to stay on the island for at least another night.

The first thing the two of them did was collect dark-colored rocks, situated them on the white sandy beach, and spelled a large "SOS." They hoped a plane would fly over and radio in their location. Once they were done making an SOS on the beach, they unloaded the boat and set up the tent in the same spot as it had been the night before. Cayman reestablished the water collection system on the tent, and they collected more bananas and coconuts for extra food and drink.

Cayman said, "Don't worry, Sarah. Etu will find us. And we have plenty of access to food and water, if needed." Whenever he and Etu had gone on overnight trips, they always took a lot of extra food for Boone. They knew they could catch fish and find food and water for themselves, but not so easily for Boone. Fortunately, this trip was no different; Cayman had brought enough food for Boone to last a week.

The first night stranded at sea went by as the other previous nights. The next day, all they could do was wait and hope that someone found them. But the day turned into night, and no one came. They didn't know it, but Etu and a friend had spent the entire day searching for them. The next morning, Sarah and Cayman waited again. While they were stranded and waiting, Etu had arranged for more help to continue the search.

Chapter Four

Two days earlier, as Etu helped prepare Sunday lunch with his parents, they wondered if Cayman and Sarah were going to make it in time. They sat at the table on the back patio and talked about the weekend and the week ahead, but there was no sign of Sarah and Cayman making it to lunch. They weren't too worried; they figured that Sarah and Cayman were having so much fun that they decided to spend the afternoon on the water. By dinner time, Sarah and Cayman still had not yet returned. And now Etu was a little worried. It would be dark soon and too late to go out on the water to search for them.

Etu knew that Cayman was as experienced as anyone, when it came to spending overnight trips at the Ten Thousand Islands. He also had helped Cayman load extra fuel and all of the necessary safety supplies and equipment on the boat. What Etu didn't know was that Sarah and Cayman had loaded their boat and pushed off to head back to the village, when their boat motor wouldn't start. Etu didn't know that they had taken their boat back to shore, where they were stranded on one of the Ten Thousand Islands somewhere southeast of the Poaceaehatchee Village.

By Monday morning, Sarah, Cayman, and Boone still hadn't returned home. Etu told his parents that he was going to have one of his friends from the village go with him to try to find them. They loaded up Etu's boat with extra fuel and food, and headed out to find Sarah and Cayman. They spent the morning searching all of the usual spots where Etu and Cayman had fished and swam. They circled the islands one by one with no sign of Sarah, Cayman, and Boone, or their boat. Etu stopped for a late lunch and to put the rest of the fuel in the tank.

Etu decided to search in another area he and Cayman had talked about several times. Again, Etu and his friend circled the new islands, one by one, and as before, there was no sign of Sarah, Cayman, Boone, or their boat. By now it was evening; it would be dark soon and he was getting low on fuel. Etu called it a day, and headed back to the docks. He was worried, but he knew that Sarah and Cayman were tough and up to the challenge. Etu knew that they could catch fish for food, and they could capture and filter nighttime rain water for drinking.

The next morning, Tuesday, Etu and his parents were awoken by knocking at the front door. It was Sarah's friend Mila wondering if they had heard from Sarah and Cayman or knew where they were. Mila told them that Sarah's parents, Vicki and Henry, called her yesterday and again early this morning wanting to know if she knew where they were. By now, they were all worried. Unless they were in trouble, it was not at all like Sarah or Cayman to not let their families and friends know where they were.

Mila told Etu, "We need to get the boat and go look for them – NOW." Etu knew that she was right, yet they needed to eat before heading out on the water for the day's search. His mom made breakfast, while Mila helped him pack food and water for them and extra for Sarah, Cayman, and Boone.

Etu asked some of his and Cayman's friends from the village to help with the search. They all met at the boat docks and loaded three boats with supplies, fuel, and food. They knew that searching for a lost boat in the Ten Thousand Islands was like looking for a needle in a haystack, but they weren't coming back until they found them.

Mila was riding with Etu, and each of the other two boats carried two villagers. They made a plan about what to do if they did or didn't find Sarah and Cayman. If one of the three groups found them, that boat was to send up two flares. Otherwise, they were to search until noon, then meet on the north side of Sand Piper Island. It was an island well known by the villagers for the large numbers of sand pipers that nested on the beaches during spring. No flares were shot into the air that morning, and they all met at Sand Piper Island.

They ate a quick lunch and made plans for the afternoon search – determining what section of the islands each boat would take. Again, if anyone found them, they were to send up two flares. Otherwise, they would meet back at the village docks before sunset. Each boat headed off to search its assigned area. Etu and Mila searched a southeastern section of the islands.

Etu didn't say this to Mila, but he wasn't confident that they would find Sarah, Cayman, and Boone in the area they were searching. It was an area of the Ten Thousand Islands that he and Cayman didn't visit often. Etu and Mila motored around the islands for hours. They were hot and exhausted, but they knew they couldn't give up trying to find their friends. Etu and Mila agreed that it was getting late and they were getting low on fuel, and believed they had just enough time and fuel to get back to the docks before dark.

At that moment, their choice was between making it back to the docks or potentially getting stranded themselves. As they began turning the boat around to head northwest toward the docks, Mila caught glimpse of a single flare launched into the sky. She screamed as she jumped to her feet, grabbed Etu, and pointed toward the flare. Cayman had faintly heard their boat motoring around the islands, and he sent up a single red flare, signaling distress.

Etu turned the boat back toward the direction of the flare and sped around the island. As they rounded the island, they first saw Cayman's boat beached on the sand, then a large SOS made from dark-colored rocks. They heard Boone barking and saw Cayman and Sarah waving their arms above their heads as they got closer to the beach.

Etu asked Mila to steer the boat while he launched two red flares into the air, signaling to the others that they had found Sarah and Cayman. Etu beached his boat next to Cayman's boat. He and Mila were so excited they

hugged, then jumped out of the boat and ran up to Sarah and Cayman to hug them, while Boone barked and wagged his tail with joy.

They all sat for a moment, Sarah and Cayman exhausted from being stranded for two days, and Mila and Etu exhausted from searching for them. They all eat the extra food and drank the water that Etu and Mila had brought. When they finished eating and loaded both boats, they were ready for the boat ride back to the village docks. Sarah, Mila, and Boone climbed into Etu's boat, while Etu and Cayman tied a long rope to Cayman's boat. They hopped into Etu's boat for the long, slow journey, pulling Cayman's boat, to the village docks.

By then the sun was setting, and there was no way they would make it back to the docks before dark. While they had running lights on the boat and a large spot light used for night fishing, it was going to take every bit of Etu's and Cayman's navigation skills to get them safely home.

They decided they should shoot another pair of red flares in case the other searching boaters hadn't seen the first signal. It was well past nine p.m., and completely dark by the time they entered the bay. A large group of their family and friends from the village were waiting for them to arrive. The villagers tied up both boats and hugged the stranded boaters and their rescuers in a warm welcome home. It was an experience in which the entire village had played a part.

Every year there were more hotels and homes being built along the shoreline in Cypress Cove, and the summer of 1960 was no different. There was a concern expressed by several locals that the extra people on and around the beaches would disrupt the sea turtles during their nesting season. As a result, the town council initiated a volunteer program to monitor and record sea turtle nests during the nesting and hatching season, from May 1 to October 1.

Volunteers, in groups of two, selected two days a week to walk the beach in the early morning and to record the number of new turtle nests. As nesting season progressed, volunteers would also record the nests that hatched. As soon as Sarah learned about the turtle watch program, she asked Cayman if he would like to volunteer two days a week with her. Of course, she knew he would say yes, since he loved all animals. And she was right. Sarah and Cayman were excited to be part of a team that was helping protect the sea turtles.

Sarah and Cayman were in for a real treat as volunteers of the turtle watch for Cypress Cove. It was going to turn out to be her most adventurous summer so far. They knew they were supposed to find and log new turtle nests, but they did not realize they would see so much more than turtle nests. As usual, Sarah brought her camera hoping to get some special photos during their early-morning beach walks. And she was not disappointed. Sarah and Cayman began their walks half an hour before sunrise. It took about three hours to walk their assigned section of the beach, record the new nests, and walk back.

Their first noteworthy sighting was on their fourth day of volunteering, just as the sun was rising in the eastern sky. They were walking south along the beach at the water's edge, when they noticed a large, seven-foot-long shark swimming south at the same pace as they were walking. Cayman recognized it as a nurse shark, which was not typically aggressive. They continued walking south to finish counting the new nests on their assigned beach, and their new friend, the nurse shark, swam less than two feet away from them for another thirty minutes. Sarah got a few interesting photos of the shark to put in their Sacred Moments photo gallery in the Poaceaehatchee Village.

The nurse shark wasn't the last of the special treats they would encounter during their turtle walks. On every morning walk, they saw dolphins and manatees swimming in the Gulf of Mexico. Sometimes the dolphins were swimming and playing, and other times, they were chasing fish for breakfast. Often the manatees just swam slowly along the shore in the warm waters of the gulf. On one of their nest-counting mornings, they saw a large fever of cownose stingrays swimming just off shore. There must have been more than 500 stingrays! What a sight!

It wasn't just the prospect of seeing large sea life that kept them motivated during their walks. There were many smaller forms of sea life, as well. They saw sea stars, sand dollars, crabs, a variety of fish, and beautiful shore birds. Finding newly laid turtle nests was why they were there, and it was certainly a delight. Yet with all of the other sightings, it seemed like they were always on a treasure hunt.

While Cayman had seen these same sea creatures when fishing with his brother Etu, they somehow seemed more special when seeing them with Sarah. She was curious about everything, laughing with excitement, at the same time getting great photographs.

It was mid-summer and they were about half-way through their turtle watch volunteer assignment. It was a warm morning and the gulf waters were perfectly calm. The sun was just starting to rise in the eastern sky when Sarah and Cayman noticed movement coming toward the water's edge. Cayman knew right away that it was a sea turtle swimming to shore. He had seen the same thing a few years earlier while surf fishing one night with his brother Etu. They stopped walking and stood perfectly still while they watched the water for more signs of movement.

Within a few minutes, they saw a huge momma loggerhead sea turtle swimming toward shore. She ever so slowly crawled from the shallow water onto the sandy beach. Once on the beach, she crawled up to the edge of the grassy dunes and began digging a nest in which to lay her eggs. The female sea turtle spent about twenty minutes digging the nest, then slowly turned around and began laying her eggs in the hole she had dug. Sarah and Cayman stood in amazement while watching from a distance. When she was done laying her eggs, she began covering her nest with sand.

The momma loggerhead slowly crawled toward the water, once the nest was covered with sand and the eggs were protected. She crawled past some seaweed and seashells on the beach and back into the Gulf of Mexico to swim away.

They watched her swim away, as she occasionally popped her head out of the water and took a breath of air. Cayman was excited that Sarah got to witness such a dreamlike miracle of a sea turtle nesting. The remainder of the turtle nesting season flew by for Sarah and Cayman, yet the moments they experienced together were etched in their memories.

While Sarah and Cayman were enjoying their summer on turtle watch patrol, Cypress Cove was continuing with off-season improvements and growth. Many of the improvements made during the summer of 1960 were traffic-flow improvements and aesthetics. With the continued growth in full-time residents, as well as tourists during the dry season, the town council was investing heavily in the town's infrastructure.

Several streets and roads were widened and resurfaced, as well as turn lanes added in high-traffic locations. There was a concerted effort to beautify the landscaping along the streets. Palm trees and flowering shrubs were planted along sidewalks and in median strips. There were more job openings than workers, and Cayman took advantage of the opportunity to work and make some money. It didn't hurt that working for the town of Cypress Cove allowed him to spend more time with Sarah.

As summer came to a close, it was time for seventeen-year-old Sarah to prepare for her senior year at Cypress Cove high school. It was her last year of high school and she had mixed emotions. She was excited to begin planning for college, but a little sad knowing next year she would no longer see her friends every day.

It was her last year to work with Mila and Avery on the school newspaper. The three of them met a few times over the summer planning for their first few stories of the new school year. Sarah, Mila, and Avery were also volunteers for the summer turtle nesting watch program. They agreed that they would write the first few stories about the many changes taking place in Cypress Cove and the volunteer turtle watch program.

Chapter Four

During the first few months back in school, the girls published several stories they planned over the summer. They hoped the turtle watch story would promote awareness for the care and consideration of the environment. The team had also taken photographs and conducted interviews with town council, residents, and workers regarding the rapid growth and changes in Cypress Cove. They released stories to make students aware of how their town was growing and how the growth might impact them for jobs and careers after high school.

During the summer, Sarah also had noticed a loss of the natural vegetation on the beaches due to all of the new condominiums and hotels being built. Because of Cypress Cove's growth, more and more of the mangroves, sand dunes, sea grapes, and sea oats were being removed and replaced with new, non-native landscaping.

She wanted to find a way to protect the natural environment, without negatively impacting development. Sarah knew that developers had a lot of pull with town council, and she must have their support to make it successful. She also realized that what she wanted to do was much bigger than her, and she'd need some high-powered help.

Sarah asked her mom and dad if they had any suggestions about how she should start her conservation effort. Her dad told her that he had written a story a few years ago about a local attorney who fought and won against a planned expansion into a portion of the Florida panther habitat. Sarah asked her dad if he would introduce her to the attorney.

Henry reached out to the attorney, sharing with her what his daughter wanted to accomplish. He asked if the attorney would be willing to meet with Sarah. The attorney liked what she was hearing from Henry, and agreed to meet with Sarah for lunch the following day.

Henry got Sarah excused from school for an hour the following day, and the two of them met the attorney at a small deli near Henry's office. Sarah told the attorney that she would like to find a way to convince builders to leave the natural foliage, instead of tearing it out to put in non-native plants and trees.

The attorney told Sarah that none of the plants she wanted to save were currently protected from trimming or removing. She also said that there were several groups working with the Florida Department of Environmental Protection to put regulations in place, but it was going to take time. It was that moment when Sarah realized that Cypress Cove needed a conservancy to advocate for the land, water, and animals – in town and the surrounding areas. Sarah thought she wouldn't be able to make big changes, but she was not going to give up.

By the time Sarah was mid-way through her senior year of high school, she was completely focused on getting into college. She applied to the Glades University of South Florida; her specific interest was in its Bachelor of Science in Environmental Policy and Management degree program. Sarah had excellent grades and she didn't think there was any reason she wouldn't get accepted.

While she loved and always would love photography, she had found a new passion to pursue. With Cayman's encouragement, her eyes and heart were opened to another passion: protecting nature. Sarah was drawn to finding ways she could make a difference for the Southwest Florida environment. She was excited to start her college studies and a new chapter as a catalyst for change and improvement for all things living.

It had been three weeks since she applied to the Glades University of South Florida, and the letter had finally arrived. She was nervous about opening the letter – what if she hadn't been accepted? She let the letter sit on her dresser for two days before she summoned the courage to open it. As she sat at the dinner table with her parents, she opened the letter, and with a huge smile on her face, she let out a sigh of relief. Sarah had been accepted into the Glades University of South Florida, and she was going to start in the fall. She couldn't wait to tell Cayman. She knew he would be happy for her.

It was spring of 1961, and nearing the end of Sarah's senior year high school. The senior prom was in a couple of weeks, and other than graduation, it was the last big event for Sarah in high school. She had so much fun at the spring dance with Cayman during her junior year, she couldn't wait to go to the senior prom with him. She didn't know it, but Cayman was as excited about the prom as she was.

While the Tutelar had celebrations throughout the school years, they weren't the same as the Cypress Cove dances. Sarah asked Cayman to go with her, and he gladly said yes. Since he met Sarah, Cayman had made quite a few friends in Cypress Cove. He had taken some of them on fishing trips in the Gulf of Mexico and hiking on trails in The Everglades and Cypress Forest. Cayman was most excited about going to the prom with Sarah, yet he also looked forward to seeing his friends.

The day had arrived, and Sarah's mom spent the afternoon helping her get ready. They styled Sarah's hair in a classy updo style, with a few strands of her long, dark hair flowing down her back. She put on the dress they made for her special day. It was a long, light-blue, sleeveless dress with thin shoulder straps.

She was nearly ready when Cayman knocked on their door. Sarah's dad welcomed him in to sit and wait a few minutes, while Sarah finished dressing. This year Cayman had his own suit; it was a light-gray suit, and he wore a white shirt and a light-blue tie. He sat patiently waiting for Sarah, while he and her dad talked. Soon Sarah and her mom appeared from her room, and Cayman jumped from the chair. A little embarrassed over his excitement, he told her how nice she looked. Cayman placed a corsage on Sarah's wrist – one he had made before he left the village. Sarah pinned on Cayman's jacket lapel a single flower that she had picked from the park across the street.

Sarah's mom wanted to take a few outdoor photographs of Sarah and Cayman before they left for the prom. The four of them walked a short distance to a small park near the town center. The park's gazebo, with a small picnic table, was shaded by a large banyan tree. Sarah and Cayman posed there for several photographs for her mom.

Her parents were so proud of the two of them, how they had grown into good friends and respectable young adults. Sarah's parents had become quite fond of Cayman, and they trusted the two of them to be careful and always do the right thing. Even so, it was prom night, and her parents relayed the rules for the night before hugging them both and sending them on their way.

Cayman was still borrowing his friend's pickup truck to go back and forth to Cypress Cove and that night was no different. They hopped into the truck and headed off to dinner before the prom. They had heard about a new restaurant that had recently opened on the edge of the Pavati River. It was known for its excellent seafood dishes and open-air dining, both of which Sarah and Cayman enjoyed.

Cayman had made reservations in advance, so they would be sure to get a well-situated table on the deck overlooking the water. They talked all through dinner about how Sarah would soon be graduating and going to college. They enjoyed dinner while the sun was setting, then headed out of the restaurant for the prom.

Chapter Four

The prom was held at the Cypress Cove Yacht Club, located near the town docks on the Pavati Bay. The yacht club was a two-story building with a grand ballroom and an outdoor balcony on the second floor. The balcony overlooked the bay where there were several sail boats and motor boats docked. The ballroom was decorated for the prom. An entire wall in the ballroom, facing the balcony, had sliding doors open to the outside.

It was a picture-perfect location for the high school prom. Sarah and Cayman talked and laughed with friends and danced all evening. Cayman drove Sarah back to her parents' apartment and kissed her goodnight before driving back to his home at the Poaceaehatchee Village. It had been an even more perfect evening than either of them anticipated it would be. Neither of them slept that night, thinking about how much fun they had and how much they enjoyed being together.

The next two weeks flew by as the Cypress Cove senior class finished their exams and prepared for graduation. It was a beautiful, warm, sunny day for the graduation ceremony of the Cypress Cove High School seniors. Sarah was excited to graduate high school and start her next chapter in life's journey, yet she was sad that she would not see her friends every day like she did during the school year.

Sarah's parents, Cayman, and his family were all there to support Sarah during her graduation ceremony. There were 89 senior students graduating as the class of 1961. The graduation ceremony took place on the football field next to the high school. The attendees were seated in the grandstands. Chairs and a stage were set up on the fifty-yard line for the graduates to receive their diplomas. Sarah was the class valedictorian; she shared a moving graduation message with her fellow graduates.

"Teachers, administrators, parents, and Cypress Cove High School class of 1961. I welcome you to our

graduation ceremony on this beautiful spring day. It's an exciting time for all of us. We are about to leave the sanctuary of high school, where we have spent the last four years, to enter the world as adults. As we move on to the next chapter in our lives, many changes are coming our way. Some of us will stay friends forever. Others will move away from Cypress Cove to start their lives. Some will go to college, and some will get jobs directly out of high school. Some will get married and have children, and some might never get married or have children. No single one of these options is right for everyone. Each of us is on an individual journey in life, and each will find a path and figure out how and where to travel in this journey.

What I would like all of us to consider is this. We are the next group of stewards – caretakers – of the planet on which we live. While we move into this next chapter of our adventure in life, please consider how each one of us impacts the land, water, and air upon which we rely. Please also remember that we share this planet with the animals, birds, and sea life, and we have a responsibility to ensure that we provide a safe and clean environment for all. Every job we take, every decision we make, has an impact on our planet and how we leave it for the next generations to come. As you get married and have children of your own, please remember to instill in them these same values of stewardship. We only get one planet, and it's up to us to take care of it and make sure others get to enjoy the things we've enjoyed as we've grown up.

In closing, I would like to remind you that we

will always have our four years together at Cypress Cove High School. Never forget the adventures you had and the friendships you made during your four years of high school. I congratulate you for your accomplishments, and I wish each of you a joyful, successful, and happy life. It's up to you to make your dreams come true. Congratulations!"

Chapter Five

The storyteller tells her daughter, "Honey, I think we should take a break for now." Her daughter replied, "Mom, please, please keep going."

"Okay, honey. Well, this is where they find out that Cayman was, I mean is Grayson Taylor."

Little did Sarah and Cayman know that the summer of 1961 was going to be a turning point in their lives. The population of Cypress Cove had doubled in the past few years and with the growth came a demand for people to help during the busy season. Men and women from the Poaceaehatchee Village were coming to Cypress Cove to work many of the jobs the locals could no longer support.

They worked in restaurants, on fishing charters, and in the hotels. They would tell visitors and tourists stories of their village and of the Tutelar people. One of the stories often told was that many years ago a plane crashed near their village, and a little boy was taken in and raised by their people. Sarah had heard the stories and was certain that Cayman was the boy they were talking about.

Realizing she caught a single photo of a boy five years earlier, she frantically searched through her old photographs. She found the photograph with the boy standing behind the Tutelar elders. There was no doubt in her mind that the boy they were talking about in the stories and the boy in the photograph was the same person, Cayman. She rushed to the village to ask Cayman if he was the boy from the plane crash. They talked and cried for hours about things Cayman had never shared. He told Sarah about the crash and his mom's final request of the Tutelar: "Please take care of my son Grayson." Cayman told Sarah his mom's last words to him were, "Honey, follow your heart and your dreams. You can be whatever you want to be and whatever you chose to be." He described his parents' funerals, and how the Deere family took him in as their own son.

Sarah and Cayman were uncertain about what to do next, but they knew they needed help. They decided it would be best to talk with the Tutelar elders and their parents to get advice. Since they were already at the Poaceaehatchee Village, Cayman and Sarah met with the elders first. They explained that the story about the plane crash was being told to the people in Cypress Cove and it was only a matter of time until others would figure out that Cayman was the boy in the story. The Tutelar were simply honoring his mother's dying wish, "to please take care of my son."

The Tutelar knew that this day would come, and they were prepared to have this conversation when Cayman was old enough to understand. Cayman ran home to get his parents to join the elders in this conversation. The Deeres brought with them a box of the Taylors' belongings from the crash. The box contained family photographs and his parents' jewelry. Also in the box was the original flight plan, information about the land they owned in Cypress Cove, and documents about Taylor Tire.

The elders told Cayman and Sarah that it was time for Cayman to follow this path to find out who he was and where he came from. Sarah and Cayman were relieved to have had the conversation with the Deeres and Tutelar elders. Grateful for the conversations and advice, they went to Cypress Cove to talk with Sarah's parents.

Sarah and Cayman sat with Vicki and Henry Cooper at their home in Cypress Cove to explain these new-found facts. They started the conversation by telling Sarah's parents that Cayman's given name was Grayson Taylor. Cayman explained that he was born in Dimerling, Ohio, and lived there until he was five years old. He told the Coopers that his parents were the founders of Taylor Tire and

Rubber Company. The two of them showed her parents the box of his parents' belongings from the crash.

Sarah and Cayman paused while the Coopers grasped what they just heard. After a long pause, Cayman went on to explain what he remembered and understood from the crash in the summer of 1948, when he was just five years old. He described the traditional Tutelar funerals for his dad and mom, including the spreading of their ashes at the crash site. Cayman told them about his mom's last words to him and her final request of the Tutelar. He told the Coopers how the Deere family had taken him in as one of their own. He described growing up and living with his brother Etu. The Coopers sat in silence, often with a tear running down a cheek, while Cayman told his story. He was relieved to finally talk about his past, and also to ask the Coopers for their guidance.

Cayman showed them the official papers from the box of belongings gathered from the crash site. Sarah's dad found a document that listed the Taylors' family attorney as Aubrey Hayes. They decided it would be best to call Aubrey and tell her Cayman's story. Surprisingly, Cayman was successful in reaching Aubrey on his first attempt. After sharing his story with Aubrey, Cayman asked her what he should do next. She immediately cleared her schedule and took the first flight to Cypress Cove to meet Cayman, Sarah, the Deeres, and the Coopers.

The Coopers, Sarah, and Cayman picked up Aubrey from the airport, took her to dinner, then to the Clearwater Inn to spend the night. Cayman stayed the night at the Coopers. No one slept at all that night. The next day, Henry collected Aubrey from the hotel and brought her to the Coopers' apartment for Cayman to tell her his story.

Cayman told Aubrey everything he had told the Coopers a few days earlier. He also showed her the box of belongings from the crash. Aubrey was quiet as she went through the box and remembered her very good friends, the Taylors. She always believed the Taylors might still be alive and she never petitioned the courts to declare them deceased. Aubrey was so happy that Cayman had survived the crash. As Cayman would later learn, Aubrey was his godmother.

The next day, the Coopers drove Cayman and Aubrey to the Poaceaehatchee Village to talk with the elders and the Deeres. The Tutelar described details of the crash and subsequent events just as Cayman had described the previous day. They told her about the plane crash near where some of the villagers had been fishing. How they brought Mary, Robert, and Grayson back to the village. The elders told Aubrey that Mary Taylor's final request of them was to take care of her son. They described the Tutelar funeral they had conducted for his dad, then again for his mom only a few days later.

The Deeres described how they raised Grayson with their son Etu. They told Aubrey that Grayson – now Cayman, was a respected member of the village, and he had proven himself as a Tutelar adult man by completing the rite-of-passage ritual. They were proud to call him Tutelar. Aubrey was thoroughly convinced that Cayman was Grayson Taylor.

Aubrey, Cayman, and the Coopers drove back to Cypress Cove to plan next steps. Henry and Aubrey developed a plan for releasing Cayman's story to the public. Hearing Cayman's story once in the Coopers' home and again with the Tutelar elders, Henry was the most informed and appropriate person to write the story. He would be much more sensitive to Cayman's privacy and feelings than a stranger.

Aubrey requested that Henry write the story, then send it to her for presentation to the Taylor Tire and Rubber Company Board of Directors. She and Henry agreed to a plan – she would notify him when it was the just the right time to release the story to several news outlets at the same time as she was presenting to the company's board. Aubrey wanted to make sure that the Taylor Tire board and leadership team were informed prior to the news hitting the headlines. Henry wrote a brilliant story, balancing the details of the events of the crash in 1948 with the remarkable life Cayman led as a Tutelar.

Aubrey was not going to let Cayman travel to Ohio alone. She spent the next couple of days in Cypress Cove helping him prepare for the trip. She made arrangements to have Cayman's childhood home in Dimerling opened and prepared for his arrival.

During the last few days in Cypress Cove, Sarah and Cayman spent several hours talking about his trip to Ohio and her leaving for Glades University of South Florida. Neither of them had left yet, but they already missed each other. They made plans to write each other regularly and to call each other when possible.

Sarah and her parents said goodbye to Cayman and wished him luck as he and Aubrey drove away to the airport. Cayman had only been on an airplane one time in his life and it was 13 years ago when he and his parents had crashed in The Everglades. In the Poaceaehatchee Village, he was known for being brave, but he was anxious about the flight. Aubrey was able to help Cayman get comfortable with the prospect of flying as they made their way to the Cypress Cove Airport. The flight went off without a hitch and they made it to the Dimerling, Ohio, airport smoothly.

Chapter Five

Upon landing at the Dimerling airport, Aubrey drove Cayman to his family home and helped him get settled. Even though Cayman was 18 and an adult, he was not accustomed to living outside of the Poaceaehatchee Village. Aubrey made arrangements for a driver and someone to help at his home until he felt comfortable on his own.

There was a lot to do over the next several days. As the Taylor family attorney, Cayman's godmother, and executor of the family trust, Aubrey cleared her schedule to focus solely on helping Cayman. She informed the other partners at her law firm that she was taking care of Cayman for as long as he needed her. Perhaps she felt a strong obligation to the Taylors, maybe she was captivated with the mystery, or perhaps she was making up for lost time. Either way, Aubrey was all in for whatever Cayman needed.

Cayman was trying to get used to living in his parents' home, where he spent his first five years as a child. He had memories of living in Dimerling with his parents, but he had not remembered how enormous their home was.

The Taylor Estate was three stories tall, with what seemed to be an endless number of rooms. The two large, wooden front doors opened into a large foyer entryway and a ceiling that was two stories tall. At the end of the foyer was a large wooden staircase with carpet in the center of each step.

The steps rose to the second floor, where there was an open mezzanine that overlooked the first-floor foyer. Several bedrooms and bathrooms surrounded the outer edges of the mezzanine. Cayman imagined how many families from the Poaceaehatchee Village could easily live in this grand home. It was a lonely place for one person to live. He was grateful to have Boone with him.

The outside and surrounding property was even more grand. The estate was set on twelve acres of land with woods and a lake. There were two pools – one a large swimming pool and the other a shallow wading and reflection pool. The grounds included several flower gardens with different themes and were connected by gravel and grass paths.

The garage was so large it could hold eight vehicles, and it was full of cars, tractors, and equipment. It was all so much more than what Cayman was used to growing up in the Poaceaehatchee Village. While Cayman was thankful that his parents had been prepared for the potential that someday they would be gone, he wasn't sure that this place was for him. Out of respect for his parents, he mustered all of his courage and energy into honoring their legacy, their home, and their company.

Getting Cayman and Boone safely and comfortably to Ohio had been Aubrey's top priority. Her next priority was to notify the Taylor Tire and Rubber Company Board of Directors and the company leadership team that Grayson was alive and in Dimerling. The Taylor Tire board and leadership team did not know him as Cayman, so she needed to refer to him as Grayson. Aubrey's and Henry's plan was to release Grayson's story to several national news outlets, once she had told the board and leadership team that he was alive and in Dimerling.

Aubrey contacted the Taylor Tire and Rubber board chairman and requested a special meeting with the board and leadership team for the evening of August 15, 1961. Once she confirmed the meeting time and date, she contacted Henry, in preparation for releasing Grayson's story to the media. The board meeting was scheduled to start at six p.m. Henry and Aubrey agreed that he would release Grayson's story to the news wire at eight p.m. that same night.

Aubrey waited patiently as the chairperson confirmed that there was a quorum and called the meeting to order. Then Aubrey proceeded to tell the Taylor Tire board and leadership team that Grayson Taylor was alive and staying at his parents' estate in Dimerling. She read to them the prepared news release written by Henry Cooper.

Aubrey shared with the board and leadership team how the Tutelar found the Taylors after their plane crashed in The Everglades. She described Robert Taylor's funeral, followed by Mary Taylor's funeral only a few days later. She shared Mary's final request to the Tutelar: "Please take care of my son Grayson." Aubrey described how Grayson was taken in and raised in the Poaceaehatchee Village by the Deere family. She explained how he went to the Poaceaehatchee school and completed the rite of passage to become a Tutelar adult. She told the board and leadership team that Grayson's story was going to be released to the news wire later that night.

Nearly half of the board and a few of the leadership team were new to Taylor Tire and Rubber, and they did not personally know the Taylors. They only knew of them through conversations with company employees or what they had read in the newspaper over the years. Even so, they all sat in quiet amazement while Aubrey shared with them Grayson's story.

At that moment, no one knew what Grayson's return meant for Taylor Tire and Rubber Company. Those who were longtime friends of the Taylor family were looking forward to meeting Grayson. Others were skeptical of what they were hearing. They tried to

convince Aubrey to hold off on releasing the story, but she pushed
back. She told the board and leaders that she was certain that he was
Grayson Taylor, and that the news would certainly get out and they
needed to manage the messaging.

As previously planned, at eight p.m. that evening, Henry went
into the Cypress Cove Chronicle news desk to release Grayson's
story. Under his name, he sent Grayson's story to print in Cypress
Cove, and transmitted it nationwide to the major news outlets. Aubrey
knew that once his story was released, reporters would flock to
Grayson to get more of his story. She let him know to be prepared and
that she would be with him every step of the way.

Even though the board had an open mind to the news they had
just heard, they knew that they had a duty to their shareholders to
verify the story. They decided to launch an independent investigation
to determine the authenticity of Aubrey's and Grayson's story. The
Taylor Tire board hired South Florida Investigation Services from
Miami, which was the original investigative services company that
looked for the Taylors in 1948. The board assigned an internal point
of contact to work with a team of two from the investigative services
company. Bonnie Hope, the head of human resources, was assigned
as the liaison and point person to work with South Florida
Investigation Services.

Bonnie shared the newspaper story and had several
conversations with the investigative team. She described the details
about Aubrey's presentation to the Taylor Tire board, regarding the
Taylors' plight on July 4, 1948, and the time that followed. She told
them about the crash and how the Tutelar conducted funerals for
Robert Taylor, and a few days later for Mary Taylor. Bonnie
explained how the Deere family had raised Grayson in the
Poaceaehatchee Village.

Chapter Five

Bonnie instructed the investigative team to start by going to the Poaceaehatchee Village to meet with the Tutelar elders. She told the team that the Tutelar had been open to and helpful with Aubrey. She wanted a full and detailed report from the time the Taylors left Dimerling on July 2, 1948, until the current date. Bonnie told the investigative team that the report needed to include details about the crash, what happened to Mary and Robert Taylor, and Grayson's life with the Tutelar. She instructed them to go to the crash site and verify that it was, in fact, the Taylors' Cessna 170 airplane.

The investigative team felt that they were well informed and clear about the scope of their assignment. The team of two investigators drove from Miami to the Poaceaehatchee Village to meet with the Tutelar elders. The Tutelar were welcoming, open, and cooperative with the investigators. To them, Grayson was one of their own and they felt obligated to help others understand and support his story.

The elders began the story of the Taylors by recounting Mary Taylor's final request, asking them to, "Please take care of my son Grayson." They wanted the investigators to clearly understand that everything they did for Grayson, was to honor his mother's dying wishes.

The elders described how a few of their villagers were out fishing when they saw the plane crash into the mangroves. They were fishing on the edge of The Everglades a few miles east of the Poaceaehatchee Village. They rushed to the site of the crash to find Mary, Robert, and Grayson Taylor, along with Grayson's dog, Luna. They carefully extracted the Taylors from the plane and collected any personal belongings that they could salvage. Then, as quickly and carefully as possible, they brought the Taylors and their belongings back to the village.

The elders told the two investigators that Robert Taylor had died during the plane crash. They explained how they tried to save Mary Taylor, but she survived only four more days. The elders described the Tutelar funeral they held for Robert Taylor, followed by another funeral a few days later for Mary Taylor.

The Tutelar elders offered to take the two investigators to the crash site to see the plane. They told the team, in advance, that the crash site was now a sacred burial ground and they could not disturb it. The two investigators wanted to go to the crash site to verify the identification of the plane by its tail number. The crash site was only reachable by water, so two of the elders guided the investigators to the village docks to get a boat. The four of them traveled to the crash site a few miles east of the village. The investigators were able to confirm it was the Taylors' Cessna, by matching the tail number with their flight plan from July of 1948.

Upon confirming that it was the Taylors' plane that crashed in The Everglades, the investigators wanted to meet with the Deere family. They wanted to learn about Grayson's childhood and growing up in the Poaceaehatchee Village. Sakari and Alo Deere met with the investigators. They described Grayson's life – from the plane crash when he was five years old, until he completed his rite-of-passage ceremony. Etu described how he and Grayson went to school together and grew up together as brothers.

Having spent time with the Tutelar elders and the Deere family, the investigation team believed that they had all of the information they needed to create and submit their report. The evidence was overwhelming that Aubrey's and Grayson's story was true, and that Grayson was who he claimed to be. The two investigators submitted their report to Bonnie Hope at Taylor Tire, confirming the story of the Taylor family's crash and Grayson's life in the Poaceaehatchee Village.

Chapter Five

While the investigators were in Florida conducting their investigation with the Tutelar, Bonnie set up meetings with Aubrey and Grayson. She wanted to hear Grayson's story directly from him, and she wanted to examine the papers, photos, and other possessions kept from the crash.

Bonnie knew the Taylors well, and she had met Grayson several times at his home and at the Taylor Tire offices, when he was a young boy. There were often occasions when Mary and Robert brought Grayson to their offices, while they worked. She had also met Grayson at the Taylor Estate during company picnics and holiday parties.

Early the next morning, Aubrey and Grayson arrived at Taylor Tire and Rubber to meet with Bonnie. Bonnie wanted Grayson to feel at ease, so she had scheduled the meeting to be held in the company library room. It was a comfortable room; she had arranged for refreshments and brought in large, soft chairs.

Bonnie didn't recognize him as Grayson right away, but it didn't take a lot of time and discussion for her to notice his mannerisms, which reminded her of Mary and Robert Taylor. She asked Grayson questions about his childhood home in Dimerling and his memories from visiting his parents' company. While Grayson was only five years old, he did describe a few memories from visiting the company. Yet, the most vivid memories he described were of playing and swimming with his dog Luna at their home. Grayson shared with Bonnie the box of possessions saved from the crash. He showed her photographs, papers of the Cypress Cove property, and documents regarding Taylor Tire.

Between Bonnie's meetings with Grayson and Aubrey and the South Florida Investigation Services report, there was no doubt that it was Grayson Taylor in her office. Bonnie and Aubrey met with the

Board of Directors and the leadership team to present the findings and to determine the next steps.

The board and leadership team quickly accepted Bonnie's conclusion that Grayson Taylor was alive and that they needed to welcome him into the Taylor Tire and Rubber Company. Bonnie volunteered to work with Aubrey and the leadership team to develop an orientation plan that would welcome Grayson into the organization. The board agreed and asked the other department heads to support her in developing an orientation plan for Grayson.

The next several days were consumed with Aubrey getting Grayson settled in to his home in Dimerling. She told him that he would go by the name Grayson while in Dimerling and at Taylor Tire and Rubber Company. There was a lot of information coming at Grayson from all directions. He and Aubrey met every day to ensure he was not getting overwhelmed and to adjust his responsibilities and activities, as needed. Aubrey told Grayson that she would help him manage any questions from the news media. Aubrey turned out to be a lifesaver for Grayson. Certainly, his parents would have been pleased with how she committed herself and her time to help him succeed.

Over the next few days, Aubrey had set aside time to review all of the family and company legal documents with Grayson. It was a lot of information, but he was up to the task. They first reviewed his parents' will and trust. Since his mom was an attorney, all of the legal documents were well thought out and complete with detailed instructions. Even though Cayman had not gone by Grayson for many years, of course all of the legal documents were under his given name, Grayson Taylor. Aubrey told Cayman, that from a legal perspective

Chapter Five

and for now, he would need to go by Grayson when signing legal documents.

The will and trust were set up with Aubrey as the executor and power of attorney. The documents stated that in the event of Mary's and Robert's deaths, everything was to go to Grayson. Since the majority of their belongings were in the Taylor Family Trust, it was a rather simple process to transfer the property and assets.

Even though they had not been heard from for all of those years, Aubrey always held on to the hope that the Taylors were alive and would one day be found. Since they were never found, she didn't petition the court to declare the members of the Taylor family deceased. Since, in the court's eyes, Grayson was living in Southwest Florida – not dead and never really lost, there was no issue with executing the will and trust as written.

The property element of the trust included the family estate with twelve acres of land in Dimerling and a seventy-five-acre tract of land on the south side of Cypress Cove. Grayson was surprised to learn about the land in Cypress Cove. He knew exactly where this land was located, and had no idea it was his parents' property.

Also included in the property was all of the furniture and belongings in the home and several vehicles and pieces of equipment in the garage. There were various pieces of small equipment, two tractors, and four vehicles, which included a 1948 Dodge pickup truck, 1947 Chevrolet Fleetmaster Convertible, 1947 Cadillac, and a 1946 Ford Super DeLuxe Tudor sedan. Aubrey told Grayson that his parents supported their largest customers from each automobile manufacturer – that's why they had four vehicles! All of the vehicles were more than fifteen years old, and they had sat in the garage without being driven since 1948. They all had low mileage and were in new condition.

Additional assets included Mary's and Robert's life insurance policies, as well as their savings, checking, and investment accounts. Grayson also inherited his parents' stake in Taylor Tire and Rubber Company, which represented fifty-one percent of the company stock. Aubrey took her time explaining the documents, answering questions, and defining what all of this meant for Grayson. It was a lot for Grayson to take in and to think about. While Aubrey was processing the signed documents, Grayson's next step was to start learning about Taylor Tire and Rubber Company's products and business.

Chapter Six

It was a confusing time for Grayson. When he was talking with Sarah and his family, he was Cayman. Yet, when he was involved with Taylor Tire and Rubber Company business, he was Grayson. For the next three years, Grayson worked at Taylor Tire and Rubber Company, while Sarah attended her freshman, sophomore, and junior years at the Glades University of South Florida. They arranged to spend time together in Dimerling, Cypress Cove, and Miami, and they wrote each other every day. Sarah updated Cayman on her college studies, and Cayman updated Sarah on his new life at Taylor Tire and Rubber Company.

In the fall of 1961, 18-year-old Grayson was acknowledged as the major shareholder at Taylor Tire and Rubber. The leadership team accepted and welcomed him into the company. Bonnie worked with others to arrange an office space for Grayson – one that would make him feel welcome and at home. She arranged to have several items of his mom's and dad's taken out of storage and placed in his new office.

With input from the leadership team, Bonnie defined a three-year orientation program for Grayson. The program was designed so he would receive training on all aspects of the company. The first year of the plan Grayson was scheduled to work in the plant operations. During the second year he would spend his time in various office functions. For the final, third year of orientation, Grayson would be working directly with the leadership team.

The first year of orientation was underway; Grayson spent it in plant operations, working two months in each of the six key manufacturing departments: compounding and mixing, component preparation, tire building, curing, final finish, and shipping and receiving. Grayson was not afraid of hard work and he put everything he had into learning how tires were manufactured. He wanted very much to be considered one of the team. Grayson worked extra hard to keep the same pace of work, and the same high-quality levels as the other workers in manufacturing.

Grayson soon found a daily routine as one of the workers in a manufacturing facility. He got up early to make his breakfast and pack his lunch. Whenever the morning weather was nice enough, he sat outside with Boone to eat his breakfast. Boone and Grayson went for walks around the gardens and in the woods before Grayson left for work.

Each morning he went out to the garage and looked over the vehicles to choose from. Every time, he chose the 1948 Dodge pickup truck. It was one of the few things in Dimerling that reminded him of home in the village. He drove the truck to the company, worked in the plant for ten hours, then drove back to the estate for the evening.

Grayson spent every spare minute he could outside with Boone in the gardens and woods. The next day, he did it all over again. He was raised to not give up and to own his responsibilities, and while he was not yet sure that this was a life for him, he tried to make it work.

The first manufacturing department Grayson worked in was compounding and mixing. There he learned how to properly mix the raw materials necessary to make rubber for building tires. Huge quantities of sulfur, carbon black, synthetic rubber, oils, and other chemicals were delivered into the plant by railcars. He measured batches of raw materials that were mixed multiple times in preparation for the next steps in manufacturing tires.

Once he was properly trained on compounding and mixing, he moved to the component preparation department. Grayson and others in the department prepared and arranged the mold components and tooling necessary to build the tires. His next assignment was to build tires. To build a tire, he took rolls of rubber and other components and used a tire building machine to form a raw tire. After a few months of building raw tires, Grayson moved into the curing department and final finish. There he vulcanized the rubber for flexibility, engraved the sidewalls and tread pattern for the final shape of the tire.

Grayson's yearlong orientation in manufacturing was completed by spending two months in shipping and receiving. While in receiving, he logged, moved, and stored raw materials and building components. He also delivered materials and components to departments when needed for production. In shipping, Grayson pulled finished tires from inventory and loaded trucks for customer delivery. He set high standards for himself and he worked hard to complete the manufacturing portion of the orientation program. With his hard work and dedication, he earned the respect of his fellow workers in those six key manufacturing departments.

While Grayson was working through his orientation journey with Taylor Tire, Sarah was attending her freshman year at the Glades University of South Florida. They wrote each other daily letters. When writing and talking on the telephone, they both referred to him as Cayman, not Grayson. In every letter, Cayman included a sketch to Sarah and Sarah included a photograph to Cayman. They talked on the telephone every chance they could get. They talked about her classes at the Glades University of South Florida and how work was going at Taylor Tire. They reminisced about their Southwest Florida adventures that they desperately missed.

The two of them talked about the beautiful, green scenery, the crazy and funny things the birds and animals did, all of the things in nature that they both loved. It was a confusing time for both of them; they missed their homes in Southwest Florida and they missed each other desperately.

While they hadn't said it yet, they could feel that they were deeply in love with each other, and their love was growing stronger every day that they were apart. They were able to spend time together during the holidays, when Sarah went back to Cypress Cove and Cayman went back to Poaceaehatchee Village. They didn't miss a chance to see each other and were together as much as possible.

This was their first year apart from each other and away from home since first meeting four years earlier, during Sarah's school newspaper assignment at the Poaceaehatchee Village. While it was difficult being apart for both of them, it was much easier for Sarah than it was for Cayman. Sarah was still in sunny, warm Florida, and she loved her environmental management studies at the Glades University of South Florida.

Cayman spent most of his life growing up in the warm outdoors of Southwest Florida. He had forgotten what the dramatic changes in weather – from spring, summer, fall and winter – were like in Ohio. He thought spring was pretty, when the trees sprouted their leaves and the plants were popping up from the ground. He loved the hot summer, and the fall colors were amazing. It was the cold and gray winter that bothered him the most.

Eighteen-year-old Sarah settled in to her freshman year of the Environmental Policy and Management degree program easily during the fall of 1961. She liked the school, professors, and she made many new friends. She found the classroom portion of her degree program interesting and informative.

Most of her freshman classes were basic, setting the foundation of learning about the two key components of her degree program. The science component included a variety of classes focused on the interactions between the biological, chemical, and physical elements of the global natural environment. There was careful study and investigation of the human impact on the environment. The policy component utilized the learnings from science to define, develop, and implement policy-level solutions to environmental issues.

One of the environmental science classes that struck Sarah was "Human Impact to South Florida." It was a two-semester class on the human impact to the land, birds, and animals of South Florida. Sarah found the entire class captivating, but one topic that captured her interest in particular was the plight of the snowy egret. The snowy egret was one of Sarah's favorite birds to see and photograph. After learning about its challenges from human interactions, Sarah's respect and admiration of the snowy egret grew even more.

She learned that in the late 1800s and early 1900s, snowy egrets were nearly wiped out by hunters. There was a high demand for the egrets' snowy white feathers. Women used the feathers as stylish trimmings for their hats. By 1910, there was prohibition of the plume trade, and the snowy egrets' numbers rose. By 1950, they had recovered to their peak population numbers.

While the snowy egret was recovering from hunters, they faced new challenges from humans. Construction and development was booming on both coasts in South Florida, pushing all wading birds, like the snowy egrets, out of their natural environments.

The sugarcane industry was also booming and expanding south of Lake Okeechobee. It was taking over more and more of The Everglade wetlands for expanded planting fields. Wetlands and rivers were either drying up or becoming contaminated with pesticides, heavy metals, or other runoff contaminants. For the snowy egret, finding new habitats meant facing new dangers and predators.

After learning about the difficulties the snowy egret faced over the last seventy-five years, Sarah hoped to share her fondness of Florida birds with her classmates. It took very little convincing by Sarah to recruit a few of her classmates to be involved in weekly bird-watching explorations. They met each Saturday morning at the university campus and drove to different parks or locations.

Each location was within a short, thirty-minute drive from campus. Ready with binoculars, cameras, drinking water, and hiking gear, they found and logged a variety of birds in their native habitats. While walking near shallow water, Sarah snapped a photograph of a snowy egret that just caught a small fish for breakfast.

Sarah was the only student in the Saturday morning bird-watching group who lived in Florida. The others in the group were new to Florida, and had never seen most of the birds they were finding and logging. Within the first three Saturdays, they found and logged more than fifteen species of South Florida birds.

During the first week, they logged great white egrets, snowy egrets, white ibises, seagulls, a snail kite, and a blue heron. On the morning of the second Saturday, they documented pelicans, double-crested cormorants, tricolored herons, and a rarer find – three Roseate spoonbills. The next Saturday, they added wood storks, anhingas, cattle egrets, woodpeckers, and a red-shouldered hawk to their list.

While driving back to the campus, one of Sarah's classmates pointed to the sky at two birds flying along with the car. She asked Sarah, "What are those two, giant pink birds flying over there?" Sarah saw the birds her classmate was pointing to, and with excitement told the others, "Those are flamingos, and very rare to see flying in the wild!"

Seeing how interested her classmates had been during the Saturday bird-watching expeditions, Sarah asked if they would be interested in driving about twice as far the next Saturday. She described Marsh Trail and how hundreds of snowy egrets and other birds perched on the trees until sunrise, when they all took flight to begin their day. They agreed to meet the next Saturday at the campus about ninety minutes before sunrise for the one-hour drive to Marsh Trail.

Word must have spread to others in their class. When Sarah arrived at their meeting place on Saturday morning, her two bird-watching classmates were there waiting. With them, were two additional students who wanted to see the egrets at Marsh Trail. Sarah was pleased to see that more students were taking an interest in the Florida birds. The larger group of students piled into one of the cars and headed west on the SoFlo Trail. After driving for an hour, Sarah pointed ahead to a sandy, limestone parking lot, and she told the driver to park in the lot.

When they got out of the car to stretch their legs, it was still thirty minutes before sunrise. Sarah explained it was a fifteen-minute

 walk to the lookout tower, where they were going to see the egrets and watch the sun rise. She and her classmates arrived at the lookout tower fifteen minutes before sunrise.

As they gazed across the open expanse,

they saw hundreds and hundreds of white birds perched in the tree tops. Sarah took a photograph of the white tipped trees as they all watched in wonderment.

As the sun was about to rise, Sarah pointed east, out over The Everglades. They watched the sun begin to rise above the horizon. It was a giant orange ball of fire, over a low-lying fog in The Everglades.

They turned back around, to look south at the trees, just in time. They saw what looked like a choreographed dance of hundreds of snowy egrets, great white egrets, and blue herons taking flight at the same time. First, they saw the birds take off, then a few seconds later they heard the sound of the flapping of their wings, while the birds chirped their morning songs. They talked the whole way back to campus about the spectacular morning it was! Sarah was delighted that her classmates enjoyed the morning bird-watching adventure at Marsh Trail.

Sarah's freshman year flew by quickly for her, and soon she was back in Cypress Cove for the summer of 1962. During her first summer back in Cypress Cove, between her college freshman and sophomore years, Sarah visited the Sacred Moments Photo Gallery at the Poaceaehatchee Village.

Her idea was to submit several new photographs to sell in the gallery, and to meet with the two young Tutelar ladies running the gallery in her absence. She had been training and mentoring Aiyana and Elu to eventually take over running the gallery. She had taught them how to take and develop photographs, and she had given them some of her photo equipment – camera, tripod, lenses, and flashes – to get started.

Chapter Six

The two of them were becoming proficient photographers, and they were adding many of their own photos to the gallery walls. Visitors and tourists to the village regularly purchased their photographs. Aiyana and Elu agreed that they would take over running the gallery, paying the rent, and selling Sarah's photographs, while retaining a small fee. They were all happy with the new arrangement. Sarah had planned give the two ladies full control of the gallery once she graduated from college and started her own career.

Cayman took two weeks off from Taylor Tire and Rubber to spend the Fourth of July in Cypress Cove with Sarah. They were excited to finally get to spend time together again. Cayman had missed Sarah and everything about warm, sunny Southwest Florida.

He was looking forward to seeing his family and friends, too, and, quite honestly, getting back to nature. He was so excited to get to home; he and Boone hopped into his dad's 1948 Dodge pickup truck, and drove twenty hours straight through. They arrived at the Poaceaehatchee Village on Sunday, July 1, 1962. He was exhausted when he arrived, but happy to see his family.

Cayman slept for a couple of hours, then drove to Sarah's house to see her and to prepare for their two weeks together. He talked with Henry and Vicki for a while, telling them about how he was adjusting to Dimerling, Ohio, and Taylor Tire and Rubber. Then he and Sarah left for a walk and to catch up on everything that had happened since they last saw each other.

For the next couple of days, Sarah and Cayman visited friends in Cypress Cove and at the Poaceaehatchee Village. On the Fourth of July, they arranged to watch the fireworks from the beach at the Kendrick Pier, with both of their families.

Sarah, Cayman, and Etu, along with Boone, arrived at the pier earlier than the rest. They spent the afternoon enjoying some time swimming in the gulf and relaxing on the beach. They brought food and drinks for lunch and extra snacks for in the evening, when their parents arrived.

Sarah's mom and dad arrived at seven o'clock, and joined them near the pier on the beach. They talked about how nice the gulf water was, and what a fine day it turned out to be for the fireworks. Cayman's and Etu's parents arrived about an hour later. They all hugged and sat down on the beach in preparation for the fireworks. They all shared the snacks and drinks they had brought.

The Fourth of July had a special meaning to Cayman and his adopted family. It was 14 years ago, on July 4, that the Taylors' plane had crashed into The Everglades near the Poaceaehatchee Village. Cayman would never forget that time; both of his parents had died tragically. It was also the day that his new life began with the Tutelar in the Poaceaehatchee Village, when Sakari and Alo Deere took him in to live with them and their son Etu.

It was almost dusk, and the fireworks would be starting soon. Cayman's adopted mom, Sakari, asked if it would be okay to say a Tutelar spirit prayer in honor of his parents. They all said yes, and were quiet and thoughtful as Sakari shared her prayer.

"Great Spirit, who brings us air, water, and food. We know that Mary and Robert Taylor are with you in the spirit world now, and we miss them dearly. We know that they are watching over us and that they are proud of how their son, Cayman, has grown into a man. We are happy that he met Sarah, and that Vicki and Henry Cooper are in his life. We are grateful for the privilege to have had Cayman live in our home and teach us his excitement of life. We ask that you watch over him and Sarah as they continue their journey together."

Chapter Six

They all thanked Sakari for her beautiful words. Sarah snapped a photo as they watched the fireworks in wonderment. Sarah and Cayman were thankful for their families and that they were able to enjoy the day together on the beach.

The two of them were enjoying their two-week vacation together, hiking on the trails, walking on the beach, and swimming in the gulf. Sarah had been planning a surprise for Cayman. On July 9, she told him that they would be going on an adventure, and it would begin at eleven p.m. that night. He curiously asked Sarah what she had planned. She said to Cayman, "It's a surprise! You'll have to wait and see!"

Sarah and Cayman packed food and drinks for the surprise Sarah had planned. They headed north out of Cypress Cove a few minutes before eleven p.m. Sarah was driving the pickup truck, while Cayman and Boone sat beside her wondering where she was taking them.

Sarah drove straight through, for four hours, until they arrived at Cape Canaveral on the east coast of Florida. Cayman still didn't know why they were there and what she had planned. Sarah finally told him that they were there to see an early-morning rocket launch. Cayman had read and learned about rockets, but he had never seen one launch. He was thrilled that Sarah planned this new experience and was sharing it with him.

Sarah told Cayman about the article her dad Henry had written recently, and how it gave her the idea to take him to see the launch. She shared with Cayman that Henry wrote a story about an historic

rocket launch scheduled for four-thirty-five a.m., on July 10. The article described a Thor-Delta rocket that would be launched into Earth's orbit from Launch Complex 17B, at Cape Canaveral Air Force Station. It was a three-stage, liquid-fueled rocket that would launch a Telstar I satellite into orbit. It was the first-ever communication relay satellite that would relay through space television pictures, telephone calls, and telegraph images, as well as a live transatlantic television feed.

Sarah wanted to share this important moment in history with her best friend, Cayman. She found a place to park the truck, leaving them a little more than an hour before the rocket was scheduled to launch. They quickly walked out onto the beach and walked north toward the launch site to find a good spot to watch the launch. Sarah, Cayman, and Boone walked half a mile, when they came to a small sandy inlet 12 miles south of the launch site. There was a full moon shining over the calm water and an old rowboat beached next to a palm tree. It was perfect spot for viewing the rocket launch.

They sat on the beach to await the launch. And then they saw the glow of the rocket igniting at the launch pad. Cayman jumped up in excitement and Boone let out a bark. It took about thirty seconds before they could hear the roar of the rocket's sound and feel the rumble as it lifted high in the sky, then arched out over the Atlantic Ocean. They saw the reflection of the rocket as it flew high over the calm ocean water, disappearing in the dark, early-morning sky.

Chapter Six

Sarah and Cayman sat on the beach, talking about what they had just witnessed, until the sun rose over the Atlantic Ocean on the eastern horizon. It was a magnificent sunrise, and Cayman thanked Sarah again and again for the surprise she had shared with him. They walked back to the pickup truck, and Cayman drove home to Cypress Cove while Sarah and Boone took a nap next to him.

There were only a few days left before Cayman would be driving back to Dimerling, Ohio, and to resume work at Taylor Tire and Rubber. Even though he hadn't left yet, he already missed Sarah. They spent their few remaining days together swimming in the gulf and resting on the beach.

On the next-to-the-last evening together in Cypress Cove, Cayman and Sarah surprised her parents with a cookout. They held the cookout in the park near her parents' apartment. Sarah arranged the picnic table, while Cayman prepared the food. The four of them and Boone enjoyed the evening together in the park. The next evening, and Cayman's last before heading north, the two of them prepared a nice dinner for his parents and brother at the Deeres' home in the Poaceaehatchee Village.

The following morning, Cayman got up early and stopped by Sarah's place so he and Boone could say goodbye before the long drive back to Dimerling. Sarah and Cayman were thankful for these two weeks they had gotten to spend together and with their families.

When Grayson returned to Dimerling that summer, he completed his rotation in the plant. For his second rotation, he moved into the office. Once there, he spent the year working in several different office functions, rotating to a new department every two months.

Grayson didn't mind working in the plant; he liked hard work and he liked working with his hands. He suspected that being cooped up in an office every day was going to be difficult. At least working in the plant meant having large overhead doors open, and being able to feel and smell the outside air, even if sometimes it was cold air. In the office, it was perpetually chilly, and there was no outside air to feel or smell.

For Grayson, one of the more difficult aspects of working in the office was wearing dress clothes every day. Back home in Southwest Florida, he seldom wore a dress shirt, let alone a jacket and tie. At times, he felt like he was smothering in his office attire. Grayson kept telling himself – out of respect for his parents – he must try to make it work.

His office rotation included working in accounting, purchasing, human resources, sales and marketing, and legal. While in accounting, Grayson learned to invoice customers and make entries in accounts receivables. He also paid suppliers' invoices and made entries for payables. Grayson prepared several financial documents, such as the Taylor Tire and Rubber income statement, balance sheet, and financial forecast.

From the accounting department, Grayson moved to the purchasing department. Once in purchasing, he worked closely with suppliers, creating purchase orders, modifying delivery schedules, and addressing quality issues. Grayson worked with scheduling to ensure that purchased product was received as planned and on time to meet production deadlines.

His next department assignment was human resources (HR). Once in HR, Grayson was exposed to recruiting and hiring, conducting orientation and onboarding, and even terminating employment. Terminating a Taylor Tire and Rubber employee was the hardest role Grayson had served thus far. He kept his head down and did the job that was assigned him, but there were times when he felt employees were unfairly terminated. Grayson didn't know yet what to do about it, but he knew he would figure out a solution. Growing up in the Poaceaehatchee Village, he never experienced someone being told they weren't good enough to do a job. The culture of the Tutelar was that every member lifted up the others, to help them get better at what they do.

After two months in human resources, Grayson moved into sales and marketing. There he learned about promoting Taylor Tire and Rubber product lines and applications. Grayson met and worked with many of Taylor Tire's customers. He enjoyed working with customers and finding solutions that fit their needs.

His final stop on the yearlong office rotation was the legal department. It was a little emotional for Grayson since it was the department his mom once led. Working in legal helped Grayson learn more about his mom, and made him feel closer to her. He listened to stories from employees who knew his mom and how they enjoyed working with her. Grayson worked hard every day, learning the Taylor Tire and Rubber business inside and out.

While Cayman was working through his yearlong office rotation, Sarah was attending her sophomore year at the Glades University. She was doing well and getting good grades in her environmental policy and management classes. Sarah enjoyed the theoretical studies in the classroom, and she especially liked the hands-on lab and field work. She volunteered for lab assignments and field trips every chance she got.

During the fall semester, Sarah was assigned to a three-person team by Professor Bakshi to collect and analyze saltwater samples along the beach. There were five, three-person teams, and each team received a different assignment. Sarah and her teammates collected and analyzed samples at six locations along the beach between Fort Lauderdale and Miami. They tested the water for evidence of red tide, blue-green algae, nitrates, and other potential contaminants.

For four months, Sarah and her team plotted the results for each sample by location, date, and time of day. At the end of the semester, the three team members presented their findings to their classmates and Professor Bakshi. Each team member presented elements of the report. One team member presented the results, another the conclusions, and Sarah presented recommendations for environmental policy changes. Each team presented their assignment's results, conclusions, and recommendations.

When the spring semester began in January 1963, Professor Bakshi gave Sarah's team a new assignment. Her team was assigned to support the South Florida park rangers, while they monitored and surveyed shorebird nesting habits. The three team members were assigned to visit specific shorebird nesting beach locations. They were instructed to accompany park rangers and help count and document the numbers of each type of bird over a four-month period.

Every spring, sandpipers, terns, and plovers scooped small spots in the sand to lay their eggs. The eggs blended into the sand and were nearly undetectable. Beachgoers rarely noticed the nests or the babies as they hatched; they blended into the sand so discreetly.

Sarah was thrilled when she learned her team's assignment, and she called Cayman right away to tell him. Sarah remembered him taking her to a secluded beach near the Poaceaehatchee Village three years earlier to see hundreds of shorebirds nesting. Cayman was pleased to hear about Sarah's spring semester assignment. He knew she would do well and that she'd have fun while doing it. At the end of the semester, the five, three-member teams presented the results of their assignments as part of their final grade.

Sarah finished her sophomore year at Glades University; she had received good grades and had enjoyed learning all she had learned. And now she was looking forward to spending the summer at home in Cypress Cove with family and friends. Unfortunately, Cayman was going to be staying in Dimerling for the summer, to complete his office rotation. He wasn't able to get away as he had the previous summer, so they planned for Sarah to visit Cayman in Dimerling for two weeks in July.

Sarah didn't want to wish part of her summer away, but she couldn't wait to go to Dimerling to be with Cayman. When July 1963 finally arrived, Sarah traveled to Dimerling to spend two weeks between her sophomore and junior year with Cayman and Boone. She took a flight from Fort Myers to Dimerling, where Cayman and Boone were patiently waiting for her at the airport. As soon as she walked out the doors of the airport, Boone barked and wagged his tail and Cayman ran over to greet her.

They were excited to spend the first two weeks of July together in Dimerling. Boone seemed as excited to see Sarah as Cayman. While Sarah was staying in Dimerling, Cayman took a few days of vacation time from Taylor Tire and Rubber to be with her. They both had made plans for things they wanted to do and share while spending this time together. Sarah made plans to take Cayman to Westwood, Illinois, to see her childhood home.

Cayman had plans to show Sarah his childhood home in Dimerling and to tour Taylor Tire and Rubber Company. Sarah was overwhelmed by his parents' home. She'd never been in such a large house with so many rooms. Cayman showed her around the estate and they walked through the gardens and the woods.

After Sarah unpacked and got settled in, they went out to the garage to get a car to drive into Dimerling for dinner. Again, Sarah was stunned at the size of the garage and all of the cars. She smiled that, given the four cars in that huge garage, Cayman selected the 1948 Dodge pickup truck to drive into town.

They found a nice little restaurant in downtown Dimerling for dinner. While they ate, the two of them made plans for places they wanted to go and sights they wanted to see. They talked about how much they had missed each other, with Sarah at college and Cayman at Taylor Tire and Rubber. After dinner, they strolled through town, before getting in the pickup truck and driving home for the evening.

When they returned to the estate, they sat on the large patio at the back of the house. It overlooked the wading pool, which was lit, with a fountain in the middle. It was a beautiful night to sit outside under the stars. The spray from the fountain shimmered from the reflection of the lights. The sky was clear and full of stars. Sarah and Cayman talked into the night, while Boone laid at their feet.

Sarah shared with Cayman all about her sophomore year at the Glades University of South Florida. How she loved her studies and she knew that conservation was the field she was meant to be in. Cayman told Sarah how things were going at Taylor Tire – he was working in the different office departments and functions, and he was learning so much about his parents' business. They talked until they could barely keep their eyes open. They both had the best night of sleep in a long time.

The next morning, Cayman made breakfast for himself and Sarah. It was a warm, sunny morning. They sat with Boone on the patio looking out upon the gardens and the woods as they enjoyed breakfast. After breakfast, they took Boone for a walk on the paths through the flower gardens and into the woods. Later they would be going to see where Cayman worked at Taylor Tire.

Sarah, Cayman, and Boone went to the garage to get the pickup truck and drive to Taylor Tire and Rubber Company. Cayman reminded Sarah that while at Taylor Tire, people would be calling him Grayson. Other than Aubrey and Bonnie, no one at Taylor Tire knew him as Cayman.

The two of them started their tour in the plant. Cayman showed Sarah the different departments and jobs he worked during his first year of orientation. He introduced her to several Taylor Tire employees who had helped him learn how to do the jobs safely and correctly.

From the plant, they went into the offices, where Cayman introduced Sarah to several employees, many of whom had known his parents. Sarah was astonished by the size of the company and the number of people working there. It was also quite touching for her to hear about Cayman's parents and how much everyone respected and loved them. They stopped by Cayman's office, and Sarah took a photograph of him sitting at his desk. After spending the morning at Taylor Tire and Rubber, they were hungry. They hopped back into the pickup truck and drove to downtown Dimerling for lunch.

After lunch, they drove around Dimerling, so Sarah could see where Cayman had lived with his parents until he was five years old. He wasn't able to describe much from memory, because he was very young when he left at age five. Cayman drove Sarah past the hospital where he had been born and the school where he had attended kindergarten. It was getting late in the afternoon, so they headed back to the house for dinner.

Sarah and Cayman prepared a pasta dinner together and enjoyed it while sitting on the patio. While they were eating dinner, Sarah told Cayman what she had planned for the next couple of days.

She wanted to take him to Westwood, Illinois, to see where she grew up and where her mom's Special Moments Photography Studio was located. Sarah also wanted to show Cayman some special spots in Chicago, like where her dad worked at the Chicago Tribune. It would be a seven-hour drive to get to Westwood, so they decided to get to bed early and get a good night's sleep.

The next morning, they got up early for the trip to Illinois. They had breakfast on the patio, then they took a leisurely walk in the flower gardens, before returning to the house to pack for the trip. Sarah and Cayman packed enough clothes and food for four days. They decided that they didn't want to stop, other than for gas and bathroom breaks, on the way to Westwood. So, they packed sandwiches and drinks for on the road.

Sarah suggested to Cayman that they could take the 1947 Chevrolet Fleetmaster Convertible for their trip. The weather was supposed to be nice for the next several days, and she wanted to drive the convertible with the top down. Cayman liked the idea, so they loaded the car and left Dimerling at nine a.m. The two of them, along with Boone, headed across Ohio, through Indiana, then on to Illinois. Cayman was used to the flat land and straight roads in Florida, and he couldn't get over how winding and hilly the roads were in the Midwestern United States.

Stopping only for fuel and short breaks, they arrived in Westwood at four thirty p.m. It was a fun drive – sightseeing with the convertible top down. Yet, it had been a long day of driving. Upon arriving in Westwood, they checked into a small hotel with a swimming pool. Cayman gave Boone some food and water, then the two of them unpacked their suitcases. Hungry from the long drive, they went in search of a place to enjoy dinner.

After dinner, they returned to the hotel for the evening. Before going to bed for the night, Sarah described some of the places and things that they would see over the next few days. When they got up the next morning, the two of them went for an early-morning swim in the hotel pool. Showered and dressed for the day, they were off to tour Westwood.

Sarah's first stop was breakfast at a small diner, where her parents used to take her when she was younger. Sarah and her parents had moved from Westwood to Cypress Cove four years earlier. Even though four years wasn't a long time, she had grown from a fifteen-year-old girl to a nineteen-year-old young lady. She wasn't sure if the Westwood folks would still recognize her, or if she would recognize anyone at the diner, but she always like eating there when she was younger.

As soon as they walked inside, Sarah recognized some of the staff from when she used to go there. Everyone that worked there was nice to her when she was younger, so she was happy to see that some were still there. Sarah introduced them to Cayman, and told them what had been happening over the last four years. So much had happened since they moved to Cypress Cove. She met Cayman, had experienced exciting outdoor adventures, graduated high school, and completed her second year of college. Sarah enjoyed telling them about her life and adventures, and Cayman enjoyed hearing her reliving their fun times together.

They left the diner, and Sarah drove Cayman and Boone to where her mom's Special Moments photography studio. It had been converted to a small clothing store, but they stopped in and talked for a bit with the new owners. Sarah told them that her mom's photography studio had been in the same space, and that she used to help her mom when she was younger. The new owners were happy that Sarah and Cayman stopped in to see them. They'd been saving a box of things accidently left behind by her mom for the last four years. Sarah took the box before thanking them and saying goodbye.

She decided they would go through the box when they returned to the hotel later that day.

The next place Sarah wanted Cayman to see was where she went to school and the library where she studied. He was surprised at how large her school building was. He was used to his small school at the Poaceaehatchee Village. Even the school at Cypress Cove didn't compare in size to Sarah's old school in Westwood.

They drove around Westwood to see some of the other places that Sarah and her parents had visited for dining and entertainment. Sarah picked one of her favorite restaurants for dinner. The food was as good as she had remembered.

When they returned to the hotel, the two of them opened the box that the owners of the clothing store gave Sarah. In it were some photographs of people Sarah didn't know, and several photographs of her, when she was much younger. Cayman had not known Sarah when she was a young girl. He enjoyed seeing the photos of her, often grinning as he looked at each photo. There was also some old camera equipment and a few other odds and ends in the box. Sarah thought it would be fun to share the box and the story of their visit with her mom, when she returned home to Cypress Cove.

The next morning, after breakfast, Sarah and Cayman drove into Chicago to see more places from her childhood. Sarah had been to Chicago many times, and she lived in Miami while going to college, so the big city did not surprise or intimidate her. Cayman, on the other hand, was in complete amazement over the tall buildings. The largest city he had experienced was Dimerling, and it didn't compare to the size of Chicago.

Sarah took Cayman to the Chicago Tribune where her dad had been a reporter when they lived in Westwood. The two of them spent some time talking with several of the reporters and staff who were her dad's former colleagues.

Chapter Six

Some of them were especially interested in talking with Cayman. It had made national news when the Taylors were lost in July of 1948, and most of the Tribune staff remembered the story. They also remembered that Sarah's dad released a story, only two years ago, reporting that Grayson Taylor was alive and living in Southwest Florida.

When Sarah introduced them to Cayman, they realized he was Grayson Taylor. Their journalistic instincts kicked in, and they had so many questions for him. Sarah quickly stepped in and asked them to please respect Cayman's privacy and to not ask questions about his parents and his past. They had great respect for Henry Cooper and, while it was difficult to suppress their curiosity and withhold their questions, they did so out of regard for Cayman's privacy. Sarah and Cayman thanked the staff at the Chicago Tribune for showing them around and said goodbye as they headed to the next stop.

They went back to the car, got Boone, then walked to one of Sarah's favorite places in Chicago, the Navy Pier. When Sarah said they were going to the pier, Cayman imagined the Kendrick Pier in Cypress Cove. When they arrived at the Navy Pier, Cayman was astounded at the sheer size of the pier. It was nothing like the pier in Cypress Cove.

Even though the Navy Pier was huge and a bustle of commerce, there was something calming about being near the water again. And although it was on a lake, it looked to be a big as the gulf back home. They walked around, exploring the pier with Boone for a while, before stopping for a late lunch. The two of them sat on a bench looking at the water while they enjoyed their lunch, before making the drive back to the hotel in Westwood.

When they returned to the hotel, they changed into their swim suits and swam in the hotel pool. After swimming, they sat on the poolside lounge chairs to dry off, while talking about what they had seen the last two days. Boone laid happily beside them while they talked and until they all went back to the room for the night.

The next morning, they enjoyed a swim before breakfast and packing their suitcases for the journey back to Dimerling. Upon returning to Dimerling, they realized that a week of their two weeks together was already gone. Sarah and Cayman agreed to spend their last week together at the Taylor Estate, hiking, swimming, playing with Boone, and just plain relaxing.

They needed a break from the pressures of Sarah's schoolwork and Cayman's work. The Taylor Estate was a perfect place to rest. Each morning, Sarah and Cayman enjoyed breakfast on the patio with Boone. They went for hikes through the woods and around the estate property, always making their way back to the flower gardens. The two of them spent the afternoons swimming and relaxing by the pool. Each evening they got dressed and drove into Dimerling for dinner. Occasionally, they would see someone that Cayman worked with at Taylor Tire, and sat and talked a while.

The storyteller tells her daughter, "Do you remember asking me if they were in love? Well, you are about to find out."

On the afternoon of the Fourth of July, 1963, Sarah and Cayman drove into Dimerling for dinner and to watch the city's fireworks display. It was their last night together, they talked about how it had been a wonderful two weeks. That night was the first time they confessed their love for each other. This time they spent together in Dimerling took their relationship to a new level; they were more than just friends.

On their last morning together, Sarah packed for her trip back to Cypress Cove. Before leaving, she took several photographs of the Taylor Estate – Cayman's childhood home. She knew that someday he would want to go back and look at those photos. That morning, Cayman drove her to the airport.

Chapter Six

As they were driving to the airport, they talked about how much fun they had these two weeks together. And they were already planning on how and when they would see each other again. Their emotions were all over the place, they already missed each other, and Sarah hadn't left yet. When they arrived at the airport, they longingly kissed each other goodbye, and expressed their love. They both felt happy and sad at the same time.

Sarah had returned to Cypress Cove, and 20-year-old Grayson began his third and final year of the Taylor Tire and Rubber orientation program. During his next yearlong rotation, he was assigned to shadow several of the executive leaders at Taylor Tire. He was collaborating with and shadowing leaders in operations, engineering, finance, and the chief executive office.

This assignment was where Grayson learned the most about how things were done at Taylor Tire and Rubber Company. He enjoyed being around people at Taylor Tire who knew his parents and told him stories about them. Grayson learned about how much his parents cared for the employees, and how they had been good stewards of the company and the environment. Often, he would hear stories about how much his parents cared about making sure their employees and customers were happy and satisfied.

What Grayson noticed was that the stories he heard from the folks at Taylor Tire didn't match with what he had seen and experienced while working there the past few years. When he worked in the plant operations, Grayson saw many examples of waste and landfill disposal of scrap materials and products. He had seen employees get terminated without, what he believed to be, a fair plan to help them improve and develop. He knew in his heart that what he was seeing and experiencing was not how his parents would have run their company if they were still living.

Almost a full year had passed since Sarah and Grayson had spent two weeks together in July in Dimerling. By late-spring 1964, Grayson was nearing the end of his three-year orientation program at Taylor Tire. Over the past three years,

he had come to the realization that Dimerling and Taylor Tire were not for him.

Grayson knew he needed to talk with Aubrey and Sarah about a plan for his future and for the future of Taylor Tire and Rubber Company. He didn't want to feel like he let his parents down, but he remembered that his mom told him to follow his passion and his heart. It was clear to him that Taylor Tire and Rubber Company and Dimerling, Ohio, were not where his passion or his heart were.

Grayson arranged to meet with Aubrey before heading to Cypress Cove to spend the summer with Sarah and his family. The two of them met at Aubrey's office and talked for hours about how Grayson felt about continuing his role at Taylor Tire.

Aubrey listened carefully as Grayson shared with her what he saw and felt during his three-year orientation program. She suggested that Grayson take the summer to think about their conversation. She asked him to come to her first thing upon returning to Dimerling in the fall, and she would help him with whatever he decided was right for him. Grayson felt good about how he left it with Aubrey, and he couldn't wait to talk with Sarah about their future.

During fall of 1963, 20-year-old Sarah started her junior year of Environmental Policy and Management at Glades. She was enthusiastic and excited to enter her junior-level classes and field work.

Sarah had created a personal project to which she needed to apply all of her learnings, if she was to be successful. Over the summer, Sarah and her friends had spent a lot of time at the beaches in Cypress Cove. Summer was the rainy season in Southwest Florida, and she noticed the impact that the town's runoff water was having close to shore, where the rain water dumped into the gulf waters.

Sarah met with Professor Bakshi, who had assigned her team the water analyses project during her sophomore year at Glades University. She explained what she noticed during the summer, and asked if Professor Bakshi would sponsor her on an assignment for extra credit. Sarah shared her hypothesis with her professor. She explained that she thought the system wasn't capable of handling the increased volume from the town's runoff water. As a result, it was contaminating the shallow water near the beaches and harming the sea life.

Sarah had done her research, and she explained to her professor that the water runoff system at Cypress Cove was built in 1938. At the time it was built, the town's population was 1,253, and now the population was approximately 5,000. Since 1938, there had been several new condominiums, hotels, and roads built to accommodate the many visitors during the tourist season. She believed that the water runoff system simply had not kept up with the construction boom and population growth in Cypress Cove.

Sarah proposed to Professor Bakshi that she would like to collect water samples before, during, and after rainfalls at specific locations near the runoff drains on the Cypress Cove beaches. She would analyze the samples for contaminants and plot the data over time. She described that she would also record visual observations of changes in water color and impacts to sea life close to runoff culverts and between runoff culverts.

Once she had collected and recorded a valid number of sample data, her plan was to draft a report and present it, along with her analyses and recommendations. Then, with her professor's feedback, Sarah agreed to draft a proposed improvement plan and policy to present to the Cypress Cove town council. Professor Bakshi liked Sarah's idea and approved her plan as an extra-credit project, as long as it didn't interfere with her other coursework.

Sarah collected water samples from September 1963 through March 1964. She collected, analyzed, and plotted the samples taken at Cypress Cove beaches, from six runoff locations and six non-runoff locations. She compiled the results into a report, which included conclusions and recommendations. Sarah presented her findings and recommendations to Professor Bakshi, along with two other professors who taught environmental coursework at Glades University.

The data Sarah had collected and analyzed indicated that during and after rain storms, the contaminant levels in the Gulf of Mexico rose significantly above defined safe levels. Her visual observations indicated that sea life in the runoff areas was in near-constant distress, as she often observed dead sea life in the water and on the beach. Sarah concluded that the Cypress Cove water runoff system was no longer capable of ensuring that the water running into the Gulf of Mexico was within the recommended safe levels.

Chapter Six

Her summarized recommendation to the professors was that Cypress Cove should upgrade the current water runoff system to sustain safe contaminant levels. The upgrade should include extending the large runoff drain pipes 1,000 yards into the Gulf of Mexico. Her report indicated that the extended drain pipes would allow the runoff to enter the gulf in deeper water, which would more easily handle the fresh water dilution of the salt water.

Sarah also recommended that the Cypress Cove water management group put a procedure in place to monitor the water quality regularly, and that they define a policy that trigged a water system upgrade before unsafe contaminant levels were met in the future. All three of the Glades University professors agreed with her findings, conclusions, and recommendations.

The next step was for Sarah to share her analysis with the Cypress Cove Town Council. She knew it wasn't going to be easy, so she asked her sponsoring professor to attend the meeting with her. Professor Bakshi agreed that it was the right thing to do, and she told Sarah she would support her during the presentation to the Cypress Cove council. Professor Bakshi reminded Sarah to be concise and informative in her presentation, and to be well rehearsed and prepared for probing questions – and potentially strong pushback – from the council members. Sarah knew it was good advice, and she practiced over and over, trying to think of every question she might have to defend.

Sarah arranged to present to the town council on Friday, May 1, 1964, only a week before her junior year ended. Sarah's mom and dad were there to support her, and had helped to get her message out to the broader community. Sarah's mom took photographs and her dad took notes to publish an article in the Cypress Cove Chronicle. Her parents hoped that if the town council knew that Sarah's presentation was being published in the newspaper, they might be more apt to support her recommendations.

Professor Bakshi stood next to Sarah when it was her turn to address the council. Sarah opened by thanking the council for their time, introduced Professor Bakshi, and told them she loved Cypress Cove – the town where she lived. Sarah reminded the town council how important tourism was for business and how the beaches were major attractions for tourists. The council listened as Sarah presented her approach, analyses, and recommendations. She shared with the council the same things she reported to her professors at Glades University.

Sarah suggested an upgrade to the water runoff system to reduce contaminants, extending the runoff drain pipes 1,000 yards into the gulf. The reduction of contaminants and introduction of fresh water further out into the gulf would drastically reduce the risk to sea life. To sustain the improvements, she recommended to the council that water management personnel test the water on a regular basis and define a system upgrade trigger, in the event contaminants reached risk levels.

The members of the town council asked her question after question, and Sarah responded to every question without wavering. The council members seemed quite impressed with Sarah's clarity and thoroughness in her approach to the study and to her delivery of the results and recommendations. Sarah thanked each member of the town council for taking time to listen to her, and asked that they take her recommendations into consideration.

Nearly every one of the Cypress Cove residents who had attended the town council meeting stood up and clapped as Sarah concluded her presentation. Several residents took turns addressing the council in support of Sarah's recommendations. Concerned residents said that if the council did not take action soon to fix the water runoff system, they were in danger of losing their beautiful beaches and crystal-clear waters. They felt that if that happened, word would spread and tourism would drop, hurting local businesses.

As Sarah and her professor drove across the state, back to Glades University, Sarah stated to Professor Bakshi, "Thank you for supporting me at the council meeting today. I'm also thankful for the support expressed by the town residents. I believe we accomplished what we set out to do. It's now in the hands of the Cypress Cove Town Council. I really hope they do the right thing and upgrade the water runoff system."

It was the summer of 1964, and 21-year-old Sarah and Cayman were back in Cypress Cove for the summer. Sarah's spring semester was finished, and she returned home from Miami. Cayman took the summer off from Taylor Tire and Rubber to spend in Cypress Cove with Sarah. They were both very excited that they would be spending the summer together.

The two of them decided to kick off their summer adventures with a day of hiking in the Cypress Forest near the Poaceaehatchee Village. Sarah borrowed her parents' car and headed to Cayman's parents' house to meet shortly before sunrise. His parents invited Sarah in to have breakfast with them. After breakfast, Sarah and

Cayman helped wash the dishes, then packed food and drink for a picnic during their hike. They waved goodbye, as they headed out the door with Boone to make their way to the hiking trail.

Their hike started on the trail at the edge of The Everglades, before reaching the Cypress Forest. Sarah had her camera with her, of course, and she was ready to take lots of photographs. While hiking the trail along The Everglades, they saw and photographed several different bird species.

One of Sarah's favorites was the Roseate spoonbill. There were several of these pink birds wading in the shallow waters, foraging for food in the mucky bottom. The birds sweep their heads back and forth through the shallow water with their bill slightly open, trying to catch shrimp, insects, and fish. The spoonbills, in their varied shades of pink, were interesting to see and beautiful to photograph.

They hiked to the edge of the Cypress Forest, where they chose to sit and enjoy their picnic lunch. They found a dry spot in the shade of the cypress trees. They ate lunch while Boone drank some water and played curiously in the woods. Sarah shared with Cayman that she was really pleased to have snapped a few good photographs of the Roseate spoonbills as they were searching for food.

She took a photograph of the small pond near where they were picnicking. It was surrounded by cypress trees that were covered with blue-gray Spanish moss. The pond was covered over with swamp lettuce; ferns and tall swamp lilies

133

surrounded the pond's edges.

As they were gathering up their picnic items, they were startled by nearby rustling in the brush. A few seconds later, a large Florida black bear stepped out into the clearing very near where they were standing. As the bear walked toward Sarah and Cayman, Boone moved to stand in between them and the bear. Boone took a defensive stance, emitting a deep growl while facing the bear. The bear stopped in place and looked squarely at them and Boone.

It wasn't Cayman's first encounter with a bear. He knew that Florida black bears rarely attacked humans, and he knew what they needed to do to stay safe. He stepped in front of Sarah, as he whispered to not move or make a sound. They both stood very still and quiet, yet they feared for Boone. They knew that he did not stand a chance against a bear weighing nearly four times his weight.

Boone continued to growl in a deep, low, threatening sound. The bear stomped the ground and shook back and forth a few times. Then, as if no longer interested, the bear slowly walked back into the woods. Sarah raised her camera and snapped a single photograph of Boone standing proudly as the bear retreated. She had hoped she held the camera steady enough to get a clear photo.

Boone must have been pleased with himself, because he barked twice then turned and ran to Sarah and Cayman, wagging his tail. They decided they had enough adventure for one day, and hiked back to the village to tell Cayman's brother and parents what had happened. It was yet another experience they would never forget.

After Sarah and Cayman shared their bear story with his parents and brother, they all hugged and said goodbye. Sarah drove back to Cypress Cove, arriving home just in time for dinner with her parents. She told them about how wonderful it was to hike on the trail along the beautiful Everglades and into the Cypress Forest. She described all the amazing birds they saw, and showed them the photograph of the Roseate spoonbills searching for food.

Sarah told her parents about their picnic, while sitting in the Cypress Forest, and how Boone enjoyed running and playing in the woods. What Sarah didn't tell them was that Boone saved them from a large Florida black bear. As far as Sarah's parents knew, she, Cayman, and Boone had a picturesque, fun-filled day of hiking – with no dangers.

The encounter with the bear wasn't going to be Sarah's and Cayman's only adventure that summer. It was the Fourth of July holiday weekend, and Sarah was spending the day at the beach with some of her old high school friends. While she was at the beach with her friends, Cayman went to her parents' house. He wanted to ask for their blessing on an important question he planned to ask Sarah that evening.

Cayman told Vicki and Henry Cooper that he loved their daughter more than anything, which was something he had told very few people. Cayman shared with the Coopers that his mother's last words to him were, "Honey, follow your heart and your dreams." He told Vicki and Henry that in his heart, he knew that he and Sarah were meant to be together.

Cayman went on to tell the Coopers that he wanted to build a home in Cypress Cove, and to spend his life there with Sarah. He asked Vicki and Henry for their permission to ask Sarah for her hand in marriage. The Coopers didn't have to think long before answering his question. They had known Cayman for many years. They had seen how the two of them were together, and how they had grown from kids into fine young adults. They knew that Cayman would be a good husband to Sarah, and someday, they hoped, a good father. The Coopers cheerfully gave Cayman their blessing to ask Sarah to marry him.

Cayman was thrilled that Sarah's parents gave him permission to marry their daughter. He had it all planned. He invited Sarah to the beach to watch the Cypress Cove fireworks with him on July 4, 1964.

The fireworks were going to be launched from a barge near the Kendrick Pier. He and Sarah would watch the fireworks from the beach a few miles south of the pier on the north edge of the Pavati River. It was the property his parents had purchased many years earlier. Cayman had prepared a picnic dinner for them to share on the beach.

Just before the fireworks began, Cayman, clumsily and beautifully, proposed to Sarah. He said, "Sarah, you are my best friend, and I love you deeply. It would make me the happiest person alive, if you would agree to let me spend the rest of my life with you. I want us to build our home together right here on the beach where we are standing, and to spend our lives together in Cypress Cove. Would you please allow me to be your husband?" With tears in her eyes, Sarah gleefully said "Yes!" and made Cayman the happiest person alive.

At that moment, he couldn't help but to think of his mom, and how he wished she was alive to meet Sarah and come to their wedding. He took solace in what he had been taught by the Tutelar elders – that the spirit lived on and his parents were always with him. Boone must have been happy, as well, because he barked a few times while wagging his tail and trying to get in on the hug.

Cayman presented Sarah with an engagement necklace, especially made for her by a jeweler in the Poaceaehatchee Village. The necklace was made from a design Cayman had sketched and given to the jewelry maker. It was a pendant inlaid with turquoise and coral stones, hanging from a silver chain. Central to the pendent was a single oval turquoise stone, surrounded by

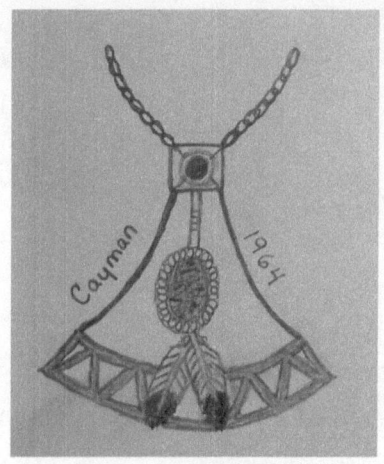

tiny coral stones, with two feathers dangling below. The feathers were inlaid with white quartz and a bit of black fossil coral only at the tips. The pendant consisted of a quarter circle of silver suspended below the oval stone; the quarter circle consisted of triangular webbing. Sarah remarked more than once how much she loved the pendant – especially the feathers.

In the Tutelar culture, a turquoise and coral engagement necklace meant peace, tranquility, and spiritual commitment, bringing love into the wearer's life. Cayman helped Sarah put the necklace in place around her neck, and they sat and watched the fireworks together, while dreaming of their future and lives together.

The next morning, Sarah and Cayman got up early for their volunteer assignment. It was their day to count new turtle nests on the beach south of the pier. As they were walking along the beach, looking for new turtle tracks and evidence of new nests, they noticed something wiggling in the shallow surf ahead. They both saw it at the same time. As they neared the wiggling surf, they saw it was a creature about seven inches long, struggling to move in the wet sand, where it got washed up by the tide onto the beach.

Chapter Six

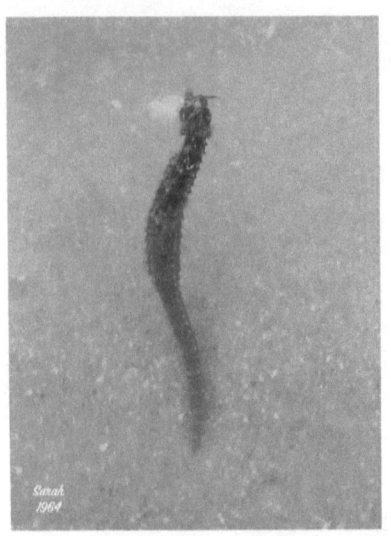

Sarah screamed, "It's a seahorse, it's a seahorse!" She gently picked up the seahorse and placed it back in the water. The seahorse floated on its side for several seconds, then its head tilted upward. Soon the seahorse was straight up and down in the water and swam away, just as Sarah snapped a photograph. They watched it swim away, until they could no longer see it in the gulf's clear water.

In Tutelar culture, seahorses were considered mystical sea creatures. Only one in one thousand seahorses survived to adulthood. Thought of as half fish and half horse, they were believed to bring good fortune. As a spirit animal, seahorses represented a precious event that happened rarely, like finding true love. Seahorses reminded the onlooker to treasure their partner and always remember the qualities that made them fall in love. Having just become engaged the evening before, Sarah and Cayman believed their chance encounter with this seahorse to be a sign of a beautiful future together.

The summer of 1964 came to a close, and Sarah and Cayman had many deep conversations about their future together. They both desperately wanted to live in Cypress Cove after they were married.

Sarah was soon entering her senior year at the Glades University of South Florida, where she would graduate with a Bachelor of Science degree in Environmental Policy and

Management. She wanted to utilize her degree and passion to be a steward of Southwest Florida's natural resources.

Cayman had completed is three-year orientation at Taylor Tire and Rubber Company. He knew that staying at Taylor Tire in Dimerling was not his passion or where he belonged. He missed Southwest Florida and everything it represented to him. When working at Taylor Tire, he felt he had lost his identity; he was stuck between Grayson and Cayman.

Together, Sarah and Cayman made plans for their careers, marriage, home, and Cayman's inheritance. They made a plan for Cayman to return to Dimerling and Taylor Tire and Rubber one last time to transition out of his late family's business. As part of his separation from Taylor Tire, he and Sarah had decided that they would build a nature conservancy on part of the seventy-five acres his parents left him in Cypress Cove. The conservancy would be commissioned to serve and protect the land and animals of Southwest Florida, and Sarah would serve as its executive director.

Cayman wanted to gift his parents' Ohio property to the Dimerling historical society as a museum. He planned to relinquish his fifty-one percent stake in Taylor Tire and Rubber Company and to establish a charitable foundation that Sarah would help him develop and manage.

Their plan was for Cayman to return to Cypress Cove to live by the winter holidays. Once he returned to Cypress Cove, he would begin building their home on the beach that they had been planning and sketching since they got engaged. Upon graduating from Glades University in the spring of 1965, Sarah would also return to Cypress Cove. Once they were married, they would move into their new home on the beach.

Chapter Six

During the fall of 1964, Sarah returned to Glades University to finish her degree program, and Cayman returned to Ohio to request Aubrey to help him with their plan.

Sarah began her senior year at Glades University engaged to Cayman. She was excited it was her last year at the university and that she would soon be starting a new adventure in her life with Cayman as her husband. Over the summer, Sarah and Cayman put a plan in place for him to leave Taylor Tire and Rubber, and return to Cypress Cove where they would be married and where they would live. Sarah was looking forward to getting married and living with Cayman in Cypress Cove, but it didn't deter her from putting all of her efforts into finishing her senior year strong.

During her senior year, Sarah took a full load of all the classes that she needed to graduate in the spring. Sarah and two of her classmates were assigned a senior project; it was to monitor, measure, and report the impacts on The Everglades and the local wildlife of the sugarcane industry. The three of them made weekly trips from Miami up through the sugarcane fields to Lake Okeechobee. They measured the water flow, tested water quality, and evaluated impacts to the wildlife habitats.

The team's project wasn't without drama. Often, they were yelled at by the field workers and local townspeople. They were told, "You don't belong here." And "Go away, and don't come back." There were several occasions when their vehicle was vandalized when they were out along the canals and rivers collecting samples and data. It didn't deter Sarah and her two teammates from doing what needed to be done for their college assignment and for the environment. They were, however, more careful from then on when near the sugarcane fields and small towns along the route. They made sure no one traveled alone and always stayed together as a group.

By the end of their senior year, they had created a comprehensive, two-hundred-page report on the impact of the sugarcane industry to the natural Florida environment. Their final report included photographs, data, tables, and graphs. It showed that the sugarcane industry was having a negative impact on the water quality, water flow, and ecosystem of South Florida. The team's summary indicated that sugarcane production had polluted the South Florida freshwater ecosystem with sludge and fertilizer. The contaminants washed into the water, along with chemical sludge from the sugar mills.

The Everglades were able to filter out some of the harmful effects, but not all. Contaminants flowed into the rivers harming fish and animals, and out to sea damaging coral reefs. The highlights of their report, along with the photographs, were picked up and published in the Glades News. Little changed as a result of their report's findings, and that was quite frustrating, Yet, the three team members were proud that their work got noticed.

Sarah's senior year at the Glades University was now down to the last week before final exams. She was excited that she would soon be back in Cypress Cove for a couple of days, then she would return with her family to Miami for her college graduation ceremony. She was even happier that Cayman was leaving Taylor Tire and Rubber Company to be with her in Cypress Cove. Their plans were to build their home over the summer, get married in the fall, and live and work in Cypress Cove.

While Sarah was completing her senior year at the Glades University, Grayson was back at Taylor Tire in Dimerling. He spent

Chapter Six

Sarah's entire senior year, the fall of 1964 to the spring of 1965, in Dimerling acting on their plan.

Once back in Dimerling, Grayson contacted Aubrey to ask her to help him put his and Sarah's plan into action. He hoped Aubrey would understand and not be disappointed in him. They had talked about his feelings before he left Dimerling for Cypress Cove at the end of last spring. Aubrey wasn't surprised or disappointed that Grayson had decided to leave Taylor Tire and return to Cypress Cove. She remembered Grayson as a small boy playing in the woods, swimming in the lake, and his intense curiosity of the outdoors. Deep down, Aubrey knew that working in a plant or office was not going to be the life for Grayson.

Grayson reminded Aubrey of his mom's last words, "Honey, follow your heart and your dreams. You can be whatever you want to be and whatever you chose to be." And he shared that his dreams were in Cypress Cove with Sarah. The plan that Grayson and Sarah put together included him leaving Taylor Tire and Rubber under certain conditions – one of which was to create a foundation with the majority of his assets. Aubrey listened carefully to understand his wishes. She told Grayson that his parents would be proud of him. The two of them – Aubrey and Grayson – agreed to put Sarah's and his plan into action in phases.

The first phase was for Grayson to separate from Taylor Tire and Rubber Company. Aubrey and Grayson worked on putting together a proposal to present to the Board of Directors at Taylor Tire. At Grayson's request, Aubrey crafted a fair and honest proposal in such a way that the company's board would not want to turn it down. As majority shareholder in Taylor Tire, Grayson was in a strong position, but he wanted to be fair to the board that kept the business running and growing over the many years he was away. The day had arrived for Aubrey and Grayson to present their proposal to Taylor Tire's Board of Directors.

The proposal included four key elements. Taylor Tire must agree to provide funds to build, and financially support for ten years, the Southwest Florida Nature Conservancy. The conservancy would be built in memory of Mary and Robert Taylor, and its work would be to preserve the land, animals, and water in Southwest Florida. It was to be built on 68 acres of land donated by Sarah and Grayson. Taylor Tire was to assign one member to the six-member Conservancy Board of Directors for the ten years of its funding.

The second key element was for Taylor Tire to commit a percentage of annual profits to sustainability. The commitment included finding new and better ways for ecologically friendly manufacturing of tires. Taylor Tire must also implement environmentally safe cleanup and disposal of scrap rubber and tires. The proposal spelled out that the company must measure, monitor, and take action for negative impacts the manufacturing process had on the local air and water ecosystems.

The third key element was that Taylor Tire must define and implement a formal onboarding, orientation, mentoring, and continued employment training program. The program must ensure employees had opportunities to grow, advance, and to be developed to their full potential. Prior to termination, Taylor Tire must ensure that employees had opportunities for coaching and additional training, as necessary.

The fourth and final key element was for Taylor Tire to purchase Grayson's fifty-one percent share in the company. The stock purchase was to be completed by Taylor Tire and Rubber Company, transferring the value of Grayson's stocks into the Jumpstart Foundation. Aubrey helped Grayson form the Jumpstart Foundation to promote entrepreneurship and children's education in Southwest Florida.

The board pored over the documents for two days before unanimously accepting Aubrey's and Grayson's four-point proposal.

The second phase of Sarah's and Grayson's plan was to disposition the personal property and assets Grayson had inherited in Dimerling.

Grayson transferred ownership of the three-story, twelve-acre Taylor Estate to the Dimerling historical society. The turn-of-the-century estate was designated as an historical landmark. He wanted it to be open to visitors to enjoy and learn the history of the rubber industry and the earlier industrial era. The historical society was grateful for Grayson's donation, and committed to the preservation and sharing of the property.

Aubrey helped Grayson establish a new Taylor Family Trust for Sarah and him, to protect the remaining property and financial assets. Grayson asked Aubrey to stay on as legal counsel for the Southwest Florida Nature Conservancy, Jumpstart Foundation, and the Taylor Family Trust. Aubrey was impressed with how Grayson had thoughtfully planned his departure of Taylor Tire and Dimerling. And she was proud of him. Aubrey gladly agreed to his request to continue to work with him.

His final request for Aubrey was to help him formally and legally change his name to Cayman Grayson Taylor. He would go by Cayman, and he did not want to disrespect his parents or lose that family connection.

Sarah and Cayman had originally intended that he would be able to complete their plan and be back in Cypress Cove by the winter holiday seasons. The details of the plan took much longer than they anticipated, and Cayman remained in Dimerling until the spring of 1965.

Cayman and Boone were finally ready to drive back to Cypress Cove about the same time that Sarah returned home from Glades University. They drove back in his dad's 1948 Dodge pickup truck. The truck made him  feel close to his dad, and it reminded him of friends from his village.

Chapter Seven

It was spring 1965, and Sarah's big day – graduating from Glades University of South Florida – was drawing near.

Cayman and Sarah's parents were so proud of all of her accomplishments over the last four years. In addition to completing her college coursework, Sarah took on the Cypress Cove Town Council, lobbying for an improved water runoff system to reduce contaminants from entering the gulf waters off of the town's beaches. Additionally, her team at Glades University brought awareness to South Florida about the effects from the sugarcane industry on The Everglades ecosystem.

It was a warm, sunny day in Miami – perfect conditions for an outdoor graduation ceremony. Cayman made arrangements for a chartered bus to take their families and friends the 95-minute ride from Cypress Cove to Miami to attend Sarah's graduation ceremony. Sarah was one of 107 seniors scheduled to graduate that sunny day.

As the dean called the seniors' names to award their degrees, the graduates walked across the stage and accepted their diplomas. Once graduates received their diplomas, they moved their tassels from the right side of their caps to the left indicating that they had completed all necessary steps to graduate. When the dean announced Sarah Cooper, her family and friends jumped to their feet cheering and clapping; as she walked across the stage, she held her head and arms high. On Saturday, May 15, 1965, Sarah graduated from the Glades University of South Florida, with a Bachelor of Science in Environment Science – Natural Resources and Conservation.

After the graduation ceremony, Sarah's mom took photographs of Sarah, along with several of her college friends. When her mom was done taking photographs and Sarah had congratulated all of her friends, she, her family, and her friends all loaded on the chartered bus for the trip back home. The first stop was to the Poaceaehatchee Village, where the locals had prepared lunch and a Tutelar celebration for Sarah. It was a shortened version of the celebration they had had for Cayman when he had completed the rite-of-passage ceremony.

After the festivities were over in the Poaceaehatchee Village, Sarah thanked and hugged all of her Tutelar friends. Some of her Tutelar friends and the rest of the Cypress Cove folks reboarded the bus to go to her graduation party at the beach. Cayman and her friends, Mila and Avery, from the high school newspaper, had a beach celebration planned for Sarah back in Cypress Cove.

They had set up umbrellas and volleyball nets on the beach, along with food, drinks, and music. They all swam, danced, and played volleyball well into the evening. It was an exciting day for Sarah. She was happy to be with her friends, proud of her accomplishments, and excited to begin the next phase of her life's journey with Cayman in Cypress Cove.

Graduation was behind them, and the summer of 1965 was underway. Sarah was out of college and Cayman was back from Dimerling and Taylor Tire and Rubber. They had developed their plans and were ready to build their dream home on the beach in Cypress Cove.

Sarah and Cayman had had lots of exciting adventures together since they first met when they were both 14 years old, in the fall of 1957. Building their dream home and getting married was their main focus for the summer.

The two of them had been planning their home since they got engaged last summer. They had worked with a builder over the winter to finalize the plans and to schedule the construction.

Cayman had never built a house, yet he helped workers in his village build homes for locals. He had also helped crews repair homes after the tropical storm in July 1959. Cayman wanted to be part of the building crew for the house being built for Sarah and him. He made arrangements with the builder to be able to help as a volunteer member of the construction crew.

Sarah's parents and Cayman's brother Etu also wanted to help in any way they could. There was plenty of work for everyone who wanted to help. Cayman and his brother worked on preparing the building lot, while Sarah's parents planned to help paint inside the home. Sarah and Cayman were grateful that their families wanted to participate in building their home.

The house was being built on the remaining seven-acre lot that Sarah and Cayman retained, after donating 68 acres to the Southwest Florida Nature Conservancy project. The seven-acre lot was located at the south end of Palm Lane and the Cypress Cove beach. It bordered the beach and the Gulf of Mexico on the west side and the Pavati River on the south side. It was a two-mile walk or drive from their lot to the Kendrick Pier.

Sarah and Cayman were careful to design and build the house so as not to disturb the natural landscape and beauty of the surrounding land. It was designed as a one-story, cottage-style home, to be built on three-foot-tall stilts

148

to mitigate storm surges.

The house was designed to include a verandah encompassing the entire home. From the verandah, stairs descended to a natural walking path onto the beach on the water side, and stairs and a limestone-packed sidewalk to car parking spaces on the street side. There were two large doors that opened onto the extended verandah on the beach side.

The outside of the home had wood siding with shutters and a tall, metal, hip-style roof. Cayman added a carving of his signature feather to the arch of the overhang on the back verandah. Sarah and Cayman included a boat dock on the Pavati River with a natural walking path from the house to the dock.

The two of them believed that one day they would have a baby, so they designed the inside with two bedrooms and two bathrooms. Sarah's and Cayman's bedroom and their kitchen overlooked the verandah on the beach side of the house. A laundry room was situated between the main bedroom and the second bedroom on the street side of the house. The living room area extended from the open kitchen to the street side. Even though it was not a large house, it was going to have an open, spacious feel.

The construction crew began working on the house in early June 1965. Sarah and Cayman enjoyed working with the construction crew. The two of them arranged to have lunches and dinners prepared daily for the construction crew and family members. Everyone was involved, chipping in when they could to help build Sarah's and Cayman's home on the beach. Even Boone seemed to enjoy spending the day on the beach while the house was being built.

Cayman rented a small apartment in Cypress Cove, so he wouldn't have to spend time driving to and from the Poaceaehatchee Village. While he was helping the construction crew, Sarah and her mom were picking out paint colors and fixtures. Cayman's parents worked in the Poaceaehatchee Village, but they helped whenever they could, usually on weekends.

By early September, the crews were putting finishing touches on the landscaping and outside painting. Furniture was in place and the final details were completed by the second week of September. Sarah and her mom hung up several of Sarah's photographs throughout their home. Sarah's and Cayman's home was complete and ready to move into by mid-September, only a few weeks before their wedding.

Cayman decided to stay in the apartment he rented, and wait to move in with Sarah on their wedding day. The two of them invited their family, friends, and the construction crew to their new home to celebrate its completion with a cookout on the beach.

Even during construction, Sarah and Cayman didn't miss opportunities to take their morning walks on the beach. Now that they were both living in Cypress Cove, they were able to volunteer for turtle watch during the summer nesting season once again. They loved getting up before sunrise and walking the beach, counting new turtle nests and seeing the birds and sea life wake up for the day.

During one of their early-morning walks, Sarah caught a photo

of the full moon descending on the western horizon, when at the same time there was a lightning strike out at sea. It had proved to be a magical summer, and they were looking forward to their upcoming wedding day.

It was October 6, 1965, and Sarah's and Cayman's wedding day had arrived. Their wedding was to take place at their new home on the beach in Cypress Cove. Their home opened onto a backyard of sandy dunes, sea oats, and palm trees. From the back verandah, leading to the beach, was a natural, sandy path, lined with palm trees.

It was a picture-perfect, warm, sunny day for a beach wedding. Sarah and Cayman had set up chairs on the beach for their parents and a few guests. Neither of them were concerned about fancy things, so an unpretentious beach wedding was a perfect fit.

The Tutelar spiritual leader, accompanied by a few villagers playing drums and flutes, were there to perform the ceremony.

Sarah's mom, Cayman's mom, and two of Sarah's best friends, Mila and Avery from the high school newspaper, were there to help her get ready for her special day. Sarah's dress was perfect for a beach wedding. It was a simple long, white, sleeveless linen dress. It had lace inserts of flowers on the shoulder straps and at the waist and knees. She wore a light-blue, wide-brim wedding hat, with a large light-blue silk bow and ribbon hanging down the back. Sarah's long, dark hair flowed down her back under the silk ribbon.

The men – Sarah's dad, Cayman's dad, and Etu – helped Cayman get ready for the ceremony. He wore a light-blue, button-down linen shirt with white, light-weight linen pants. Cayman and the other men left the house and headed to the beach to wait for Sarah to walk down the sandy path. The Tutelar drummers and flautist were already playing traditional Tutelar wedding songs. Cayman was jittery and anxious to see Sarah come walking down the sandy path.

The women soon appeared on the path and made their way to their chairs on the beach. The moment had finally arrived, and Sarah was walking slowly down the path toward Cayman. He was overcome with emotion as she appeared to be floating toward him. Neither Sarah nor Cayman were wearing shoes during the ceremony. Once she made it to her spot on the beach, the Tutelar spiritual leader began the ceremony.

While there were similarities to that of a traditional Anglo wedding ceremony, the Tutelar ceremony was much more spiritual. When it came time to exchange their vows, they each placed a ring on the other's finger. The rings were designed and sketched by Cayman, and crafted by a Tutelar jewelry maker. The rings were wide silver bands, each having a single silver feather carved in the center of a dark recessed section. The single feather stood for honor, trust, and to protect one another. The year of their wedding, 1965, was carved into the inside of each ring.

As Sarah placed Cayman's ring on his finger, she recited her wedding vows to him. "Cayman Taylor, you're my best friend. You opened my eyes to a part of our world I had never seen and didn't know existed. You showed me the living world around us – the plants, trees, and water. You helped me see how important the birds, animals, and fish are to us. Because of you, I have found my true calling and purpose in life. I know now that I can make a difference in the world in which we live. I can't imagine life without you, and I am ready to start our new adventure together. I love you so much."

As Cayman placed Sarah's ring on her finger, he recited his wedding vows to her. "Sarah Cooper, you are my best friend. You helped me become part of the bigger world around me. I promise to take care of you and to cherish you for the rest of your life. A very wise woman once told me to follow my heart, and it led me to you. I can't imagine life without you, and I, too, am ready to start our new adventure together. I love you so much."

Their wedding day culminated with a celebration and picnic on the beach, under the palm trees, at Sarah's and Cayman's new home. It wasn't a big fancy reception; rather, like Sarah and Cayman, it was a simple family festivity. Sarah's mom, Vicki, made a congratulatory toast to Sarah and Cayman. "Henry and I always knew that you and Cayman would be together. We could tell by the way you smile when you see each other and the way you look when you are apart. You have already had more adventures than most people, and I am sure there are many more to come. We are so proud of the adults you have grown to be and we wish you many, many more years of love and joy."

Cayman's mom, Sakari, made a toast to the newly-wedded couple in Tutelar fashion. "Cayman and Sarah, you have respected the Tutelar culture by getting married today in a traditional Tutelar wedding ceremony. Cayman, you came to our village a scared young boy, and you have grown to be an honorable member of the Tutelar tribe. Sarah, you came into Cayman's life when he needed you most. You didn't try to separate Cayman from the Tutelar; instead, you learned and embraced our culture. Alo and I are happy you chose Cayman to be your husband. We wish both of you all the best."

Cayman's brother, Etu, also made a toast. "Brother, since the day you joined our family, when we were just kids, you have been my best friend. Sarah, Cayman deserves the best, and you are the best. I am so happy you two found each other, and I am glad that I now have a sister. I can't wait to see what comes next."

They all enjoyed the picnic, and danced and talked until the stars and moon shown over the gulf waters.

The day was simple and the ceremony was heart-felt. Sarah's mom took wedding photos throughout the day. She snapped shots of

Chapter Seven

Sarah getting ready and of Cayman nervously waiting for the ceremony to begin. Vicki took photographs of Sarah walking down the sandy path to the where Cayman was waiting. She took several photographs during the ceremony and picnic. Sarah picked up the camera and took photographs of her mom making the toast and her mom and dad dancing barefoot in the sand. They all left for home after a wonderful day.

Sarah and Cayman didn't go on a traditional honeymoon; they couldn't imagine any place nicer than where they lived in Cypress Cove. Cayman got up early the next morning and made breakfast for his new wife. They sat outside on the verandah and enjoyed breakfast together, while watching the beach and water as the sun came up over the front of their house.

After breakfast, they went for a walk on the beach. They talked and talked, until they ended up walking two miles to the pier. The two of them took a short break on the pier before heading south toward their new home. While resting at the pier, they noticed a mother manatee with her calf alongside, swimming under the pier below. The adult manatee looked like she was about nine feet long and the calf was a third of her size. Sarah snapped a photograph as the pair of manatees swam under them.

Walking back home, they pledged to start every morning with a walk on the beach. Turtle nesting season was over for the year, yet they would be out next year volunteering for turtle watch. Boone was happy to join their tradition of daily beach walks. From that morning on, Boone planned to wake up Sarah and Cayman early to take him along on their beach walks. He made sure they knew it was time to get up and that he was going with them.

During one of their early-morning walks, as they approached the jetty at an inlet, they noticed a large blue heron standing among the rocks. It stood there unconcerned that they and Boone were nearby. Sarah snapped a photograph of the heron as it stood proudly watching over the stretch of the beach.

They were enjoying their morning beach walks, talking over their plans for launching the Jumpstart Foundation and the Southwest Florida Nature Conservancy. They had lots to do, and they couldn't wait to get started.

Chapter Eight

December 1965, Sarah and Cayman, with Aubrey's help, founded the Jumpstart Foundation for entrepreneurship and children's education. The foundation was funded by the Board of Directors of Taylor Tire and Rubber Company, which had approved and executed the buyback of Cayman's fifty-one percent stake. Funds in the amount of the value of his stock were transferred into the Jumpstart Foundation's financial account. The value of Cayman's share in Taylor Tire was significant enough that, with wise financial management and smart grant assignments, the Jumpstart Foundation could operate into perpetuity.

The mission of the foundation served to promote entrepreneurship and child development in Poaceaehatchee Village and Cypress Cove. By law in the state of Florida, they must state the names, and have a minimum, of three directors on the board of the foundation. Cayman Taylor served as the board chairman; Aubrey Hayes and Sarah Taylor served in the other two director roles. The foundation board approved three immediate grant awards – a new school for the Poaceaehatchee Village, a scholarship program for underprivileged children of Poaceaehatchee and Cypress Cove, and a photography lab and studio for Cypress Cove Schools.

The first piece of business taken up by the Jumpstart Foundation was to provide grant monies to the Poaceaehatchee Village for the construction of a new school for the Tutelar children. Cayman had spoken with the Tutelar council of elders to make them aware of the grant application process so they could build a new school. The council was thrilled with Cayman's gesture and assistance, and looked forward to getting the school completed and opened for the Tutelar children. The council of elders formed a core team of elders and teachers to oversee the project. They set the expectations of the core team to define and execute a plan to build and open the school by the beginning of the next school year.

Sarah and Cayman envisioned underprivileged children of the Poaceaehatchee Village and Cypress Cove to have the opportunity to go to college. The foundation's second act of business was to develop a scholarship fund for the children of Cypress Cove and the Poaceaehatchee Village. They requested leaders from both schools to come together for the purpose of defining criteria, a process, and an organization to manage the scholarship program. The school leaders were tasked with defining a program that treated the students of the two schools fairly and equally. Sarah and Cayman shared with the leaders of the program, that once the Jumpstart Foundation board felt comfortable that proper governance was in place, it would fund the program.

The third grant that the Jumpstart Foundation planned to award was for the provision of a photography lab and studio in the Cypress Cove High School. Sarah's mom was a professional photographer, and Sarah had been an amateur photographer since she was a child. Sarah believed that photography helped her to see the world around her in a deeper, more significant way. She wanted to share that way of seeing the world with other children in Cypress Cove.

Sarah asked her mom if she would lead the design and implementation of a photography lab and studio in the Cypress Cove High School. Sarah also thought her mom would be the perfect person to teach photography. Vicki was excited about the idea and couldn't wait to get started.

Sarah and her mom scheduled a meeting with the Cypress Cove school board to discuss the Jumpstart grant proposal. The board voted unanimously to move forward with the photography lab and studio. They assigned a team to work with Vicki Cooper to build and equip the lab, design the class curriculum, and launch a pilot class during the next school year. Vicki's team consisted of school staff representing maintenance for the lab, purchasing for equipment, a teacher for curriculum development, and an administrator for course scheduling.

These first three Jumpstart grants were what Sarah and Cayman had determined to be the most important and immediate actions needed by the Poaceaehatchee Village and Cypress Cove. All three of these grants awarded by the foundation were in the area of children's education. They had not yet identified a grant opportunity in the area of entrepreneurship. The two of them knew that there would be more actions taken by the foundation, awarding more grants over time.

Sarah and Cayman wanted to do something for his adopted parents, the Deeres. They had taken Cayman into their home when he was five years old at the scariest, saddest time of his life, and raised him as their son. They encouraged him and guided him as he grew from a boy to a man.

Sakari and Alo were modest, and Cayman knew that they would not want anything big, fancy, or elaborate for themselves. It was not the Tutelar way or custom to accept large gifts, unless it provided for the entire village in some way. He and Sarah talked it over, and they decided his parents would be happiest if they did something for Etu instead.

Etu knew better than anyone in Southwest Florida where to find the best fishing spots in the shallow backwaters and in the deeper gulf waters. Since he and Cayman were young boys, Etu had talked about starting a fishing charter business for tourists and locals. Sarah and Cayman believed that helping Etu start a fishing charter business, on behalf of their parents, would be the perfect gift to give him.

Sarah and Cayman talked it over with Sakari and Alo. His parents were very pleased with and grateful for this plan to help Etu establish a charter business. Etu's dream had always been to be a charter captain, yet Etu was a proud man, and Cayman knew he must carefully plan how to present the idea.

Cayman met with Etu the next day to discuss the charter business idea. He asked Etu if he remembered talking about wanting to start a fishing charter. Etu quickly said, "Of course! I would love to find a way to get it started!" Cayman told Etu that he and Sarah would like to jumpstart his fishing charter business by investing in his idea and providing him with his first charter fishing boat. Etu was thrilled with the idea. He shook Cayman's hand, and told him he was going to name his boat Fish-Hawk, meaning osprey. It was to honor Cayman's parents' by naming his boat after their Cessna 170 airplane.

The next day Cayman and Boone picked up Etu at the village then drove to the Cypress Cove train depot. From the depot, they took the train to Fort Myers. From the Fort Myers train depot, they took a taxi to the Boat and Marine Center on the Caloosahatchee River.

Cayman knew that Etu had always wanted a 28' Sport Fisherman boat. He had contacted the marina in advance to make sure they had a new boat prepped and ready for when they arrived. Cayman and Etu took the Sport Fisherman for a test drive on the Caloosahatchee River and out into the Gulf of Mexico. They both knew immediately that it was the perfect boat for Etu to launch his charter fishing business. The boat had eight rod holders and two fishing outriggers. It was the right size for chartering eight people out to the best fishing spots in Southwest Florida and the Gulf of Mexico.

They purchased the Sport Fisherman, along with a dozen rods and reels, life vests, safety equipment, coolers, fishing tackle supplies, and other necessities for Etu's charter business.

The two of them took turns driving the boat during the five-hour trip back to the Poaceaehatchee Village. They talked the entire trip about how exciting it was that Etu was finally launching his fishing charter business.

Together, they defined a rough business plan, a mission statement, and company name. Etu came up with the name Seabright Fishing Charter. Seabright was a Tutelar word for glory at sea. They defined the Seabright Fishing Charter mission to be, "The Seabright Fishing Charter mission is to provide customers with a one-of-a-kind fishing experience, while striving to sustain the natural balance of sea life in Southwest Florida."

To support the mission, Etu came up with talking points to deliver to passengers while they were on the way to the best fishing spots. He would cover the basic safety points, such as staying seated while the boat was moving, the location of life jackets, and safe handling of the fishing poles and lines.

Etu, the charter captain, would also share some of the Tutelar cultural elements of fishing. He decided that he would tell passengers that, "while the Tutelar get enjoyment from fishing, we do it to sustain life through food. We respect the fish and all animals, and we protect them by only taking what we need, and we safely return back to the sea what isn't needed." He would also tell his passengers what type of fish they would be catching during the charter, and he would share the Florida Fish and Wildlife Conservation Commission rules for fishing.

Cayman and Etu determined that a key element of the business plan was to help drive more business and opportunities to the Poaceaehatchee Village. Not only did Etu and Cayman want the charter business to be successful, yet in Tutelar custom, they wanted other villagers to benefit, as well. To do so, Etu determined that he would promote the village as part of the overall fishing experience. He planned to dock the boat at the village docks so that customers would walk through the village to reach the boat. It would provide an opportunity for other businesses to prosper, as well.

By docking at the village docks, early-morning charter customers could come to the village before fishing and enjoy breakfast. After the passengers were done fishing, they could have lunch and do some shopping for handmade Tutelar jewelry and clothes. Afternoon charter customers could come to the village before their charter appointment to enjoy lunch and shop before getting on the boat.

Most of the kids in the Poaceaehatchee Village were skilled at filleting fish. Etu thought that they could offer to fillet the fish caught during fishing charters. He planned to talk with the village eateries to see if they would be interested in preparing customers' filleted fish for lunch or dinner at a modest fee. The whole way back to the village docks the two of them talked about ways to help the village prosper, along with Etu's fishing charter business.

As Etu pulled the boat into the dock at the Poaceaehatchee Village, he looked at Cayman with a big smile and gave him a hug; they both knew that they would be doing something good for the villagers.

Chapter Eight

In January 1966, Sarah and Cayman officially announced the plans, location, and mission of the Southwest Florida Nature Conservancy. "The mission of the Nature Conservancy is the preservation of the land, animals, and water in Southwest Florida." Sarah and Cayman donated 68 acres of the 75-acre tract of land his parents bought in Cypress Cove during their honeymoon in 1938.

The Southwest Florida Nature Conservancy was a non-profit organization that relied on donations from visitors, wealthy donors, and corporate donors. Sarah and Cayman asked Aubrey to serve as board chairwoman of a six-member board of directors and as legal counsel to the conservancy.

To ensure fair and balanced representation, Sarah and Aubrey recruited two board members from the Tutelar tribe and two from Cypress Cove. Their intent was to bring together villagers of Tutelar and people of Cypress Cove, for a common cause of protecting the animals, clean water, and a healthy environment. Due to Taylor Tire and Rubber Company's ten-year commitment to fund the conservancy, Sarah added one board member from the company. Sarah was designated to serve as secretary to the board and executive director of the conservancy. She would hire and lead the staff members, manage communications, define initiatives, and secure donor funding.

Cayman was to serve as operations director, overseeing day-to-day operations of the facilities and grounds. He would also lead the implementation of four phases of building and development. The first phase of construction was the main building for exhibits and learning. The second phase was utilizing the lake and grounds as an outdoor adventure area for hiking and boating. The third phase of construction was to build and staff a conservancy hospital to rescue and rehabilitate animals, birds, and sea life in distress. The final phase was to open a thirty-acre botanical gardens for visitors to see and learn about a variety of plants and trees native to the region.

During the winter of 1966, Sarah and Cayman broke ground to begin construction of phase one of the conservancy. It took six months to build and open the main building, which included an information center, schoolroom, gift store, photo gallery, and exhibits with descriptions and explanations of local plants, animals, birds, and sea life. The conservancy was built to allow space for teaching children about the land and animals in Southwest Florida, with a classroom that would be shared by Cypress Cove and Poaceaehatchee children.

The gift store sold books, photographs, posters, and drawings of animals, birds, sea life, plants, and trees. There was a variety of clothing with animal, bird, and fish imprints, such as hats, tee shirts, jackets, and scarfs. For the kids, the store sold toy animals, birds, and fish. There was a variety of related costume jewelry and other knickknacks that could be purchased. Refreshments, such as drinks, sandwiches, and snacks, could be purchased and enjoyed in the shaded picnic area on the conservancy grounds.

The photo gallery, named Sacred Moments II, was a place for visitors to enjoy photographs taken in Southwest Florida. There were photographs of animals, birds, and sea life in their natural habitat. Several of the photographs were taken by Sarah over the years, as well as new photographs she had taken for the gallery. Sarah provided space in the gallery for Aiyana and Elu, the proprietors of Sacred Moments I gallery in the Poaceaehatchee Village, to display their photos. All of the photographs exhibited in the gallery were made to have reprints available for purchase in the gift shop.

Sarah framed and hung the sketches that Cayman had drawn and included with his letters to her over the years. His sketches of animals and scenery fit perfectly with the other exhibits in the conservancy.

The exhibit hall included nearly one hundred life-sized photographs, renderings, and replicas of a variety of animals, birds, and sea life from Southwest Florida. Each exhibit included a written and a recorded explanation of the exhibit. Exhibit explanations described the animal's natural habitat, how it migrated, its food source, its size and life span, and what its natural enemies were. The exhibits hall's primary purpose was to provide hands-on learning and awareness for children and visitors to Southwest Florida.

The Southwest Florida Nature Conservancy was dedicated on July 4, 1966, in memory of Cayman's parents, Mary and Robert Taylor. It was the 18-year anniversary of their plane crash on July 4, 1948, in The Everglades.

The second phase of the conservancy construction was to create an outdoor adventure area positioned around the eight-acre lake on the northeast section of the land. Work on this phase started during the construction of phase one, and it was opened to the public on Sarah's birthday, September 3, 1966.

Sarah
1966

It included a three-mile hiking trail around the lake, through the Cypress Forest and mangroves, and over the wetlands. Over a mile of the trail was boardwalk over wetlands, where hikers were treated to sights of alligators, river otters, and a variety of fish and birds. An information center, picnic area, and dock were built near the edge of the lake. Visitors went to the outdoor adventure area to relax, enjoy picnics with friends and family, or feed the birds and fish. More adventuresome visitors rented small paddle boats or took group rides on pontoon boats. There was something for everyone.

During the spring of 1967, phase three of the conservancy opened. It was the conservancy hospital for animals, birds, and sea creatures. It was a place to bring sick or injured creatures for care, recovery, and release back into their native habitats.

Visitors were invited to come to the hospital to see and learn about the animals. They learned about where the animals lived, what they ate, and how to protect them from accidental injuries by human interactions. The hospital was designed to allow visitors to view the animals while veterinarians provided care for their injuries and the animals were recovering.

Often the conservancy hospital would announce information about an upcoming release. Lucky spectators could see birds – eagles, ospreys, pelicans, and others – being freed back into the wild. They might also get to see a dolphin, sea turtle, or stingray being released into the Gulf of Mexico. On rare occasions, a lucky few spectators would get to see a panther being taken back to the Cypress Forest to run free. The conservancy hospital drew thousands of visitors from all over the country and some from outside the United States.

Thirty acres of land was set aside for the botanical gardens – the fourth and final phase of the conservancy. The gardens opened on two of the thirty acres in the fall of 1967, with exhibits and descriptions of mostly local plants and trees. The two-acre gardens began with ten trees central to the gardens, including five palm trees, and five other local trees. The palm tree exhibit included cabbage palm, royal palm, thatch palm, pygmy date palm, and the areca palm. Other local trees included large banyan, bald cypress, live oak, longleaf pine, and Sarah's favorite, a royal poinciana.

Chapter Eight

The Florida State tree – the cabbage palm – was also known as the sabal palm. It grew to about 35 feet tall, with large fan-shaped leaves, or fronds. The cabbage palm was an evergreen tree shedding the older fronds as they grew out. The trunk of the palm was made up entirely of stalks from fronds that feel off.

The royal palm was a tall, noble, native palm to Southwest Florida and it grew rapidly to 60 feet tall. The trunk was light gray with a smooth-looking surface. The palm fronds spread up to 25 feet. The thatch palm was a slow-growing native, and the fronds were used on thatched roofs. It grew to 20 feet tall and had weepy fan fronds, with a skinny gray trunk.

The pygmy date palm was often used in landscaping and it grew to six or seven feet tall and five feet wide. It was often seen in clumps of three, with fine fronds and a well-manicured trunk. The areca palm, also called the butterfly palm, was sometimes used as a tropical privacy border. It had long feathery fronds reaching up to 30 feet from bamboo-looking stems. The feathery look made it one of Cayman's favorite trees.

Banyan trees were members of the Ficus family, and were one of the world's largest trees. Banyans grew 100 feet tall and hundreds of feet wide, with roots growing down from the branches as they spread. Bald cypress trees were slow-growing trees with a tapering trunk. They grew to 100 feet tall in wet, dry, or salty soil, and had a three-foot diameter trunk. Live oaks were huge, wide-spreading trees, that formed canopies of shade. They had large limbs of crooked shapes. They were often seen shading streets, park areas, or yards.

Longleaf pines had a course, brownish-orange bark and grew to 90 feet tall. They had eighteen-inch-long soft needles, with large ten-inch pine cones on upward growing branches. Sarah's favorite, the royal poinciana, had a wide canopy covered in small soft leaves, that looked like bright, orange-red flowers. The canopy of the poinciana was wider than the tree was tall.

Several of the plants in the exhibit included firebush, coreopsis, honeysuckle, jasmine, black-eyed Susan, liatris, swamp lily, and yucca.

The firebush was a 12-foot-wide tall shrub with greenery and bright orange-red tubelike flowers. Coreopsis grew in clusters and had green leaves and yellow daisy looking flowers. Honeysuckle was a shrub with tubular flowers, yellow, pink, red, or white in color. Jasmine was a climbing plant with sweet-scented white flowers.

Black-eyed Susans were a wildflower that grew three feet tall with a three-inch-diameter yellow flower. In the middle of the flower was a dark ball holding the flower pedals. Liatris was a tall spiky plant with purple thistle-like flowers on top of the green stem and foliage. Swamp lilies grew best in water, up to three feet tall, with spidery-shaped white flowers. Yucca plants had a single thick stem growing up from spiky leaves at the base. At the top of the stem was a large cluster of white bell-shaped flowers.

Sarah and Cayman opened the botanical gardens with ten local species of trees and several local plants. Their ten-year plan was to fill all thirty acres of the gardens with hundreds of different plants and trees on display. They envisioned it becoming a popular destination for locals and tourists.

Even with all they had done in the last two years – getting married, building their house, launching the foundation and the conservancy – Sarah and Cayman didn't slow down. They had always planned to build a home near theirs, on the beach, for Sarah's parents.

Chapter Eight

Her parents had sacrificed a lot for Sarah, moving to Cypress Cove and living in their small apartment for the past ten years.

Sarah and Cayman wanted to do something for them in return. With Sarah's input, Cayman sketched a rough design of the house they wanted to build as a surprise for her parents. During the winter of 1967, Sarah and Cayman met with the builder who had built their house.

The two of them designed a simple one-story, cottage-style home. They planned to build it on a one-acre, beach-front lot near their home, and arranged to have that split from their seven acres and deeded to her parents. Her parents' house was going to be built on the lot just north of their home on Palm Lane.

It was designed to be built on three-foot stilts to protect it against potential storm surges. The design included a verandah that wrapped around the entire house, with stairs going down to ground level on the beach side and stairs on the side next to the street.

The floor plan was open, with the living room and kitchen situated on the beach side of the house. There was a set of double doors from the living room and kitchen that opened onto the verandah for access to and a view of the beach. There were two bedrooms on the street side of the home with a shared bathroom. A small laundry room and a storage room sat between the spare bedroom and the kitchen.

The builder finished site preparation late winter, with requests from Sarah and Cayman to maintain as much of the natural foliage as possible. The construction crew started building the house on the first day of Spring 1967. Sarah and Cayman kept the construction a secret from Vicki and Henry, wanting to surprise them when it was complete and ready for them to occupy.

Sarah checked on the construction progress every day to make sure it was on schedule and met the original design. When she was visiting with her mom, she asked her questions, to try to figure out what she would want if she were designing her own home. She tried to asked questions in a way as to not give away their secret construction project. Cayman often took Henry out fishing in the backwaters and in the gulf. When they were fishing, Cayman tried to discretely figure out some of Henry's preferences for building a home. Sarah and Cayman used the information they gleaned from her parents to select paint colors, fixtures, lighting, appliances, and furniture.

The construction crew completed the home early summer, and scheduled a walk-through inspection with Sarah and Cayman in late June. By mid-July, the remaining items from the walk-through were corrected, and they were ready to have the furniture and appliances delivered. The house was completed and ready to move into by the end of July. Sarah and Cayman were excited and couldn't wait any longer to show the home to her parents.

The two of them invited Vicki and Henry to join them downtown for dinner on August 1, 1967. After dinner, Sarah and Cayman invited her parents back to their house to talk and watch sunset.

On the way there, they stopped at the new home, next door to theirs. Sarah and Cayman told her parents that they wanted to show them the new house that was built next to theirs. As Vicki and Henry were walking through the home, they began noticing that things looked strangely familiar. To Sarah's parents, it was almost as if they had picked out the colors, furniture, and fixtures themselves. By now, her parents were becoming curious and suspicious as to why they were looking at this house.

Sarah couldn't wait any longer. She told her parents, "Cayman and I appreciate everything you've done for us. We appreciate how you sacrificed for me to live in Cypress Cove and to attend Glades University. How you have always been good to Cayman, and let us go on amazing adventures. In return, we wanted to do something for you two. We built this house for you, and we hope you will make it your home, by living next door to us."

Vicki and Henry were beyond thrilled about the gift they just received! They loved their daughter and her new husband, and they were proud about the caring and giving adults they had become. They happily accepted this generous gift. The very next day, the Coopers notified their landlord that August was the last month they would be renting the apartment in town.

During the month of August, they packed and moved their belongings into their new home. By late August, they had moved in and were happily new neighbors to Sarah and Cayman on Palm Lane. On August 31, they invited Sarah and Cayman to dinner to celebrate and thank them.

Part Three:

Emma

Chapter Nine

The young girl said to her mom, the storyteller, "There is so much going on in Sarah and Cayman's life! What could possibly happen next?" Her mom replied, "Honey, just wait! There are more surprises to come."

During a routine doctor's visit in March 1968, 24-year-old Sarah learned that she was pregnant. Even though she had no idea she was pregnant, it was the best news she could have heard from her doctor. She could hardly wait to get back to the conservancy to tell Cayman that he was going to be a dad. The two of them had been hoping for a baby.

As soon as she left Doctor Essert's office, Sarah headed straight to the conservancy to tell Cayman the good news. When she got there, she asked Cayman to sit down, because she had some important news to share with him. Cayman knew she had been to her doctor's office, so he was nervous, not knowing what she might say. Then Sarah started smiling, and she blurted it out. "We're going to have a baby!" Cayman jumped to his feet and lifted Sarah off her feet while he hugged her. Somehow, as if it were possible, Cayman loved her even more than he already did. Boone must have known Sarah shared good news, because he started barking and trying to get in on the hugging action.

Cayman couldn't wait to start picking out names and working on preparing the baby's room. He could barely concentrate on work for the rest of the day. They were both so excited, they didn't sleep much that night. Early the next morning, they got up and went for their beach walk.

All they talked about was having a baby and all the things they wanted to do to prepare. The two of them talked about setting up a nursery. They planned how they would tell her parents, his parents, Etu, and the staff at the conservancy. They decided they would tell both sets of parents at the same time by having them over for dinner at their house that evening. Once they had told their parents, they would tell the conservancy staff the next day. Before they knew it, they had walked all the way to the pier.

As they headed south, back to their house, Sarah noticed a cockle shell situated perfectly on the beach – as if to appear to be angel wings. She knew that in Tutelar culture, when you saw angel wings, it was a message of love  and support. She couldn't resist taking a photograph of the shell that she took as a sign of good things to come.

Once they arrived home, Sarah called her parents and Cayman's parents to invite them to the house for dinner. While Sarah was calling their parents, Cayman went shopping to get groceries for dinner. They both went into the conservancy that day, but their minds were on sharing their exciting news with their parents.

The two of them got home early to prepare dinner for their families. Cayman's parents, along with Etu, arrived about five-thirty p.m., and Sarah's parents walked over from their home, and arrived a few minutes later. They all sat down for dinner and talked about their day, and other normal stuff. After dinner, Cayman collected the dishes and cleaned up the table, while Sarah asked everyone to join her on the verandah to watch sunset.

Cayman stepped out onto the verandah as the sun was setting and the colors in the sky were changing to brilliant pinks and oranges.

Chapter Nine

After the sun had set, Sarah told everyone that she and Cayman had some exciting news to share. She looked at Etu and blurted out, "You are going to be an uncle!" They all looked surprised for a moment, then they suddenly figured out what she was saying. They couldn't contain their joy! Everybody stood up and hugged each other over the very exciting news. They all sat down again and took in the beauty of the evening on the beach and of the news they had just received.

The next morning, Sarah and Cayman went on their daily beach walk, had breakfast, and then went to the conservancy to share their news. The conservancy staff had only been working together for a short time, yet they had quickly become a family. The staff was delighted with Sarah's and Cayman's vision for the conservancy and its positive impacts on Southwest Florida, where they all lived.

Sarah and Cayman asked everyone to meet them in the outdoor picnic area so they could share their wonderful news. Everyone was surprised when they heard that Sarah was pregnant; they all clapped and hugged with joy. The conservancy team knew that Sarah and Cayman would be great parents and that they would get to be part of the new baby's life.

Over the next several days and weeks, Sarah and Cayman made plans for what it meant to add a new member to their family. Their morning walks on the beach were perfect for planning all of the details of bringing a new life into their world. They discussed the conservancy, putting together a nursery, baby names, continuing their daily walks on the beach, and life after their new baby was born.

Sarah told Cayman that she wanted to continue to work at the conservancy during her pregnancy. Cayman knew that the conservancy was Sarah's first baby, and that she was determined to keep life as normal as possible. He supported her decision and told her that he would help her with anything she needed to make it work. They also discussed how she could delegate some of her duties to others on her staff. Sarah later talked it over with a few members of her team, and they all agreed that they would take on extra responsibilities to help her out. She felt good that her family, staff, and Cayman were there for whatever she needed along her journey to giving birth.

Sarah and Cayman already had shared the duties and responsibilities of taking care of their home, preparing meals, cleaning, and laundry. Even so, Cayman assured Sarah that he would take over any responsibilities that caused her discomfort during her pregnancy.

During her follow-up doctor's visit, Cayman joined Sarah to be part of the discussion about any recommended changes to physical activity and dietary modifications. Dr. Essert told them that Sarah should continue to exercise and get lots of sleep. She should continue to eat lots of seafood because it's loaded with vitamins and minerals, such as iron, zinc, and omega-3. It was all good news, since they both enjoyed fishing, preparing, and eating their catch. She told them that Sarah needed to start eating for two. There wasn't anything Dr. Essert told her that she should stop doing. On their way home from the doctor's office, Cayman told Sarah that he would like to go with her for every doctor's visit. She was pleased that Cayman wanted to be with her during her appointments, and they both felt good about what they had heard from Dr. Essert.

Sarah and Cayman felt comfortable with the plans they had made for work at the conservancy and physical activities. Now they wanted to turn their attention to baby names and getting the nursery ready for the baby's arrival. The two of them continued their turtle watch volunteer assignment by walking the beach between their house and the pier each morning, counting new turtle nests. They took advantage of their uninterrupted time together, using their daily walks to talk about plans for the nursery and ideas for baby names.

Chapter Nine

During one of their morning beach walks, Sarah asked Cayman, "Which would you prefer to have, a boy or a girl?" Cayman said, while smiling, "I hope we have a girl and that she's exactly like you." Sarah just laughed and smiled back. From then on, each morning, while walking on the beach, they each shared some boys' names and girls' names. A few names they considered were Lucas, Noah, Liam, Ethan, Owen, or Logan for a boy, and Olivia, Charlotte, Camila, Nora, Emily, or Riley for a girl. They liked all of the names they discussed, but none seemed to feel quite right. Neither of them were about to give up on finding the perfect name before the arrival of their new family member. They talked about names all of the time – morning, noon, and night. Beach walks were when they were the most creative.

While they were trying to figure out the perfect boy's and girl's name, they were also working to make the nursery just right for their new baby. Sarah and her mom had been shopping for the nursery. They looked for a crib, changing table, rocking chair, diaper pail, blankets, sheets, nightlight, pillows, storage bins, hamper, and diapers. Cayman was busy repainting the walls and adding colorful designs, like rainbows, to the walls. The two of them added colorful furniture to the nursery. Their parents were also bringing them toys, books, and supplies for the nursery. With each passing day, Sarah, Cayman, and their families were getting more and more excited for the new baby to arrive.

While they were trying to decide on baby names and get the nursery ready, Boone was showing signs of his age. Cayman was not sure just how old Boone was. Cayman had found him in 1956, so Boone was at least twelve years old. Boone wasn't eating like normal and he did not want to go on beach walks. By July 1968, Sarah and Cayman knew they needed to have Boone checked by a veterinarian. They took him to Adeline, their veterinarian friend, to see what she thought could be done. Adeline told them that 12 years was a good, long life for a large dog like Boone, and his time had come.

They knew what she meant, and they were devastated to hear that news. Boone had been their dedicated friend and protector for more than a decade, and they weren't ready for him to go. Adeline, like many people in Cypress Cove and the Poaceaehatchee Village, had known Boone for a long time. She tried to console them, telling them, "Boone has been a good dog and friend to you. He is not in pain and he has had a good life. Take him home and make him comfortable for his last few days." Sarah and Cayman were quiet the entire way home, while contemplating life without Boone. They watched over him with tenderness and love, and he died peacefully just one week later.

After Boone had passed, Sarah and Cayman invited their parents to their home for dinner so they could tell them together. They knew that they would have to tell them as soon as they arrived, since they would quickly notice that Boone wasn't around. Once they arrived, Cayman asked them to come out to the back verandah so they could talk before dinner. When they were all seated, Cayman said, "Boone died calmly and quietly last night. He wasn't in any pain. Sarah and I are sad that he is gone, but we know that his spirit is here and will always be with us." Sarah said that they had been discussing how important Boone was in their lives and that they wanted their baby to grow up knowing that friendship. She shared that they had decided they were going to get a puppy to raise as a friend and protector of their baby. Everyone was sad, but impressed with how Sarah and Cayman handled it in a thoughtful way.

Chapter Nine

Sarah's parents told her how Boone played a role in their lives and what he meant to them. The two of them told her that when she was younger and went on adventures with Cayman, they were happy that Boone was there to watch over them. Cayman's parents retold the story of how Cayman had jumped into the water and swam past the alligators to save Boone. They said that naming the puppy Boone, meaning miracle, was appropriate because Boone really saved Cayman. It was when Cayman was in a time of need, after he lost Luna a few months earlier. Etu shared a story about when he and Cayman had been lost in the Cypress Forest, and Boone got them home safely.

Sarah decided it was the right time to share the story of when she and Cayman were picnicking in the Cypress Forest. She told them that as they were turning to hike back to the village after their picnic, a bear approached them from the woods. Sarah described how Boone stepped between them and the bear, and the bear backed down and slowly walked away. Everyone had special stories to share about how Boone had touched their lives.

Like Luna in 1956, Cayman also wanted to give Boone a proper send off. He once again asked Etu to help him give Boone the same Tutelar funeral they had given Luna. The next morning Sarah and Cayman drove to the Poaceaehatchee Village, where Etu awaited. With the help of their parents, he and Etu performed a Tutelar funeral for Boone. The five of them took Boone's ashes by boat to the site in the Cypress Forest where Cayman had rescued him from the alligators 12 years earlier. In Tutelar language, Sakari sent Boone off to the spirit world. Sarah and Cayman spread his ashes next to the big limestone rock where Cayman had been sitting next to Boone the day they first met.

The following morning, Sarah and Cayman gathered the conservancy team together and told them that Boone had died. Since the conservancy opened two years earlier, Boone had been a regular member of the conservancy family. He was there every day, welcoming visitors, and curiously and calmly watching over patients brought into the conservancy animal hospital. Boone seemed to know that the animals were either sick or injured. The conservancy hospital patients liked having Boone there to offer them support and care while they recovered. The conservancy team was saddened by the news and offered their comfort and support to Sarah and Cayman.

A few weeks later, Sarah and Cayman were walking on a beach at Lovers Key State Park. It felt strange to be out walking without their friend Boone, because he had gone with them everywhere. As they were walking along the beach, they noticed a large piece of drift wood close to the water's edge. It was about eight feet tall, with branches extending in every direction.

When they got close enough, they saw that it was a shell tree. People had placed shells on almost every branch. Cayman picked up a shell and placed it on a branch, as he turned to Sarah to say, "This shell is for Boone." It's common in Southwest Florida for people to put shells on trees and branches close to the beach. For each person, it may represent something different, such as making a wish, giving a blessing, or in memory of someone. For Cayman and Sarah, it was in memory of a friend lost. Sarah took a photograph of the shell tree, and it hangs in the Sacred Moments Gallery at the conservancy, in memory of Boone.

Chapter Nine

Sarah and Cayman asked Adeline to watch for a puppy in need of a good home. A few months later, in September, she contacted them and told them there was a two-month-old black and gray, almost silver, mixed-breed rescue puppy waiting on a new home. She let them know that the puppy would grow to be as large as Boone. Sarah and Cayman were excited about getting a puppy that could be a friend to their new baby. They happily told Adeline that they wanted to pick up the new puppy right away. They named her Dakota, meaning friend. They took Dakota home that afternoon and got her settled into her new home.

The storyteller's daughter said, "Mom, I'm sad they lost Boone, but I'm glad they found Dakota. She'll get to grow up with their new baby. And they will be good friends."

Dakota was getting used to her new home with Sarah and Cayman. At the same, time Sarah's two best friends from high school, Mila and Avery, were arranging a surprise baby shower. The two of them got together with Sarah's mom, Vicki, and Cayman's mom, Sakari, to make the plans. They had already talked with Cayman about having the baby shower at his and Sarah's house. He was glad they asked, and he told them that Sarah would be happy that they had it at her home. He also reminded them that he and Sarah lived modestly, and did not need big, fancy things. Simply getting together to celebrate would put a big smile on Sarah's face. Perhaps they were shaking their heads yes, and meaning no, because the girls didn't listen to the "simple" part of the conversation.

Mila and Avery arranged for Cayman to take Sarah on an unplanned trip to the conservancy the morning of Saturday, September 21, 1968. While the two of them were at the conservancy, the ladies were at Sarah's house getting ready for the shower. Mila and Avery took care of all of the decorations. They brought balloons, streamers, photographs, and a guest book. The ladies decorated the front door, kitchen, living room, and the outside verandah. Vicki arranged for all of the snacks and drinks, and Sakari brought a cake for the baby shower. By noon on Saturday, Sarah's friends from Cypress Cove, Poaceaehatchee, and Glades University had arrived. Eighteen of Sarah's friends were in her house waiting for Cayman to bring her back from the conservancy. Some rode together and others were dropped off, so there were quite a few cars parked along Palm Lane next to their house.

Sarah and Cayman were on their way home, when Sarah noticed all of the extra cars parked along the road. Often people park along the lane to go to the beach, so Cayman, knowing about the party, fibbed and said that it must be a busy beach day. They parked in the driveway and walked around to the back, to go into the house from the beach side. At the same moment Sarah realized that there were a lot of people at her house, the double door popped open and her friends came rushing out to surprise her. She was overcome with joy and happiness when she saw all who were there. Cayman hugged and kissed Sarah as he left her to her party with her friends.

Sarah spent the afternoon talking and laughing with her friends. They played baby shower games, ate, opened gifts, and talked about old times and times to come. As the afternoon rolled on, some guests started to leave. Sarah hugged and thanked each of her friends for coming to share this special time with her. By four p.m., all of the guests had gone, except the party planners, Mila, Avery, Vicki, and Sakari. The five of them quickly cleaned up the decorations, wrapping paper, and food. They all sat and rested for a few minutes to reflect on a wonderful day. The four baby shower planners and Sarah were perfectly happy with how the day turned out. Sarah hugged and thanked them for being a part of her life, as each one left for home.

Sarah and Cayman had so much to celebrate with the many good things that happened in the past three years. On October 6, 1968, they celebrated their three-year wedding anniversary. Since getting married, Sarah and Cayman helped Etu establish is fishing charter business and built a new house for Sarah's parents. They founded the Jumpstart Foundation and the Southwest Florida Nature Conservancy. Soon they were about to welcome a new member to their family.

It was the evening of November 26, and Sarah's parents were dining with Sarah and Cayman at their house. They had a nice dinner, talking about the conservancy, and all of the things Sarah and Cayman were grateful for. Vicki and Henry told them how proud they were of the remarkable adults they had become. Cayman told them he was especially grateful that they had come into his life, and had supported and believed in him when he asked their blessing to be Sarah's husband. After dinner they all went out back to sit on the veranda and watch the sun set over the beach. Sarah and Cayman had been thinking of baby names for almost nine months and they finally

settled on a name for a girl and a boy.

Sarah told her parents that if the baby was a girl, she would be named Emma, and if the baby was a boy, he would be named Elliot. At that moment, as the sun was setting on the horizon, Sarah caught a photograph of a pelican flying in the reflection of the sun on the water. Sarah knew, that in Tutelar culture, the pelican meant attachment to the young, and the sun setting meant end of a journey. She thought it fit perfectly. They were at the end of a journey, having decided on baby names for a girl and a boy, and both names made them feel closer to their baby.

It was a gorgeous, sunny Wednesday morning on November 27, 1968. Sarah and Cayman skipped their beach walk, but went into the conservancy as usual. Cayman was working out on the grounds with the landscape crew, and Sarah was having an informal standup meeting with some her staff in the Sacred Moments II photo gallery. All of a sudden, her water broke, and she and the other ladies knew that the baby was coming.

Sarah was ready for this moment; she calmly asked one of her coworkers to tell Cayman the baby was coming, and to meet her at the truck. She asked another to call her parents and Cayman's parents to let them know, and she asked the third to get her "go bag" from her office. Sarah headed outside to their pickup truck to meet Cayman for a ride to the Cypress Cove hospital. Cayman wasn't quite as calm as Sarah; he arrived excited and breathless, running to the pickup truck in time to help her get in. They drove the short distance to the hospital and got her checked in. Soon after, Sarah's parents and Cayman's parents and brother arrived at the hospital.

Cayman went with Sarah to her room, and stayed with her during labor. When it was time to deliver the baby, the nurse escorted him back to the waiting room to stay with his family and Sarah's family. At three p.m., on November 27, 1968, they welcomed their seven-pound, two-ounce baby girl, Emma Marie Taylor, to the world. Everyone was there for Emma's arrival. Sarah's parents, Grandma Vicki and Grandpa Henry; Cayman's family, Grandma Sakari, Grandpa Alo, and Uncle Etu, were all in the waiting room.

Chapter Nine

Cayman was the first to be allowed back into the delivery room, where Sarah was holding Emma in her arms. She was a perfect, beautiful baby. Sarah and Cayman could not be any happier than they were at that moment in their lives. Soon the others were permitted in the room to see baby Emma and to congratulate Sarah and Cayman. Everyone was happy for the new young parents.

The next day, Cayman told all of their friends at the conservancy that they added Emma to their conservancy family. Everybody was ecstatic for Sarah and Cayman, and couldn't wait to see Emma. He let them know it would be a few more weeks until Sarah returned to the conservancy and they would hopefully see Emma then, too.

For the next several days, Cayman could hardly concentrate on his duties at the conservancy. All he could think about was seeing Sarah, and taking her and Emma home from the hospital. He visited Sarah at the hospital every day until she was released four days after giving birth. When it was finally time, Cayman and Dakota went to the hospital, and drove Sarah and little Emma home. They had taken good care of her in the hospital, but Sarah was really glad to be in her own home. She and Cayman tucked Emma into her new little crib and Cayman watched over her. Sarah took a moment for herself and went out on their back verandah. She sat in complete fulfillment while she watched and listened to the water rolling onto the beach.

So each could spend some time at the conservancy for the next three weeks, Sarah and Cayman took turns taking care of Emma. After only the first week at home, Sarah took Dakota and went on a beach walk. She and Dakota walked up to the pier and she talked to some of the friends she and Cayman had made over the years. She told them about Emma, and that soon, she and Cayman would be bringing Emma with them on their daily walk on the beach. She took some time to just sit contently on a bench before she and Dakota walked back home.

Cayman's parents visited them to see Emma, but none of Cayman's other friends at the Poaceaehatchee Village had seen her or Dakota yet. On Saturday morning, Sarah and Cayman loaded the stroller, Emma, and Dakota in their truck and headed to the village to introduce their new daughter and puppy to their Tutelar friends. They arrived at the village in time for lunch at Cayman's parents' house. Cayman and Etu prepared lunch while their mom and dad sat with Emma, Sarah, and Dakota.

After lunch they walked with Etu to the boat docks, to send him off with a group of three tourist couples scheduled for an afternoon fishing charter. Cayman was proud of how his brother had made his charter business into a success for the village. They spent the rest of the afternoon visiting with local villagers. They stopped in to visit Aiyana and Elu at the Sacred Moments gallery. The new gallery proprietors were excited to meet Emma and Dakota, and they took several photographs of the baby and puppy together. The two of them promised to give Sarah and Cayman prints the next time they saw them. The Taylor family headed back to their home in Cypress Cove in time for dinner and sunset on the beach.

During Emma's first couple of years, Sarah and Cayman put their efforts in balancing work, their lives, and taking care of Emma. They wanted Emma to start early experiencing and getting comfortable with the world around her. Four weeks after she was born, they took her with them when they returned to work at the conservancy. Everyone was eager to meet Emma and her puppy, Dakota. They were now part of the conservancy family.

Chapter Nine

Cayman set up a crib and play area in Sarah's office so Emma could be with them at the conservancy. It wasn't unusual for a parent working at the conservancy to bring a child to work. Sarah had established a child-friendly policy upon hiring their first team member. She and Cayman had always envisioned that the conservancy would be a place for everyone to come and learn about nature and animals. She wanted Emma to grow up seeing and learning as much as she could about the world around her, and the conservancy was a perfect place to do it.

All through Sarah's pregnancy, she and Cayman had gone on their daily beach walks and any other exciting things they could do without risking her health or the baby's. After Emma was born, Sarah's adventuresome spirit did not dwindle. In fact, it grew. Sarah wanted to take Emma on all kinds of adventures and show her all of the things she had gotten to experience. As Sarah grew stronger and Emma a little older, they resumed their daily beach walks with their puppy Dakota.

The Tutelar had been making and using on-the-body baby carriers for many years and it was starting to gain wide-spread popularity. Cayman met with one of the Tutelar garment makers while Sarah had been pregnant. He had a special on-the-body baby carrier made for either of them to wear during their beach walks. It worked perfectly, and Cayman loved carrying little Emma and having Dakota curiously walk and run along.

By the time Emma turned one year old, she was walking around the house. She loved playing with Dakota. She would hold onto Dakota's side while she walked along her. Sometimes when they were playing, Dakota would gently nudge Emma and she tumbled onto her behind while laughing. Some of Emma's first words were "Dakota, come here." She didn't have the balance and strength to walk the beach yet, but she was already learning to swim.

Sarah and Cayman took Emma out to the crystal-clear surf in the early mornings for short swimming lessons. They had first started the lessons standing a few feet apart, encouraging Emma to swim from one to the other. As Emma grew stronger and became a better swimmer, they took one step apart until they were five feet apart, then eight feet apart, then 12 feet apart. By the time Emma turned two years old, she was easily swimming 25 feet between Sarah and Cayman. She was talking up a storm, even identifying some of the common birds on their beach like ibises, pelicans, and egrets. Emma walked on the beach with her parents, and ran around on the beach with Dakota. She was really coming into her own personality.

Sometime around Emma's third birthday, Sarah and Cayman had taken her along with Dakota on boat rides. They took her when they went fishing in the gulf and on the rivers. Emma seemed to like the rocking motion of the boat from the waves; it was calming for her. She liked riding in the boat so much that she was often asking her parents to take her on another boat ride. Her personality bloomed between her third and fourth birthdays. Emma talked to everyone she saw, she swam better than many of the older children, she could comfortably go on two-mile hikes, and she loved going out in the boat.

While Emma was forming her young personality, Cayman led the Jumpstart Foundation through its busiest three years. Aubrey, Sarah, and Cayman approved six grants for entrepreneurial startups in Cypress Cove and the Poaceaehatchee Village. The foundation approved a grant for a young Tutelar couple to open a day care for underprivileged children in the village. Another grant was for a woman in Cypress Cove to start a maid service. The grant was approved under the condition that at least half of her employees were minorities. A third grant was approved for a couple to start a tile roof cleaning service. That grant was approved under the stipulation that the roof cleaning service used only environmentally safe chemicals.

The Jumpstart Foundation also awarded a grant to a Tutelar family to provide affordable lunches to the Poaceaehatchee school children. The grant was contingent on the lunches meeting specific nutritional guidelines set by the Department of Health and Human Services. The fifth grant was awarded to a couple to start a bus service for tourists. The service was a ten-passenger bus to take tourists from Cypress Cove to several stops in The Everglades, Cypress Forest, and the Poaceaehatchee Village.

The sixth grant awarded during the last three years had been to an engineer to put his fish hook removal tool kit into production in Cypress Cove. When released to consumers, the fish hook removal tool kit provided a way to safely remove hooks from fish before releasing them back into the water. Often, fish suffered severe injuries when fishermen removed hooks. The foundation board was honored to support local causes that positively impacted the lives of those living in and visiting Southwest Florida.

During the fall 1972, the nearly four-year old Emma started preschool at the Poaceaehatchee Village. Sarah and Cayman wanted her to learn about Tutelar history, customs, and language. Emma possessed a natural curiosity and strong interest in learning, and she was eager to start her first year of school in the village. Sarah and Cayman had planned for Emma to attend the Poaceaehatchee school part of each school year and to attend the Cypress Cove school part of each school following her kindergarten year.

Emma's preschool classes started at seven-thirty and ended at eleven-thirty a.m., Monday through Friday. Cayman drove Emma to the Poaceaehatchee school each morning. Depending on the day of the week, either Cayman's mom or brother met Emma at school and walked with her back to the Deeres' house. Cayman drove to the village each day and collected Emma after lunch. Sometimes he drove to the village early, and had lunch with Emma and his parents. Sarah was busy leading the conservancy, but occasionally she was able to make the trip to drop off Emma at school, or to pick her up at lunch. Sarah was pleased that Emma was able to spend more time with her Tutelar grandparents. Since Sarah's parents were their neighbors, Emma saw them almost every day, but she had spent less time with Cayman's parents.

On weekends, Sarah, Cayman, and Dakota spent every minute they possibly could with Emma. They often spent weekends with her on the beach behind their house, going for walks, fishing, swimming, and having cookouts. On many Saturday mornings, they went into the conservancy after breakfast for a few hours to check on the animals that were in the care of the conservancy hospital. The conservancy hospital typically had several animal patients in recovery.

Emma liked checking on the animal patients, but a few that she was especially fond of were the burrowing owl, a young dolphin, and female panther. The burrowing owl was injured when landscapers got too close with their equipment. The panther was struck by a car, and had a broken leg, but was doing well. The dolphin's tailfin was caught in a fishing net for a long period and it needed time to heal and rehabilitate. Emma and Dakota enjoyed being part of the animals' care team. Sarah and Cayman were happy that Emma wanted to spend time at the conservancy, as well as at the beach.

Emma's first school year at the Poaceaehatchee Village went well. She had learned Tutelar words and short phrases. She enjoyed learning about Tutelar history and customs. Her parents were pleased with how quickly, easily, and comfortably Emma adjusted to school with the Tutelar student and teachers.

While Emma was attending school at the Poaceaehatchee Village, Sarah and Cayman were busy at the conservancy. Under Sarah's leadership, it was the busiest season for visitors since the conservancy opened six years earlier. The animal hospital nursed a record number of birds and animals to full recovery and had released them back into the wild. Taylor Tire and Rubber Company had four years remaining on their ten-year funding commitment. Sarah recruited two large donors that committed to five years of funding after Taylor Tire's funding would run out. It was a good year for the Southwest Florida Nature Conservancy.

Summer had arrived, and four-year-old Emma was ready for more adventures with her parents. She regularly went to the conservancy with her mom and dad during the week, and on weekends they typically were at the beach. It was particularly busy at the conservancy animal hospital during the summer of 1973. It seemed like the conservancy was getting calls daily for distressed or injured birds and animals. Depending on the call, Cayman would usually take Emma along to watch. And Emma loved going out on the calls with her dad.

At ten a.m., on a June morning, the conservancy got a call that an alligator had crawled out of the gulf waters onto the Cypress Cove beach. It was rare for an alligator to be in the saltwater or on the beach, and only the third such call since the conservancy opened in 1966. Cayman told Emma about the alligator on the beach, and that she couldn't go along. Emma wasn't having any of that! She wanted to see the alligator, and she said so. "Daddy, may I please go? I promise I will stay out of the way." Sarah jumped in and said, "I'll go too. Let her go and watch. It'll be good for her." With Sarah's support, Cayman reluctantly gave in to Emma's plea. Emma and Sarah jumped into the conservancy van with Cayman, and two other conservancy staff members followed in another vehicle.

When the conservancy team arrived at the beach, they found that a four-foot alligator had taken temporary residence under a young tourist's beach chair. There were nearly 40 spectators standing around the alligator, pointing and taking photographs. Sarah stayed back on the small boardwalk with Emma, while Cayman and the other two conservancy team members asked the crowd to move further away from the alligator.

Growing up in the Poaceaehatchee Village with Etu, Cayman had plenty of experience with alligators, so he wasn't worried about safely removing this small one from the beach. While his two team members managed the crowd, Cayman got around behind the alligator. He quickly, almost in one move, got down on his knees over the back of the alligator and grabbed and held the alligator's jaw closed with his hands. One of the conservancy team members tied its jaw shut, so Cayman could get a better hold. The crowd took photographs and applauded as he carried the alligator to the conservancy van.

The three-person conservancy team carefully placed the alligator in a cage, while Emma watched in amazement. They determined that the gator was healthy and simply needed to be relocated to a safe place away from people. Cayman drove the van east into The Everglades where he knew several good spots to release it. He backed up the van to a river, and the conservancy team removed the alligator from the cage. Cayman held it down on the ground, while one of the others removed the rope from its jaw. Cayman stood up and backed away in a quick motion, as Sarah and Emma watched the alligator scurry into the river. During the drive back to the conservancy, Emma asked, "Daddy, weren't you afraid of the alligator?" Her dad replied, "I wasn't afraid, but I respect its strength. I didn't take any unnecessary risks that might get me or the alligator injured." Emma thanked her dad for letting her go along on the alligator rescue.

That was the first of several exciting rescues that summer. Only a few days later, the conservancy got a call that a fisherman at the pier had hooked a pelican in the wing. Emma didn't even have to ask if she could go along on that rescue mission. It had happened, unfortunately, many times before, and it was usually a fairly simple rescue. Emma and Dakota jumped into the truck with her dad, and they were off to the pier.

When they arrived, Cayman took out of the back of the truck a large shallow-scoop net, attached to a long rope. They quickly walked out on the pier to where the fisherman was holding his fishing pole. Cayman dropped the net about fifteen feet down to the water and let it sink a few feet before maneuvering it under the pelican. Once the net was under the pelican, he lifted it straight up. The pelican was sprawled out in the net. Cayman gently lifted up the net and pelican, and brought both over the rail of the pier. He gently held the pelican's beak slightly open, so it could breathe easily. He carefully sat the net and pelican on the deck of the pier. Cayman asked the fisherman to hold the pelican by the beak, slightly open and not tightly closed, while he secured its wings.

Emma was watching in admiration as her dad worked to rescue the pelican without causing any injuries. Fortunately, the hook had not pierced the pelican's wing. The wing had gotten wrapped in the fishing line. This was why the pelican couldn't fly. Emma asked, "Daddy, will the pelican be okay?" Cayman told her the pelican would be fine, once the fishing line was removed and it was released to fly away. He carefully freed its wing from the fishing line and looked it over for any potential injuries.

Once he determined that the bird was okay, he held its wings gently against its body and took hold of its beak from the fisherman. Cayman let Emma pet the pelican on its beak and back. She was thrilled to touch the pelican. He told Emma to step back so he could release it to fly away. Emma watched as the pelican stood up and tested its wings. After a moment, the bird fully expanded its wings and flew away, as Emma cheered and Dakota let out a bark of support. Emma couldn't wait to get back to the conservancy so she could tell her mom all about the pelican they had rescued. For the next few weeks, the conservancy hadn't received any rescue calls, so Emma hung out with the veterinarians at the conservancy animal hospital.

It was only a few days later, when Emma went out on an early-morning turtle watch walk with her mom and dad, that they saw a distressed momma loggerhead sea turtle. It was nesting season, and she had returned to the beach where she had been born, to dig a nest and lay her eggs. She was trying to crawl up the beach, but from a distance, they could see she was in trouble. They picked up their pace to get to the distressed sea turtle quicker. As they got closer, they saw that her right rear flipper was entangled in a fishing net.

Emma's parents knew exactly what they had to do and they jumped right into action. They had freed other sea creatures from fishing nets during their snorkeling and fishing adventures. Cayman handed Sarah his pocket knife, while he carefully secured the female loggerhead. Sarah told Emma she could watch, but to stay away from the sea turtle's head and flippers. Emma and Dakota sat and watched intently, while her parents worked to free the sea turtle's flipper from the net. Sarah gently cut the net away, piece by piece, until the flipper was unrestricted.

Chapter Nine

Emma's parents examined the loggerhead for injuries before releasing her. The momma sea turtle sat for a few moments, then looked at her rescuers as if to say "thank you," before slowly turning her four-hundred-pound body around and crawling back into the gulf to swim away. Emma asked her parents, "Why didn't she make a nest and lay her eggs?" Her mom responded, "It's not unusual for a sea turtle to skip nesting once it has had an encounter with a human. She'll be back another day to lay her eggs." They made note of their encounter with the injured loggerhead, and continued the rest of their turtle watch for the morning.

It had been an amazing summer, full of adventure for young Emma. She had lots of stories she could tell her classmates when she started kindergarten in the fall.

Nearly five-year-old Emma started kindergarten class in Cypress Cove during the fall of 1973. She was delighted to start at new school and make new friends. Sarah and Cayman took turns taking Emma to school and picking her up afterwards. Emma's kindergarten class ended a few hours before Sarah and Cayman's day ended at the conservancy. So, they brought Emma to the conservancy until it was time to go home for dinner. Emma liked spending afternoons at the conservancy where her mom and dad worked. Everyone there was nice to her, and she loved visiting patients at the conservancy animal hospital.

Emma had attended preschool at Poaceaehatchee Village, and was now in kindergarten at Cypress Cove. Sarah and Cayman arranged to meet with the school board in Cypress Cove and the elder's council in the Poaceaehatchee Village. And Emma's parents got what they sought – approval for Emma to attend both schools, splitting each school year between the Cypress Cove and Poaceaehatchee schools. They wanted Emma to grow up in both worlds, that of the Tutelar and of Cypress Cove. Sarah, Cayman, and Etu took turns transporting Emma to and from the Poaceaehatchee school. Whether Emma was attending school at Cypress Cove or Poaceaehatchee, she would go to the conservancy after school, until Saran's and Cayman's work day ended.

Emma was learning to speak and write the Tutelar's native language and the English language. She was becoming a remarkable storyteller. When they sat for dinner, Emma would tell her parents everything that happened in school that day. If the stories weren't about school, they were about the conservancy or their weekends on the beach and in the boat. She loved telling the stories and writing them in her journals. Sarah and Cayman truly enjoyed listening to Emma's stories. They were always thinking up new escapades for Emma, to help feed her passion for adventures.

When Emma wasn't going to school, Sarah and Cayman were spending time with her and Dakota on the beach or out in the boat. Sarah and Cayman were both strong swimmers, and they had taught Emma to swim when she was less than a year old. By the time she was six years old, she was comfortable swimming in the currents of the gulf waters. She often body surfed and swam with Dakota for hours. By the time Emma turned seven, she was a stronger swimmer than most of the older boys on the beach. She often challenged tourists who were older than herself to see who could swim out around the pier and back to the beach more quickly. The local girls and boys loved it and cheered her on, when at only seven years old, Emma would easily win against teenage tourists – girls and boys.

Emma valued spending time on the beach with Dakota and her parents, and she enjoyed helping at the conservancy just as much. She was only seven, but she wanted to help when she spent time there, not just waiting for the day to be over and to go home for dinner. Sarah talked with the director of the conservancy hospital about how Emma might be able to help her. The director thought Emma would enjoy helping with the care and feeding of injured animals and birds. Emma was thrilled with the idea.

Emma was mostly at the conservancy in the late afternoons and sometimes for a few hours on Saturday mornings. She spent a few weeks with one of the veterinarians, learning what and how to feed the animal patients. Emma was a quick learner, and was soon taking care of the afternoon feedings on her own. She would hand feed one of the small birds from a feeding syringe, give fish to a dolphin, and slide a food tray through an opening for an injured panther. Emma wasn't only responsible for feeding, she also had to take care of the cleanup duties. That wasn't as fun for her, but she took it in stride and did her duty. She was a hard worker, and everyone at the conservancy liked having her there. They all made her feel like she was one of the team.

Chapter Ten

Early in the spring of 1976, the Poaceaehatchee Village council of elders reached out to Sarah to ask her to join a committee to help plan a seafood festival. She was honored that they had asked and, without hesitation, she said yes. They wanted Sarah on the committee because she was a respected member of the Cypress Cove community. She was respected by the Tutelar, and she would represent the committee from an environmental-impact point of view. The elders where planning to hold a first annual seafood festival, and they needed input and support from Cypress Cove representatives for it to be successful.

The seafood committee consisted of eight members – four from the Poaceaehatchee Village and four from Cypress Cove. A Tutelar elder served as committee chair, and included members from law enforcement, community maintenance, entertainment, and the conservancy. They had several committee meetings over the next four weeks to finalize their plans. Their key agenda items included what to name the festival, when to have it, how long it should be, and where it should be held. They also determined what kind of entertainment to have, type of vendor stands to allow, and what food vendors would be included.

The Cypress Cove committee members were as eager to have the seafood festival as the Tutelar were. They decided to call it the First Annual Southwest Florida Seafood Festival. The eight committee members unanimously agreed to hold the first festival during the slow summer season, as sort of a dry run. By holding the first festival during the off season, it would give the committee a chance to work out any issues before having a larger festival crowd during the high season. They selected the first weekend in May, starting Friday, May 7, and ending on Sunday, May 9. The festival hours were to be from noon to eight p.m. on Friday and Saturday and noon to four p.m. on Sunday.

The committee determined that Langundo Park, centrally located between Cypress Cove and the Poaceaehatchee Village, would be a prime location to hold the festival. It had a large sand and limestone parking area, shade trees, and plenty of space for food vendors, merchandisers, and an entertainment stage. The council decided to have the entertainment stage at one corner of the parking lot, with several rows of chairs for spectators between the parking lot and stage.

The food vendors would be set up in two rows, extending from the right edge of the stage. There would be picnic tables and shade tents between the rows of food vendors for people to sit and eat. The merchandise vendors would be set up in three rows, with walking space between rows, extending from the left edge of the stage. A row of portable toilets would be staged at another edge of the parking lot, away from the food vendors. They planned to have plenty of trash cans near the food vendors, parking lot, and portable toilets. The committee members determined that they would need about fifty volunteers to help set up the stage, direct cars to park, provide directions, and cleanup trash.

The seafood committee promoted the festival in the Cypress Cove Chronicle, Fort Myers News, and Poaceaehatchee Village. They were advertising to rent spots to food and merchandise vendors, and to encourage people to attend the festival. Food and merchandise vendors were responsible for their own set up, tear down, and cleanup. Each vendor would be charged a flat fee for rental of ground space for the weekend. The committee members put up posters and reached out to local organizations requesting volunteers to help. Two of the committee members arranged music entertainment by local

Southwest Florida bands for each day of the festival. The bands would offer a variety of music, including southern rock, folk, blue grass, and blues bands.

Without any persuasion necessary from Sarah, Cayman and Emma signed up as volunteers. Sarah assigned Cayman to help with set up of the entertainment stage and to direct traffic in the parking lot. She recruited seven-year-old Emma as her deputy committee member and helper. Their role was to oversee the food vendors for the three days of the festival. It was mostly an honorary role, and Emma enjoyed being involved and helping.

Word about the seafood festival spread quickly, and when Friday afternoon arrived, so did people! Attendees came from the Poaceaehatchee Village, Cypress Cove, and Fort Myers. Some even came from as far away as Miami. Friday evening was a success – the stage rocked with music until eight p.m., food vendors sold out, and the merchandisers were selling their products.

The vendors got to it early and restocked for another big day on Saturday morning, and they were pleased with the activity once again. People arrived early, filling the parking lot and even parking along the road. Cayman and others were managing the traffic, while Sarah and her deputy committee member, Emma, helped the food vendors. Music started at noon, and rocked the stage until eight p.m. on Saturday night.

Sunday was a bit calmer with blues-style music scheduled on the stage. Many of the merchandise vendors sold out and were taking down their tents to leave early. By midafternoon on Sunday, there was very little food left for the vendors to serve. Once all of the vendors and attendees left on Sunday afternoon, the volunteers spent the entire evening cleaning up Langundo Park.

The seafood festival committee held a picnic for all of the volunteers a week later at Langundo Park. The committee served lunch, gave volunteers door prizes, and asked for their feedback. Emma was awarded the seafood festival volunteer medal for being the youngest volunteer. Sarah and a few other committee members gave short speeches, thanking the volunteers and letting them know that they couldn't have pulled it off without them.

When lunch was over and the door prizes were given out, the committee collected feedback from the volunteers. They wanted to collect the volunteers' observations and suggestions about how to improve the festival for next year. The majority of the feedback was positive, with a few minor recommendations for improvements. Most of the improvement suggestions were related to better managed traffic, parking, and trash cleanup. The seafood festival committee let the volunteers know that they planned to reach out to the merchandising vendors and food vendors to get their input for improvement opportunities, as well. They committed to include all of their suggestions in the planning agenda for next year's second annual seafood festival. All in all, the seafood committee members believed that the festival had been a success.

The seafood festival was over and the rainy season had begun by June 1976. It was a perfect time for planting new plants and trees in the conservancy botanical gardens. It had been ten years since the conservancy was first built and the first few acres of the botanical gardens had opened. Since that time, Cayman, the groundskeepers, and the landscapers had continued to add plants and trees to the exhibits. They had cleared and created nearly two miles of walking paths for visitors to leisurely stroll through the gardens and to enjoy the many varieties of plants, flowers, and trees. The gardens also attracted many South Florida birds, from hummingbirds to parakeets, which liked to be near the flowering plants.

Cayman had been planning for several months to plant the last batch of trees and flowering plants. The shipments had finally arrived and were ready for planting. Sarah and Cayman were excited that they might soon be able to say that the botanical gardens were complete, based on the original plans. Sarah told Emma that the next morning they would be going to the conservancy to plant new trees and flowering plants in the gardens.

Sarah and Cayman agreed that they needed help deciding where to place the new plants and trees. And they had hired landscape contractors, who would be there to help.

Each new garden exhibit had a small plaque placed in the ground near the plant or tree, describing its natural habitat, its common name, and its scientific name. Sarah thought Emma might find it exciting and interesting to help decide the planting locations and to help create the exhibit plaques. Emma spent a lot of time at the conservancy since she was a baby, and she loved being there. During the slower, rainy season, Emma often helped setting up and writing descriptions for the nature exhibits in the main hall. During the busy tourist session, she was usually at the outdoor adventure area. Emma helped people with canoe rentals, directions for hiking trails, and packaging small bags of food for kids to feed the fish and ducks in the lake.

Emma especially liked helping in the conservancy hospital where the conservancy veterinarians helped injured and sick wildlife recover. The most exciting part was when they would release the animals back into the wild. She helped release a giant sea turtle back into the gulf and helped free an osprey back into the wild. Seven-year-old Emma wasn't about to miss this chance to put the finishing touches on the botanical gardens.

Sarah, Cayman, and Emma talked about the day ahead while they enjoyed breakfast on the verandah overlooking the beach. When breakfast was over, Cayman cleaned the dishes, while Emma helped her mom pack lunches and extra drinking water for the day. They piled into the pickup truck with Dakota and headed off to the conservancy. They arrived at the conservancy maintenance yard at the back of the conservancy. The three of them met in the maintenance building with the groundskeeper and landscape contractors. There, they discussed plans and locations for planting the new plants and trees. While the grounds team was deciding what equipment was needed for planting, Sarah and Emma began making plaques for each plant and tree.

The grounds team used a conservancy truck to pull a trailer loaded with plants and a backhoe tractor to pull the second trailer. Cayman followed with Sarah, Emma, and Dakota in their pickup truck. Once they arrived at the planting site, Cayman and the grounds team unloaded the plants and set them next to the planting locations suggested by the landscapers. By lunch time, the team had planted a little more than half of the plants and trees.

Sarah and Emma took the pickup truck and drove into town to pick up some extra sandwiches and drinks for the landscapers. When they returned, they all took a break and found a seat wherever they could. While they were eating lunch, they gathered in smaller groups and talked. When they were done with lunch, they planned the rest of the day of planting. They felt they would easily finish by dinner time.

One team planted trees using the backhoe tractor to dig the holes, lift the trees in place, refill the holes, and stake the trees. After each tree was planted and staked, Sarah and Emma placed the appropriate exhibit plaque in place so that visitors could easily read it from the walking path. Another team planted all of the flowering plants using shovels to dig and fill the holes, and then used rakes to distribute pine needles for a finishing touch.

One of the last plants to go in the ground – Emma's favorite – was the lobster claw flower. It's a coral-colored flower with yellowish tips hanging in an alternating sequence from the stem. Emma asked the landscaper if it was okay if she planted the lobster claw. The landscaper was happy to let her plant the flower, while he offered a little help to make sure its roots were safely placed and covered. Emma filled in the hole and put some pine needles around the base of the stem to help sustain moisture and to provide for a finished look.

When they finished the last planting, the grounds team took the conservancy equipment back to the maintenance area to clean and put away. Sarah drove Cayman, Emma, and Dakota home in the pickup truck, where they had a pleasant dinner sitting outside on the verandah, watching the sunset over the beach.

It was a pleasant summer weekend morning in 1977, and Emma got up before the sun rose. She was almost nine years old, and she wanted to do something fun with her mom and dad. Emma ran into her mom's and dad's room and asked, "Mommy, daddy! What are we going to do today?" Cayman had already planned to go surf fishing on the beach that morning. He replied to Emma, "Let's go fishing on the beach behind our house." Sarah quickly jumped in and said, "After fishing, we'll go swimming this afternoon, and have a cookout with what you catch." Emma said, "Yes, let's do it." They enjoyed an early breakfast on the verandah, then collected their fishing equipment, and walked out their back door to the beach.

As they walked to the water's edge, Sarah reminded Emma that the Tutelar culture was to protect and respect the animals that gave them life, and they only took what they could use. She told Emma, "We'll carefully and gently release the fish we don't keep." Emma replied, "I understand, I'll be careful. Let's go fishing."

They all took a moment to enjoy in the dramatic view of the clouds in the western sky, over the Gulf of Mexico. The sun was just about to rise in the eastern sky, and it was reflecting off of the clouds in the gulf. The reflection of the sun caused the clouds to light up the sky with bright pinks and oranges. There were smaller clouds that were several shades of gray and white in color. Near one of the clouds, far out in the gulf, was a bright rainbow that stretched from the top of the cloud to the water. Emma saw the rainbow and called out to her mom and dad. "Mommy, daddy! Look at the rainbow. We learned in school that a rainbow is a symbol of protection in Tutelar culture." Cayman smiled as he remarked to Emma that she was correct; it was a symbol of protection, and a pathway to the spirit world.

The three of them and Dakota made their way to the edge of the water to set up beach chairs at their fishing spot. Cayman brought along a casting net to use to catch bait fish and a bucket for the bait fish. He casted the net a couple of times to show Emma how it was done. To cast the net, he draped one edge loosely over his left hand, and the other edge in his right hand, then tossed it away from his body in a circular motion. The net fully opened as it landed in the shallow water, before quickly sinking to the bottom, due to the net's weighted edge. When Cayman pulled in the net, the weighted edge closed around the bait fish. Cayman lifted the net out of the water and shook it a few times to let the small fish drop out of the net. Then he and Emma picked up their catch, and placed it in the bait bucket that was filled with water from the gulf.

Cayman wanted to teach Emma how to cast the net to catch bait fish. He handed her the net and helped her set it up in her hands for casting. Emma turned her body sideways, and gave it a whirl. The first cast didn't go so well. The net didn't open, and it barely made it into the water. Emma wasn't about to give up. She picked up the net again and asked her dad to help her set it up properly in her hands. She turned sideways again and tossed it away from her body, just like she saw her dad do. And this time the net opened as it landed in the water. Emma pulled the net in by its rope, and held it up to find that she caught six small bait fish. She was so happy! She screamed with delight and Dakota gave her an approval bark.

Two curious snowy egrets noticed the small fish laying on the sand, and they swooped in, landing near the bait bucket. The egrets were looking for an easy breakfast and Emma was happy to help. Before Emma could pick up her catch, the egrets quickly snatched the bait fish for their meal. She casted the net again, only to share her catch with more egrets that must have gotten the message. By now, Emma made friends with six or seven egrets

who wanted to help themselves to her small bait fish.

While the egrets were snacking on Emma's catch, a pair of frisky birds began to play. They were jumping and flying, almost as if they were sparring over their territory and who should get to snack on the bait fish. They were going at each other, sometimes jumping several feet above the water – their wings expanded and the feathers on their heads standing straight up. The egrets were face to face, trying to show each other which one owned that space on the beach. Dakota let out a bark once in a while, but the egrets were more focused on who was getting the fish, and mostly ignored the barks.

Even with the egrets snatching up snacks, Emma had soon caught enough bait fish in the bucket to start fishing. Cayman, reminded her how to safely bait the hook, and he helped her cast the line into the water. He baited his pole and cast his line out beside Emma's. Sarah relaxed on a beach chair and watched them fish. Every time Emma caught a fish, she screamed and laughed, while Dakota let out a bark or two as she reeled in her fish. Most of the fish Emma and her dad caught were smaller fish, so they were quickly and carefully released back into the water.

After fishing for a couple of hours, Emma felt a strong tug on her fishing line. She quickly jerked the pole up and back, as her dad had taught her, to set the hook. Emma soon found out that she had caught a large fish. It nearly pulled the pole out of her hands. Sarah quickly jumped from her chair and reached around Emma to help her reel in her catch.

As the two of them reeled in Emma's line, within about twelve feet of shore, Sarah quickly realized that Emma had hooked a shark. Sarah looked at Cayman to see what he thought they should do. He wanted Emma to have the full experience of bringing it in to shore. He knew it was an experience she would never forget, but he also wanted her to be safe while reeling it in. He told Sarah to stay with

Emma and to back up out of the water until there was about five feet of wet sand between them and the water. Cayman told Emma to keep reeling in the shark until it was on the wet sand but not clear out of the water. He wanted to make sure that the shark had water splashing over it the entire time, so that it could breathe and not get injured.

Once the shark was at the very edge of the shallow water, Cayman carefully removed the hook and the shark quickly swam away, just as Sarah snapped a photograph.

The three of them stood in amazement about what had just happened. Eight-year-old Emma just caught and safely landed a four-foot-long shark. It was another incredible moment. They excitedly replayed what had just happened before they got back to fishing. After a few hours, they caught enough fish for a meal and to restock the freezer. Cayman took the fish and tackle back up to the house. Sarah prepared a light snack while Cayman taught Emma how to fillet and clean the fish. They put most of the fish in the freezer and kept out enough for a cookout later that day.

After they had snacks and drinks on their back verandah, the three of them walked back down to the beach for the afternoon. They swam in the warm gulf waters, and body surfed on the waves coming into shore. Emma played ball with Dakota, running up and down the beach. The three of them tossed a frisbee back and forth, until they were all tired. They rested on the beach for a while before going back up to the house to prepare for the cookout.

Emma set the table and got the drinks ready, while Sarah prepared rice and vegetables for side dishes. She already had fresh strawberries in the refrigerator and ice cream in the freezer for dessert. Cayman prepared the fish by baking it with light seasonings and lemon butter. Everything was ready to serve just as Sarah's parents arrived.

They all sat down to dinner under the palm trees, and Emma began to tell her grandparents what an exciting day she'd had. She told her grandparents that she learned how to cast a net to catch bait fish, and how the egrets were fighting over the fish. Then she told them about catching a shark. She didn't leave out any details. "Grandma, grandpa! You should have seen it! The shark took the bait and almost pulled the fishing rod out of my hands. It bent the pole over until it touched the water. I started to reel it in, but it was too strong. Mommy had to help me reel it in to the shore. When it was almost on shore, daddy released it from the hook and it swam away. It was as big as me." They all laughed and congratulated Emma, while they ate dessert and watched the sun set.

It was the summer of 1978, and nine-year-old Emma was ready for another adventure. She asked, "Mommy, would you please take me on another one of those adventures like you and daddy went on when you were younger?" Sarah was pleased to hear that Emma looked forward to doing things with her parents. Sarah was up to the task of thinking of something that Emma would always remember. She remembered how much she had enjoyed the hike she and Cayman had taken through The Everglades and the Cypress Forest several years before. She had never forgotten that day, and wanted to share a similar experience with her daughter.

They bought Emma a bicycle several years earlier for her birthday. Sarah and Cayman remembered how excited Emma was when she saw the bicycle. She jumped on it and tried riding it right away. Emma flopped her bicycle a few times, but she didn't give up. Sarah taught her how to ride, and she often took short rides with Emma around the neighborhood. Emma enjoyed it when they went on rides together, even though they were only on the roads in her neighborhood. As time went on, they stayed out longer, riding farther distances each time. Over the first few years Emma was riding her bicycle, she became comfortable and confident. A few times, they had loaded the bicycles in the back of the pickup truck and hauled them to small, local trails to ride on smooth, blacktop surfaces. Until now, they hadn't gone on any big bicycle excursions.

Sarah talked with Cayman about taking Emma and the bicycles to the Poaceaehatchee Village and riding the trails along The Everglades and into the Cypress Forest. Cayman liked the idea. Sarah asked Emma if she would like to ride bicycles on the trails at the Poaceaehatchee Village. Emma didn't even let her mom finish, "How soon can we go?" The two of them planned out the whole day together.

Their bicycle excursion started early on Saturday morning, with Emma getting up and helping Sarah make breakfast. Emma served her mom and dad breakfast on the back verandah. While they were eating, Emma shared with her dad what she and her mom had planned for the day. While Emma cleaned up the dishes, Sarah packed a picnic, and Cayman loaded the bicycles in the back of the truck. Sarah drove, while Emma continued talking with her parents about their plans for the day. When they arrived at the Poaceaehatchee Village, Sarah parked the truck at Emma's grandparents' house. They sat outside and talked with the Deeres about their plans before getting on their bicycles and heading to the trails.

They rode the exact same trails that Sarah and Cayman had hiked several years earlier, only this time it was Dakota with them, not Boone. As they rode on the trail along The Everglades, Emma could see all of the birds in the water and flying above. They stopped for a few minutes to watch the birds, and for Sarah to take some photographs. They saw pelicans, ibises, wood storks, anhingas, Roseate spoonbills, and ospreys. Sarah took a photograph of two spoonbills standing together in the shallow waters on the edge of The Everglades. After a short break, Emma, Sarah, and Cayman continued riding until they reached the Cypress Forest.

Emma and her parents rode on the trail in the Cypress Forest for a while, until they reached the spot where Sarah wanted to stop for a picnic. Sarah said, "This is the same spot where your dad brought me for a picnic a long time ago, and this is where we had lunch." Emma thought it was neat that she was having a picnic with her mom and dad in the same spot where they had picnicked before they were married. While they ate lunch, they talked about all of the things they had seen so far on their trail ride. Emma told her mom and dad how grateful she was that they shared this experience with her.

They were almost finished with lunch when Sarah decided to tell Emma about the bear that they had seen that day 14 years ago. Sarah told Emma, "We turned to hike back to the village, when a large Florida black bear stepped out of the woods and walked toward us. Just then, Boone quickly stepped between us and the bear. We could see the hair raised on Boone's back as he made a low, deep growl at the bear. It went on for what seemed like a long time, but it was probably only 30 seconds. Boone stood his ground and the bear shook its front body side to side, pounded its front paws on the ground a few times, then turned and walked back into the woods."

Emma was so quiet while she listened to her mom tell the story about the bear. She sat for a few minutes before calling Dakota over to sit with her. She hugged Dakota, and whispered, "I know you would protect me, just like Boone protected mommy and daddy back then."

It was fall 1978, and Emma started fifth grade at Cypress Elementary School. It had become a tradition for Sarah to get a photograph of Emma on her first day of school, and this school year was no different. Sarah took a photograph of Emma standing next to her bicycle, wearing a backpack and a helmet. Her school was less than a mile from their home, and Emma had gotten quite good at riding her bicycle safely.

Sarah and Cayman had talked it over, and they agreed that it would be okay for Emma to ride her bicycle to school. Emma was inspired with the trust her parents had given her and the freedom riding her bike provided. Sarah told her that she had to wear a helmet any time she was riding, and told her to stay off of the main roads. Emma gladly agreed and waved goodbye, as she peddled off to school to start her new classes and to see her friends.

A few months into the school year, around Emma's tenth birthday in November, her teacher told the class she was going to schedule a field trip to the Southwest Florida Nature Conservancy. Emma was thrilled when she heard the news. She had practically grown up at the conservancy, and she knew that her parents had important jobs there. After school, Emma rode her bike to the conservancy to tell her mom and dad the news. Sarah had received a call from Emma's teacher earlier that day, and they had scheduled the field trip for the following week. Sarah didn't want to spoil Emma's surprise, so she acted like she was hearing about the field trip for the first time. Emma told her mom, "We have lots to plan, and I want to help." Sarah was pleased, although not surprised, that Emma wanted to be involved. Together they came up with a plan to entertain and teach the students about nature and wildlife.

The following Monday, the bus – with Emma, eleven of her classmates, and their teacher – pulled in to the conservancy parking lot. They were met by Sarah, Cayman, and Dakota. Sarah gave each of the children a conservancy tee shirt, with their choice of animal on the front. There were birds, fish, and land animals to choose from. Emma couldn't resist telling her classmates that Sarah and Cayman were her mom and dad, and Dakota was her best friend. From the bus, they went straight to the exhibit hall, where they saw life-size drawings, photographs, replicas, and sculptures of animals, along with descriptions and explanations.

One of the school children noticed a large, sandy-colored cat, and she asked Sarah, "What kind of cat is that?" Sarah explained, "That's a replica of a female Florida panther. Panthers are a type of a puma. The female panthers grow to about 75 pounds and males 115 pounds. They were almost extinct in the 1950s due to hunting. Panthers are nocturnal animals. In recent years, they have become endangered due to car strikes during dusk and dawn hours." Another child asked about a replica of a river otter. "That's a cute-looking animal. What is it?" Emma jumped in and answered her question. "It's a river otter and it can live on land and in the water. Its strong flat tail, short legs, and webbed toes make it a strong swimmer - like me! Otters can also run fast on land." The school kids giggled at Emma's response. And they remarked about how much they liked seeing these exhibits of the many different animals and birds.

The exhibit hall also included several renderings of Southwest Florida landscapes, showing how changes had taken place over the years. Some changes were natural and others occurred because of building, farming, and population movements. One of the children asked, "Why did that big grassy, marsh area change in all of those images?" Sarah told the class, "It's a progression over time of images of The Everglades. It was once three million acres in the early 1900s. Now it is one-and-a-half million acres today. Over the years, about half of The Everglades were drained for development and farming. The Everglades used to have a natural north-to-south flow of water, but today the water flow is controlled by canals and levees."

Exhibits in the main hall of the conservancy also offered recordings and headphones for visitors to listen to descriptions and explanations. After taking time to see the exhibits and to hear the explanations, the children moved into the theater room. In the theater room, there were several long bench seats and a large screen on the front wall for viewing. There, they watched a twenty-minute video about South Florida. The video showed The Everglades, Cypress Forest, and Gulf of Mexico. It also included the animals, birds and sea life that lived and thrived in the different habitats.

Emma's classmates were having fun learning about the different animals and places. The students were eager to see and hear more, and Sarah's and Emma's plan would provide that. The next stop was the conservancy animal hospital. It covered a large indoor and outdoor area of the conservancy main building. This part of the tour began in the outdoor section of the conservancy hospital.

When they all made their way outside of the animal hospital, the kids ran to the large, above-ground tank. In the tank was a huge sea turtle peering back at them through the thick plastic window. The children all yelled out at once, "What kind of turtle is that?" Emma quickly jumped in, "That's a loggerhead sea turtle. It's recovering

213

from being hit by a boat propeller. Daddy rescued her and brought her here about three weeks ago. The conservancy veterinarians are nursing her back to health. When she's healthy enough, daddy and his team will take her to the beach and release her back into the sea."

Emma's teacher asked if her class could be notified so they could go to the beach and watch the release. Sarah replied, saying that she would love to share the experience with the students. She told the teacher that Emma would know about the release several days in advance, and would share the date and time with the class. Emma was pleased that her classmates would someday soon get to see the sea turtle crawl back into the Gulf of Mexico from her back yard.

There were several smaller sea creatures being rehabilitated, which the students viewed. There was a stingray in a shallow tank; Sarah helped each student touch its back. She cautioned the kids that the stingray did not like being touched on the tail or the belly. The kids described the skin as feeling like fine sandpaper. In the same tank was a sea star that Emma gently picked up and let each of her classmates carefully hold for a moment. Sarah showed them an osprey that was on the mend from a broken wing. She described how it would be released back into the wild, when the conservancy veterinarians determined it was healthy. The children enjoyed the conservancy hospital.

From the conservancy hospital, the class went to the outdoor adventure area, where Sarah and Emma had a picnic lunch waiting for them. They sat at the picnic tables at the edge of the lake, and ate lunch under the shade of the large cypress trees. When the students had finished lunch, Cayman and Dakota took them for a boat ride on the lake. Emma told them the names of all the different birds they saw as they rode the boat around the lake.

As they got closer to shore, across the lake away from the boat dock, Emma pointed out several alligators sunning themselves on the bank. Sarah snapped a photograph, just as Dakota barked a couple times, but

the alligators weren't bothered. The kids got quite a treat, when a large bald eagle dove, talons first, into the water next to the boat and emerged with a large fish in its claws. It shook off the excess water mid-air, then flew to a nearby tree to enjoy its lunch. Sarah explained to the kids that was an example of how nature worked and animals survived. Cayman docked the boat and helped the children safely disembark.

The kids walked back to the main building where Emma gave them all a small toy animal from the gift shop. Sarah and Cayman thanked them for coming and invited them back anytime. The students thanked Sarah and Cayman, and gave Dakota a pat on the head, before walking back to the bus together. Emma gave her mom, her dad, and Dakota big hugs before climbing on the bus with the rest of the kids. Their teacher told Sarah and Cayman it was a wonderful experience, and she was sure that the children learned a lot and would remember their visit to the nature conservancy. The teacher thanked them, and told them it was more than she could have hoped for.

Chapter Ten

During the summer of 1979, one of Sarah's staff members at the conservancy told her about a family who had purchased land on a small barrier island south of Cypress Cove. The staff member went on to explain that the family had built a three-story, pyramid-shaped house, entirely out of cedar. She described the top of the pyramid as having bright mirrors that reflected the sun. One entire side was a three-story lanai with views of the gulf, and another side was entirely made of windows. The staff member told Sarah that she had heard that the family had horses, birds, and several other animals on the island.

Sarah was intrigued by the story, and she was anxious to share what she had heard with Cayman. She told him that she would like to take Dakota and ten-year-old Emma on an overnight camping trip to the island. Cayman loved the idea, and that weekend they packed their boat with food and camping supplies to go to the island. It was a two-hour boat ride to get to the barrier island.

They docked their boat on the inland waterway side of the island for overnight protection from the surf. They only had to walk a short distance from where they docked to get to where the pyramid house was built. When they arrived at the pyramid house, they saw the owners sitting in their lanai taking in the magnificent view. Sarah introduced herself and her family, along with Dakota, to the homeowners. The pyramid homeowners welcomed the Taylors to their home and introduced themselves and their daughter, who was about the same age as Emma.

Sarah told them that she had heard about their home from a member of her staff at the Southwest Florida Nature Conservancy, and that her passion and field of study were natural resources and conservation. She said that when she heard about their home, she just had to see it for herself. They were pleased that Sarah had taken an interest in their home and told Sarah they would be happy to show it to them. While the homeowners were taking Sarah and Cayman on a tour, their daughter showed Emma and Dakota the horses and other animals on the grounds.

During the tour, the homeowners explained to Sarah and Cayman how they brought supplies to and from the island and how they managed water and power. They had built a barge capable of bringing supplies and animals to the island. There were no power lines and no water that ran to the island. For water, they created a desalinization system to convert saltwater to fresh water. They also captured rain water in a cistern as an additional water source. For electricity, the homeowners had built a windmill to supply limited power. Sarah and Cayman were intrigued by the resourcefulness of these homeowners. They were able to live comfortably on the island, with very little impact to the natural environment.

What the pyramid homeowners were doing fit perfectly with the mission of the nature conservancy. Sarah asked them if it would be okay if she took some photographs to display in their exhibits at the conservancy. And she took some notes for her dad, Henry Cooper, to potentially write an article for the Cypress Cove Chronicle. The homeowners were proud of what they had created and were happy for Sarah to share their story.

Sarah shared with the homeowners that her family had planned to camp on the island for the night, before returning to Cypress Cove in the morning. The homeowners suggested that they set up camp on their land. And they invited the Taylors for dinner that evening. Sarah gladly accepted their offer. Cayman, Emma, and Sarah set up the campsite for the night.

Cayman invited the homeowners' daughter to go fishing with him and Emma. While the three of them were fishing along the shore, they noticed an osprey circling high above. It seemed as if it wanted to join their fishing party.

Sarah grabbed her camera to snap a few photographs of the magnificent bird. Suddenly it dove, talons first, straight for the water. Sarah took a photograph just before the osprey hit the surface of the water. The osprey skimmed the top of the water and lifted out a fish in its strong claws. It hovered with its catch above the water, while it shook its wings forcefully to rid itself of water, then it flew to a perch in the tree to enjoy its catch. They were in awe of the osprey's ability to catch fish so easily. Emma told everyone about the eagle she had seen, which had done the same thing at the conservancy lake a few months earlier. The group had to work a little harder than the osprey, but it didn't take long until they caught enough fish for dinner that night.

Cayman cleaned and cooked the fish, while the two young girls arranged the table. Sarah and the homeowners prepared the drinks and side dishes for their dinner. The two families sat down for dinner and talked about life on the island until the sky was full of stars. The two young girls fell asleep first, then they all retired for the night. The next morning, the Taylors thanked the homeowners for their hospitality and waved goodbye as they drove their boat out of the channel to head back to Cypress Cove.

For the last few years, Emma had been asking her mom and dad lots of questions about where they had grown up and what their childhoods had been like. Sarah spent most of her childhood in Westwood, Illinois, before moving to Cypress Cove just before she turned fifteen. Cayman had spent his first five years in Dimerling, Ohio, and the rest of his childhood growing up in the Poaceaehatchee Village. Emma was curious about their childhoods before they had lived in Southwest Florida.

Sarah and Cayman decided it was time for a road trip to Illinois and Ohio to show Emma their childhood homes. There was still plenty of time left during Emma's summer break from school for a two-week road trip. It was the first time Sarah and Cayman had left South Florida since they had gotten married nearly fourteen years earlier. The two of them began making arrangements right away for coverage at the foundation and the conservancy. There were no grants in process at the foundation, yet Cayman asked Aubrey to check in with their small staff of two a few times while they were gone. Sarah informed the staff at the conservancy that she and Cayman would be out of town for a couple of weeks. She put in charge the trusted director of the conservancy animal hospital while they were gone. Sarah had known her since they went to high school together and she was one of the longest serving team members of the conservancy.

Cayman drove to the Poaceaehatchee Village to borrow a truck camper from a friend, and to let Etu and his parents know they would be out of town for a few weeks. Etu helped Cayman and their friend load the camper onto Cayman's pickup truck, then Cayman headed back to Cypress Cove. Sarah, Emma, and Cayman loaded the camper with clothes, food, drink, fishing poles, and other travel supplies. They were confident that they had packed everything they would need. They were all eager to get an early start on their journey north, so the evening before leaving, they mapped out their thirteen-hundred-mile route to Westwood, Illinois.

The next morning, they got up early and had breakfast with Sarah's parents on the verandah. While enjoying breakfast, they sat gazing at the beach. It would be their last time seeing the gulf for two whole weeks. Sarah asked her parents to check on their house a few times while they were gone. The three of them and Dakota pulled out of the driveway and waved goodbye to Vicki and Henry. They planned to drive to Atlanta, Georgia, to camp for the night.

They took a route that meandered north through the small towns in the center of the Florida. There were orange groves for as far as the eye could see. They stopped at a roadside rest area around noon to have lunch. Emma and Dakota jumped out of the truck first to stretch their legs from sitting for so long. Emma wanted to know when they would cross the border to Georgia. Cayman said, "We're only about half-way to Georgia. It will probably be about three more hours until we're out of Florida." Emma replied, "Geeze, really? Florida sure is a long state!" After a short break, they hopped back into the truck and Sarah took over the driving. They drove all day, and finally reached Atlanta around dinner time. Sarah pulled into a small diner, where they ate dinner. Sarah asked the manager for permission to park their camper out back for the night.

The manager nodded his approval, and they pulled around back to get a good night's sleep for the next day's drive north. The excited travelers got up early the next morning and had breakfast at the diner before hitting the road for Nashville, Tennessee. They planned a much shorter four-hour drive, since they would be traveling over the Appalachian Mountains. Emma had never seen mountains, so it would be a new experience for her and for Dakota. Cayman pulled over at several scenic stops to take in the views and for Sarah to snap a few photographs. They were surprised at how cold the air felt at the higher mountain altitudes. It probably wouldn't have been that cold to most people, but for Emma it was the coldest temperature she had ever experienced.

Their camper pulled into Nashville mid-afternoon, and they drove around to explore some of the area. The three of them visited the Grand Ole Opry House and the Country Music Hall of Fame before stopping for dinner in old town Nashville. After touring the city, they found a campground with water and electricity. The next morning was going to be the last leg of their three-day journey. It would be a seven-hour drive, and they planned to pull into Westwood, Illinois, sometime in the mid-afternoon.

They awoke early on day three, and had breakfast in the camper, before pulling onto the road for Westwood. Sarah drove while Emma and her dad played "count the cows." Emma took the left side of the road and Cayman the right side. They counted the cows on their side of the road. The object of the game was to count the most cows. If they passed a graveyard on their side of the road, they had to start over with zero cows. They played the game between each fuel stop and rest stop, starting a new game as they resumed each leg of the trip. By the time they got to Westwood, Emma had won four games, Cayman two games, and Dakota zero games. (Although no one was really sure who actually won the cow-counting game.)

On the way into Westwood, Sarah found a KOA (Kampgrounds of America) on the edge of town. They paid for a reserved campsite for the next two nights, while they toured Sarah's childhood home of Westwood and explored Chicago. The next morning, they drove into Westwood. Their first stop was for breakfast at a diner Sarah used to visit when she was about Emma's age. It was the same diner she had taken Cayman, when they visited Westwood sixteen years earlier – in 1963. Sarah didn't recognize any of the people at the diner, so she asked if anyone knew what happened to the previous owners. The lady running the cash register told Sarah that they were her parents and they had retired a few years earlier. She told Sarah that she and her husband had taken over the diner when her parents had been ready to retire. Sarah told the daughter that she used to come there with her parents when she was a teenager, and the daughter's parents were always nice to her. Sarah wished her well and asked her to tell her parents hello, as they left the diner for the next stop.

They spent the rest of the day touring around Westwood, exploring Sarah's childhood hometown. They stopped where Sarah's mom's photography studio – Special Moments – used to be. Her studio and several other buildings were torn down and replaced with a shopping mall. Sarah drove to her childhood school, where they parked and walked around for a few minutes. Emma only knew one-story, open-air-style schools in Southwest Florida, and she thought the big, square, three-story-tall building was strange looking. After seeing all of Sarah's local spots, they headed back to the campsite for dinner. Cayman went fishing in the small pond at the campground, while Sarah and Emma talked about her old hometown. They enjoyed a tasty fish dinner before calling it a night.

Sarah's dad had made arrangements with some of his former coworkers for a tour of the Chicago Tribune. The last time Sarah and Cayman were there was shortly after Cayman had been discovered as Grayson Taylor. He hoped they wouldn't remember that, and start asking lots of questions again. When Sarah drove them into Chicago, Emma's eyes lit up with astonishment at all of the tall buildings. Sarah told her that the tall buildings were called skyscrapers, because they looked like they touched the sky.

After driving around the block a few times, they finally found a place to park, several blocks from the Tribune. Emma told Dakota she had to wait in the camper while the three of them walked to the

Tribune. After they signed in at the reception area, one of Sarah's dad's friends met them for a tour. He remembered Cayman, but Henry had already asked him not to pry. Out of respect, he never asked Cayman one question about his past.

Henry's friend took the Taylors on a tour of the Chicago Tribune. Emma got to see where the reporters worked and where the newspapers were printed. She was in wonderment about how the newspaper business worked. It may even have been what further sparked her passion for writing. When they had finished with the tour, the three of them walked back to the camper to get Dakota. From there, the four of them walked several blocks to the Navy Pier, where Sarah loved to go as a child. They had lunch and walked around the pier for a few hours before heading back to the camper to start their drive east toward Ohio. Emma said to her mom, "Thank you, thank you for showing me where you grew up and went to school."

Cayman drove to Toledo, Ohio, where they had dinner and parked in a shopping plaza parking lot for the night. The next morning, after breakfast, they drove along the south side of Lake Erie to Cleveland, Ohio, then south to Dimerling. It was eleven a.m. when Cayman drove down the long, tree-lined lane to the visitor parking lot at his parents' former estate. Sarah was telling Emma that this was where her dad had spent his first five years as a child. Emma's eyes almost popped out of her head when she saw the house. Her first question was, "Is that a castle or a hotel?" Her next question was, "Did dad really live here?" Sarah smiled as she told Emma about spending time there with Cayman in the summer of 1963, two years before he donated the estate to the Dimerling Historical Society.

Cayman parked the truck camper in the parking lot and they walked toward the entrance of the estate. While they were walking, Sarah told Emma that the estate was an historical landmark and a museum. People came to the Taylor Estate to take tours of the house and the property. The three of them were greeted and asked to sign the registry as they entered the front door. Sarah signed them in as Sarah, Emma, and Cayman Taylor. The receptionist saw the name on the registry and asked them if they were any relation to Mary and Robert Taylor.

Someone in the small office behind the reception area must have heard the conversation, because she quickly came out and saw Cayman standing there. Her first words were, "Grayson Taylor, you haven't changed a bit." Emma was confused and asked her dad, "Who's Grayson?" Cayman responded, "That was me a long time ago. Don't let me forget to tell you more about that later." The lady who had come out of the office was on the original committee when Cayman donated the estate to the historical society. She told Cayman how happy she was to see him and how thankful they were having the estate as part of the historical society. Cayman introduced Sarah and Emma, and asked if it was okay to show Emma around the house and grounds. She quickly responded that he was welcome to take Emma anywhere in the house and on the property that he wanted.

The three of them spent a few hours walking through the house looking at every room. Emma saw pictures of Cayman's parents, her grandparents, whom she never knew. She saw baby pictures of her dad and the room where he slept when his was a young boy. Emma was in complete amazement at what she was seeing. When they had finished their tour inside the house, Cayman went to the truck and got Dakota to walk with them in the gardens and woods. Emma just couldn't believe her dad had lived here and that her mom had spent time with him there one summer, long ago. Dakota must have somehow sensed Luna's ghost on the property, because she walked with them as if she was respecting an ancestor from the past.

Cayman took them to the huge garage where the tractors and cars were stored. Emma pointed to the old sedans and the convertible, then she pointed to the old pickup truck and said, "Dad, that looks just like our old truck." Sarah told Emma, "Your dad's was the original pickup truck from the estate. It's the only thing he kept, because it reminded him of his dad. He wanted to maintain the originality of the estate, so he replaced the original pickup with a used one that he had painted to match. Even though he doesn't drive that old pickup much anymore, he still keeps it, because it reminds him of home."

After spending the afternoon touring the Taylor Estate and grounds, the four of them loaded into the pickup truck and headed for a campground outside of Dimerling. They were exhausted from all of the driving, touring Chicago, and visiting the Taylor Estate. Everyone, including Dakota, slept well that night, and no one got up as early as usual the next morning. Cayman and Sarah loaded the supplies into the camper, and drove Emma into town for a late breakfast. After breakfast, they headed to the Taylor Tire and Rubber Company.

The three of them went into the main entrance of Taylor Tire and signed in at the front desk. Cayman asked the receptionist if she would please call Bonnie Hope in Human Resources to let her know he was there. The receptionist asked Cayman, "Who are you again?" He replied, "Please tell her Grayson Taylor is here to see her." It had been fourteen years since he had last seen Bonnie and he hoped she would remember him. Emma said, "There's that name Grayson again. Why does dad keep saying that?" Sarah replied, "It's a long story and we'll explain everything on our drive back to Cypress Cove." The receptionist was confused. She had heard the name Grayson Taylor before, but the rumor was that he died in a plane crash. She looked at Grayson and as she pointed to the name on the wall, she asked, "Are you…?" And before she could finish, he nodded his head yes.

Bonnie stepped out of the elevator, and when she saw Sarah and Grayson, and she walked quickly to them and gave them all big hugs. Bonnie asked Grayson, "Who's this beautiful young lady?"

Chapter Ten

Emma quickly stepped over to Bonnie and held out her hand, while telling her, "I'm Emma Marie Taylor, it's nice to meet you. Will you please show me where my grandparents used to work?" Bonnie smiled and said, "Come with me!" Bonnie showed Emma around Taylor Tire and Rubber Company. Emma exclaimed that she had never been in a manufacturing plant. And when the three of them were walking back to the truck, Emma said, "Dad, I can see why you don't work here anymore." Sarah and Cayman both smiled as they got into the truck.

It was getting close to dinner, and it was too late for them to drive south. They got some dinner at a local eatery, and parked the camper for the night in a mall parking lot. The first thing the next morning, they set out for Florida. Sarah and Cayman decided to take a different route going home, and left Dimerling, Ohio, for Winston-Salem, in North Carolina. It was a scenic, seven-hour drive that took them through the mountains of West Virginia. Emma was amazed at how big the mountains were, and a bit nervous about how the edge of the road disappeared into deep gorges.

The Taylors pulled their truck camper into Winston-Salem around two p.m. Sarah and Cayman took Emma to tour a couple of Old Salem Museums and Gardens. Then the three of them went for dinner on the North Carolina's Historic Barbecue Trail. Back in Cypress Cove, seafood was their typical dinner, so a hometown barbecue was a fun change. Sarah asked one of the waitresses for a recommendation on parking their truck camper for the night. The waitress said, "Just pull it around behind our building. You'll find a plug for power and outdoor spigot to hook up your water hose." All three of them thanked her for her hospitality before jumping in the truck and parking it for the night.

Cayman got up early and made breakfast before their drive from Winston-Salem to Savannah, Georgia. It was a scenic, five-hour-drive down to the coastal city. In Savannah, the streets were lined and shaded with large oak trees covered in Spanish moss. The city sat along the Savannah River, and was adorned with cobblestoned streets and horse-drawn carriages. In the center of town was a huge gothic cathedral. Sarah got carry-out food at a local eatery, and they sat in one of the manicured parks for dinner. They spent that night parked near stables at a horse farm. Emma and Dakota enjoyed watching the horses before they dozed off for the night.

Daytona Beach, Florida, was their next destination. By highway it was nearly a four-hour drive from Savannah, but Cayman took the coastal road A1A. It was a beautiful, scenic drive along the east coast of Florida. Emma had never been to the east coast of Florida, and she couldn't get over the difference in the sand and the ocean waves. The beaches on the east coast of Florida were darker sand than the white sandy beaches in Cypress Cove. The waves on the beach from the Atlantic Ocean were gigantic compared to the ripple-sized waves in the Gulf of Mexico.

When they arrived at Daytona Beach, Cayman pulled the truck camper right out onto the sand where there were lots of people and lots of parked cars. He parked the truck on the beach, and they all went into the camper to put on their bathing suits. Emma and Dakota were eager to try out the large waves that were crashing onto the beach. Emma swam out one hundred feet and body surfed back into shore. She enjoyed it so much, she did it over and over, until she was exhausted. While taking a break on the beach, Emma noticed several people further out in the water laying on surf boards. It was something that she didn't see in the gulf waters at Cypress Cove. Emma and Dakota were having so much fun, she asked her parents if they could spend the night in Daytona.

Chapter Ten

Sarah found a campground on the beach where they parked the truck camper for the night. Emma and Dakota played in the ocean while Cayman went fishing. He caught several fish for dinner, and he cleaned them while Sarah prepared a salad. Sarah and Cayman finished setting the picnic table just about the time Emma and Dakota returned to the camper. After a nice fish dinner, Emma helped clean and put away the dishes. They sat and watched the ocean waves until they nodded off as the sun went down behind them in the western sky.

Emma and Dakota were up and outside early the next morning. Emma wanted to be swimming as soon as it got light. She was surprised by the big yellow fireball of the sun rising above the water in the Atlantic. In Cypress Cove they saw sunset, not sunrise, over the water. Emma banged on the camper door and yelled for her mom and dad to come outside to see the sunrise. Sarah and Cayman stepped out of the camper, just in time for sunrise and for Sarah to snap a photograph of the bright colors over the water in the eastern sky. Emma and Sarah swam for a several hours while Cayman, with Dakota by his side, watched them swim, occasionally joining in.

By lunch time they had packed up and were driving four hours south to Miami, where Sarah had graduated from college. Sarah stopped at the Port of Miami to show Emma where the cruise ships docked. Emma was stunned at the size of the ships, saying, "Those ships sure wouldn't be able to dock at the Kendrick Pier in Cypress Cove!" Sarah parked the truck camper in Little Havana, where they had an authentic Cuban dinner and listened to Latin music. After dinner, Sarah drove west on the SoFlo Trail to show Emma where she went to college. She turned into the entrance of the Glades University campus. After seeing her old campus, Sarah drove the SoFlo Trail home to Cypress Cove. It had been a very interesting and fun-filled road trip, and they were all glad to be back at their home on the beach.

Emma turned eleven years old shortly after she started sixth grade, during the fall of 1979. A few weeks into the new school year, her teacher announced that in a couple of weeks the class would be going to go on a field trip to the Poaceaehatchee Village. The teacher wanted the students to learn about their neighbors, the Tutelar. She wanted the children to learn about the Tutelar's customs, culture, and their respect for nature. Emma's teacher knew that Emma attended school at the Poaceaehatchee Village part of each year, and that her dad grew up there. Her teacher asked Emma to see if her dad would be willing to chaperone the field trip.

Emma was thrilled about her class taking a field trip to the Poaceaehatchee Village. Since she was four years old, she spent part of each school year in the Tutelar school, learning their language and customs. At dinner that evening, Emma told her mom and dad about the field trip and that her teacher asked if her dad would help. Cayman quickly responded, "I'd be happy to help, but I need to ask my boss at the conservancy if it's okay for me to take a day off to join you all." Cayman looked at Sarah, and smiled. Sarah said, "Absolutely he will chaperone the field trip, honey."

Cayman contacted Emma's teacher the next day to let her know he'd like to help chaperone the field trip to the Poaceaehatchee Village. The teacher knew the field trip would be more fun for the children and more successful as a learning experience with Cayman involved. They talked for an hour, making plans for a full day of fun and learning. Once the date was arranged and her expectations were understood, Cayman made calls to a few people in the village.

He contacted the school administrator to arrange for the Cypress Cove children to visit the Poaceaehatchee school. Cayman reached out to the proprietor of a small outdoor eatery to arrange for the kids to have a traditional Tutelar lunch. He talked with Etu about taking the school children on a boat ride on the Fish-Hawk. He made arrangements with Aiyana and Elu for the kids to visit the Sacred Moments gallery – the gallery that he and Sarah had opened in the village many years earlier. Finally, Cayman asked the council of elders if they would speak to the class about how the council lead and supported the village. Everyone agreed to play a role in the field trip.

Cayman and Dakota rode along with the teacher and the school kids on the bus to Poaceaehatchee Village. They parked near the Poaceaehatchee school; one of the teachers greeted the bus full of students. Cayman had made arrangements with the Tutelar teacher to arrange for three of her older Tutelar students to talk with the younger Cypress Cove students. They led the young school children into a classroom in the Tutelar school. Cayman, the Tutelar teacher, and Cypress Cove teacher took chairs in the back of the room, and Dakota settled next to Cayman. The three Tutelar students stood at the front of the classroom.

Each Tutelar student introduced herself/himself, along with the meaning of each one's first and last name. They told the Cypress Cove students that it was part of their heritage that words and names had special meanings. The young school children were fascinated to hear their names and that each name had a specific meaning. The Tutelar students planned to have the visiting students introduce themselves. They knew that it was not part of the culture to have special meaning for their names, but wanted to make it fun and interesting for their visitors. So, when the Tutelar students asked the Cypress Cove students to introduce themselves, they also asked that they include what they would like their names to mean. The kids introduced themselves, creating funny, interesting meanings to their names.

After the introductions, the Tutelar student presenters talked about their history, how their ancestors had been in Southwest Florida since the 1700s. They described their culture and village norms. The Cypress Cove students were interested in hearing about culture and people, yet they really wanted to ask questions. One of the first questions asked was, "What languages do you speak?" One of the Tutelar students explained that the Tutelar speak two languages. English when around English-speaking visitors, and the native Tutelar language at home and with friends. Another student asked, "What do you eat?" The answer was easy, "We eat just about the same things you eat. Except most of our food is freshly picked or caught on the day we eat it. You are going to have lunch in a little bit, and the fish you eat will have been caught this morning. Some of the vegetables will have been picked today. We don't have a lot of prepackaged foods, like you buy in stores."

The next child asked, "What do you learn in school?" The Tutelar student told them, "We are taught similar subjects as your schools teach. We learn reading, writing, math, science, social studies, and so on. The difference is *how* we are taught. We learn from the perspective of how the subject matter fits into our lives, our families, our village, and the nature around us. We are taught that everything we do affects someone or something else. We are taught to respect the animals and the land and never to take more than we can use." The Cypress Cove children were full of questions and the Tutelar students answered each question with enthusiasm. Before they finished, one of the Tutelar student presenters told the visiting children, "We're really not that different from you. We like many of the same things. We're just kids trying to make it in the world around us."

It was almost time for lunch, and the kids were getting hungry. Cayman made arrangements to have lunch at a small outdoor eatery, a short walk from the school. The kids thanked the Tutelar students for an interesting visit, and headed out of the building for lunch. When they arrived at the eatery, the students took seats at the picnic tables under the large live oak canopy trees. Cayman, Emma, and her teacher helped the owner serve food to the kids. Emma was having fun at the village, getting a chance to practice her Tutelar language skills. For lunch, the kids enjoyed fresh fish, corn, beans, squash, and pumpkin bread. The Cypress Cove children talked all through lunch about what they heard from the Tutelar students, and especially about the meaning they had given to their names. When lunch was finished, everyone pitched in to help clear the tables, and they thanked the cook for a wonderful lunch.

The next stop on the schedule was to head to the docks for a ride on Etu's boat. Etu was there to welcome the students and help them get onto the boat safely. He went over all of the safety rules, while Cayman and Emma untied the boat. Once everyone was safely onboard, Etu backed the boat away from the dock and headed out toward the Ten Thousand Islands. It was a beautiful fall day and the water was crystal clear. Etu drove the boat slowly around the islands, pointing out some of the wildlife. One of the students was looking and pointing down at the water, yelling "stingray." All of the kids rushed to that side of the boat to see a large fever of nearly 100 stingrays passing under the boat. They saw a variety of fish swimming around the boat, as well.

Etu asked Cayman to drive the boat while he pointed at a fish and asked the kids to tell him what kind of fish it was. If they got it right, everyone cheered. If they didn't, he told them what kind of fish it was and a little about what each fish means to the ecosystem. Etu told the kids that the Tutelar enjoy fishing, but they fish for food and they only keep what they can eat. The kids were having fun learning about all of the different fish.

Etu took over driving the boat. He knew a spot where there were usually lots of dolphins, so he sped up the boat a little to see if he could get the dolphins to play. Soon there were three dolphins following the boat. Sometimes they would get up close to the side of the boat and jump out of the water, swimming in the boat's wake. The kids were screaming with joy at the dolphins playing alongside of the boat. Suddenly, one of the dolphins behind the boat swam very fast toward the boat, then jumped straight up until its entire body was out of the water, then it landed on its side making a big splash. The kids loved it, and Dakota let out a bark, signaling her pleasure with the dolphin show.

Etu turned the boat around to head back to the docks. Along the way, when he was near the shore of the mainland, he slowed the boat. He pointed to a spot on the bank, near the mangroves, where there was a large creature laying on the bank. Some of the kids yelled out saying, "Look at the alligator!" Cayman knew right away that Etu had spotted a crocodile, not an alligator. Etu told the kids what they were looking at was a crocodile. Cayman told them that South Florida was the only place in the world where alligators and crocodiles lived together in the wild. He told the kids that alligators preferred fresh water, like lakes, ponds, and rivers. Crocodiles preferred saltwater or brackish water along mangroves and saltwater tidal pools. The two of them told the kids that the easiest way to tell them apart was that alligators were more of a black color with U-shaped snouts, and crocodiles were a grayish-brown color with V-shaped snouts. The kids thought it was so cool to see a crocodile. Etu eased the boat back into the dock, while Cayman and Emma took the ropes to tie it up. All of the kids yelled thank you to Etu, as they headed back into the village.

Cayman had two more brief stops planned. The next stop was the Sacred Moments I Photo Gallery. Emma couldn't wait to stop there; it was the gallery her mom had started with her dad many years ago. When they arrived at the gallery, Emma introduced Aiyana and Elu to her classmates and to her teacher. She told them that Aiyana meant eternal blossom and Elu meant beautiful. The kids clapped about hearing the meaning of more names. The teacher asked the kids to introduce themselves to Aiyana and Elu. She also instructed the children to be careful not to touch anything while looking through the gallery. The kids were awe struck at the photographs of scenery and animals on the gallery walls. Emma described some of the photographs to the class, then Aiyana and Elu described the photographs Emma had not seen. The kids enjoyed seeing the photographs and thanked Aiyana and Elu as they filed out of the gallery for their next and final stop.

Cayman had arranged for two of the council elders to say a few words to the children before they got back on the bus to head home to Cypress Cove. They stopped at the main hall in the village center to enter the council of elders' chambers. The kids were quiet as they entered the chambers and sat before the elders. They didn't know what to expect. Cayman said a few words to the elders in the Tutelar language, then introduced the elders to the teacher and her students. Cayman asked the teacher to introduce herself and for the students to introduce themselves. Cayman told the elders about their day and thanked them for the hospitality shown the Cypress Cove students. The elders told the students a little bit about how the council of elders worked for the village and that they could loosely compare it to how the Cypress Cove town council worked. The kids were quiet the entire time, either out of respect or they were just too afraid to even ask one question. The elders told them they were welcome anytime and to please tell others about their visit. The children thanked the elders, then made their way back to the bus for the ride home to Cypress Cove. They talked about everything they had seen and done the entire way home.

During the summer of 1980, eleven-year-old Emma and her Tutelar friend Catori, from the Poaceaehatchee school, were planning an adventure. Catori meant spirit, and she was as thrill-seeking as Emma. The two girls wanted to go on a camping trip in the Ten Thousand Islands. Catori was at Emma's house for dinner, and it was their chance to ask Emma's parents to take them camping. Emma and Catori had it all planned – how they would ask during dinner that evening. As they sat down for dinner, Catori just kind of blurted it out. "Mrs. and Mr. Taylor, will you please take Emma and me camping in the Ten Thousand Islands this weekend?" Sarah and Cayman both smiled as they looked at each other and nodded their heads, while saying "sure" at the same time.

Sarah, Cayman, Emma, and Dakota left the conservancy early on Friday to load the boat and drive it three hours around the point to the docks at the Poaceaehatchee Village. They wanted the boat and supplies to be at the village, ready for an early start on Saturday morning. Cayman's parents did not have enough rooms in their home for everyone, so Etu helped them pitch their tent in his parents' backyard. Catori came over for dinner and to stay with the three Taylors in the tent on Friday night. Emma and Catori arranged the table, while Sarah and Cayman prepared dinner for everyone – including his parents and Etu. They sat down for dinner at the large picnic table in his parents' backyard and talked about where they were going camping the next day.

Remembering Sarah's and Cayman's stranded-at-sea adventure in 1960, Etu wanted to know exactly where they were going camping. Sarah said, "The girls asked for an adventure, so an adventure they'll have. We're taking them to the same island where we were stranded 20 years ago. Its large sand bar is great for swimming, the crystal-clear waters are perfect for snorkeling, there's good fishing for dinner, and a pleasantly shaded area that is nice for pitching the tent." Etu laughed and said, "Well good, at least I know where to find you, if you're not home for lunch on Sunday!" Cayman chimed in to say, "No need to worry about us, brother. We have much better equipment now than we did 20 years ago." With that, they all retired for a good night's sleep.

Emma and Catori woke up first; they were excited to get out on the water. Dakota was already up and out visiting some of her animal friends in the village. Sarah and Cayman got up next, and everyone pitched in to get breakfast ready. After breakfast, Emma and Catori cleaned up the dishes, while Sarah, Etu, and Cayman tore down the tent and made sure they had everything they needed loaded on the boat. The girls finished the kitchen duty and arrived at the dock ready to shove off. Etu waved goodbye and yelled, "Make sure you are home by lunch on Sunday." Cayman honked the boat horn, as they pulled out of the bay into the open water.

It was a two-hour boat ride to the island where they were going to camp. Cayman encouraged Emma and Catori to take turns driving the boat through the channels and around the islands. Soon they spotted their destination; it was a large island off in the distance. As they neared, the girls could see the large sandbar jutting out from the island. Cayman beached the boat on the east side of the sandbar, and everyone jumped out to swim in the warm, shallow water. Dakota played in the shallow water on the sandbar, while the others snorkeled in the deeper water. The girls were having a blast, diving down to gently pet stingrays and carefully picking up sea stars to show each other. Sarah and Cayman snorkeled a while, then returned to the sandbar and played with Dakota. They must have spent three hours swimming and snorkeling before finding a good spot on the island to set up the tent.

They cruised around the side of the island to find the same spot on the beach where Sarah and Cayman were stranded many years ago. Sarah spotted it first and pointed, "There, that's the spot, where we camped and made an SOS on the beach out of dark stones." Sarah pulled the boat into shore, while Cayman jumped out with a rope to tie it to a palm tree. The others disembarked, and everyone unloaded the tent and camping supplies.

They all pitched in to put up the tent, in the exact same spot where Sarah and Cayman had camped when they were much younger. Once the tent was up, it was time to catch fish for dinner. Often, they fished from shore, but  Cayman asked the girls if they wanted to go back out in the boat to fish. Emma and Catori were always in for a boat ride, and quickly nodded yes.

Cayman drove them to a spot that looked good for fishing, and he anchored the boat. He helped prepare the girls' fishing lines, then sat back with Sarah and Dakota, while Emma and Catori fished for dinner. It took a little over an hour for the girls to catch enough grouper for dinner. Sarah drove the boat back to their spot on the island, while Cayman helped the girls put the fish on ice and the fishing gear away. Sarah pulled the front of the boat up onto the beach and Cayman jumped out and tied it to the same palm tree as before. Emma told Catori that part of the adventure was learning how to clean fish for cooking over the fire. At first, Catori was a little squeamish, but she soon got the hang of it, and helped Emma clean the catch.

Sarah showed the girls how to cook the fish over a campfire, while Cayman prepared a couple of side dishes. The girls were really excited with their adventure, and thanked Sarah and Cayman several times during dinner. After dinner, everyone pitched in to clean the dishes and cookware for stowing away in a compartment on the boat. As they sat talking about the fun they had that day, the sun was setting, leaving vibrant colors behind. It soon became very dark; it seemed like the stars lit up the sky. The exhausted girls quickly fell asleep next to the fire. Sarah and Cayman talked a bit longer, before helping the girls make their way into the tent for the night.

On Sunday morning, Sarah and Cayman sent Emma and Catori in search of bananas and coconuts for breakfast. When they returned, they all shared in their find, while Dakota ate the food they had brought along for him. The girls went swimming, while Sarah and Cayman took down the tent and packed up the boat. Cayman had hoped to add two side trips to their adventure, but to do so, they were going to have to go back to the village docks and get a smaller boat. He told Sarah his plan, and she thought it would okay for Emma, but that they should return Catori to her family.

After Emma and Catori were done swimming, they hopped in the boat and headed for the village boat docks. Sarah drove, while Cayman told the girls they were heading back to the village docks for lunch. Upon returning to the boat docks, they unloaded the camping supplies and fishing equipment. It was lunch time and Etu was surprised to see them back so early. Cayman told him where he was taking Emma, but he wanted to have lunch first. Etu hadn't been to either location for a long time and asked Cayman if he could ride along. Cayman responded, "Absolutely, please come along."

They all had lunch, while Cayman told his parents where they were taking Emma. Sakari and Alo were glad that he was going to show Emma the sacred place where his parents' spirits were set free. Catori hugged and thanked Sarah and Cayman for taking her along on the camping adventure. She gave Emma a big hug and said goodbye. As Catori turned to walk to her parents' house, Emma said to her, "Catori, I'm really glad that we're friends." Catori said, "Me too." They both smiled as they went their separate ways.

Along with his larger charter boats, Etu had two smaller backwater boats, perfect for getting into narrow, shallow waterways. Cayman and Etu got one of the smaller boats ready while Sarah, Emma, and Dakota got on board. Etu drove the boat out of the bay, away from the dock, into the open water. He drove east along the islands for 45 minutes, then turned north into a small channel. He slowly drove the boat up the channel for 30 minutes, until he and Cayman knew they were at the right spot.

Cayman pointed to the side of the channel where he wanted Emma to look. As she looked where he was pointing, Emma noticed an airplane's tail sticking above the mangroves and a wing sticking through the  mangroves. Cayman had told Emma the story during their road trip from Ohio, on the way back to Florida. So, she knew what it was, she had just never seen it. Cayman told Emma that it was the plane that

239

his parents, he, and Luna were in when it crashed on July Fourth, 1948. Sarah had been there with Cayman before, when they went several years ago on the Fourth of July to remember his parents and Luna.

Cayman said to Emma, "You wanted to understand where and how your mom and I grew up, and this is part of the story. I don't want you to be sad; I simply hope this helps you understand a little more about our family and history." Cayman went on to tell Emma that the Tutelar saved him and Luna from the crash, but they couldn't save his mom and dad. He told Emma that the Tutelar spread his parents' ashes at the crash site. This was after holding a traditional Tutelar funeral in the village for his dad, and four days later for his mom. When Luna died, he brought her back to the same place to be with his parents. Emma was a little sad, but glad her dad had showed her this place that was so important in his life.

Cayman told Emma, "We have one more stop before heading back to the village for dinner, then for the boat ride back to Cypress Cove. I think this stop will be a little more fun for you to see." Etu drove the boat back the Aquene River that led into the Cypress Forest. He drove the boat 20 minutes up the river, until Cayman pointed and said, "Stop over there." There was a bank along the river, where several large cypress trees were standing in the water. Etu pulled the boat far enough up on the bank that it stayed without an anchor. The four of them and Dakota jumped out of the boat. Cayman led Emma and Dakota over to a large limestone rock. Emma sat down on the rock, while Dakota sat next to her on the ground. Sara and Etu stood next to her, as Cayman began to describe a story about Boone.

Cayman told Emma, "Etu and I were fishing in the Aquene River from our canoe, when we saw a puppy sitting on the edge of the water, next to this rock. There were several alligators in the river, waiting to get the puppy. We saved him, before the alligators had a chance to snatch him off of the bank. We named the puppy Boone, meaning miracle dog. When Boone died, we spread his ashes here next to this rock.

Etu immediately jumped in and tried to correct Cayman's story. "That's close, but not exactly how it happened. You see, we were fishing from our canoe over there on the river, but *we* didn't save the puppy, your dad did. He jumped from our canoe and quickly swam past the alligators to the shore. He picked up and held the puppy, until I got there with the canoe. That's the day your dad swam with the alligators, and it's why we call him Cayman, a word for alligator."

Emma sat quietly listening in wonder at the story she just heard. She turned to Sarah and asked, "Mom, whose story is true?" Sarah kind of shrugged her shoulders and responded, "Honey, only your dad and your uncle were here that day. But the legend around Cypress Cove has it the way your uncle described it."

Cayman just smiled as they climbed into the boat and Etu drove them to the village docks. When they arrived at the village docks, they all walked to the Deeres's home for dinner before the boat ride to Cypress Cove. After dinner Etu walked to the village docks with Sarah, Emma, and Cayman. The three of them climbed into their boat with Dakota to drive to Cypress Cove. As they were backing

away from the dock, Emma called out, "Uncle Etu, thank you for driving us to the site of the plane crash and for telling me the story about Boone."

As they were leaving the Poaceaehatchee docks for their boat ride back home to

241

Chapter Ten

Cypress Cove, Sarah noticed a small raised spot in the water, with a single mangrove tree that shaded the entire spot. It seemed like a message of perseverance, and she took a photograph for the Sacred Moments II conservancy gallery. They drove the boat west to round the point and head north along the coast to the Pavati River, where their boat dock sat next to their house. As Cayman pointed the boat north, the three of them looked west to see the sun setting on the horizon. It was the perfect ending to a wonderful weekend – just the kind of adventure Emma had wanted before staring the seventh grade.

Fall was approaching; it was the last weekend before Emma was to begin seventh grade. Sarah and Cayman got up early on Saturday morning to pack snacks, water, and other necessities. The two of them were taking Emma and her friend Sadie, who had slept over, on a hiking adventure at Marsh Trail. Sarah woke the two girls, and they all had an early-morning breakfast together. When breakfast was finished and the dishes cleaned up, the four of them and Dakota piled into the pickup truck. Cayman drove them to the trail head parking lot under dark skies.

Once they arrived and the truck was parked, the four of them jumped out and gathered their supplies. As they hiked toward the observation tower, Cayman and Dakota led the way. They were making sure that there were no dangers, like bears or panthers, lurking ahead. Upon arriving at the observation tower, the four of them and Dakota climbed to the top to wait for the sun to rise over The Everglades and the Cypress Forest.

It took only a few minutes until they spotted the first glimmer of the sun peaking above the trees in the eastern sky. As the sun was rising, hundreds of white birds appeared to awaken at the same time and began to fly from the trees on both sides of the trail. A few moments later, the entire sun was visible above the trees. Sarah snapped a photo, just as a heron flew through the image. Everyone was thrilled to see the all of the birds take flight and the sun rise, starting another beautiful day in sunny, Southwest Florida.

After the sun had fully risen, the four of them took the stairs back down the observation tower to the trail below. As they continued their hike to the end of the trail, they saw an occasional alligator laying just off the edge of the trail, on the bank of the marsh. They were in no immediate danger, but Dakota and Cayman took the lead to make sure there weren't any surprises. Once in a while, Dakota let out a bark and an alligator quickly ducked down into the marshy waters. They made their way to the large open field at the end of the trail, and took in the beauty of the birds on the water and in the air. When the four of them reached the trail opening, they sat on the soft, sandy grass to have a snack, take a drink of water, and to rest.

After an adequate rest, they began their 45-minute hike back to the parking lot. The sun was much higher in the sky by then, and there were many more alligators sunning themselves along the edge of the trail. They took their time hiking back to the parking area, as Dakota and Cayman cleared the way. Once they safely reached the parking lot, they hopped into the pickup truck. It was still early, and

Chapter Ten

Sarah and Cayman made plans to take the girls to the Poaceaehatchee Village. They were going to have lunch with Cayman's brother and parents, then go for a short fishing trip on Etu's boat.

Emma was excited when she learned they were going to the Poaceaehatchee Village. Sadie had never been there, and Emma wanted to share it with her friend. Cayman's parents, Sakari and Alo, and his brother, Etu, came outside to greet them as soon as they pulled up in the pickup truck. Emma introduced them to Sadie. They all hugged before having a seat outside to talk about their morning trail hike and to enjoy lunch together.

Emma and Sadie told Emma's grandparents and uncle about the thousands of birds (they might have exaggerated a little) that flew from the trees as the sun began to rise. Then they went on and on about all of the alligators along the trail and how Dakota and her dad weren't afraid, and they had cleared the way. Of course, Sakari and Alo knew that Cayman and Etu grew up around alligators. They knew that Cayman would not be afraid, but that he would respect the alligators' space and strength. Etu told the two young girls the story about how Cayman rescued his dog Boone from the alligators many years earlier. Emma had heard the story before, but it was fun for her to hear it again with Sadie.

As they all sat outside and continued their conversations, Cayman and Etu went inside to prepare a traditional Tutelar lunch. Etu prepared the fish he caught during the early-morning charter trip, which he had taken with a few fishermen. He also helped Cayman prepare side dishes of corn, beans, squash, avocados, and papayas. The two of them delivered the food, drinks, and utensils outside to a large picnic table under the shade trees. There, they sat and chatted while they enjoyed the lunch that Etu and Cayman had prepared. Following lunch, Cayman and Etu quickly cleaned up the food and dishes. Etu wanted to take Emma and Sadie out fishing on his charter boat, the Fish-Hawk.

The group walked a short distance to the docks and climbed into Etu's boat as Cayman untied the ropes. Etu piloted the boat, while the others sat in the back and enjoyed the ride. Cayman began preparing fishing poles and bait for Emma and Sadie. It was a 30-minute boat ride to get to one of Etu's favorite fishing spots.

Cayman helped Emma and Sadie put their lines in the water, and Etu anchored the boat. It wasn't long until both girls were reeling in fish. Cayman and Etu helped the two girls gently release the fish into the water and rebait their hooks. Sarah was ready with her camera to get photographs of Emma's and Sadie's biggest catches. The two girls caught several fish on this brief fishing excursion. Most were released, yet they kept a few to take home to put in the freezer.

Etu let Emma and Sadie take turns driving the boat back to the village docks. Once Etu docked the boat, everyone pitched in to clean it before walking back to the house. Emma and Sadie thanked Etu for the fishing trip and her grandparents for lunch. As they all hugged and said their goodbyes, Emma told the Deeres that it was an absolutely perfect day.

Cayman was driving back to Cypress Cove when Sarah told the girls that they had one more stop to make on the way home. Curious, Emma asked, "Mom, where are we going?" Sarah replied, "Honey, it's a surprise. Just wait and you'll see." Now Emma was getting eager to know where they were going. When they got to Cypress Cove, Cayman pulled into the parking lot at the veterinary clinic. Dakota knew where they were, and she let out a short bark. Then Emma asked, "Why are we here? Is Dakota sick?" Sarah told her that they stopped by to see their friend Adeline.

What Emma didn't know was that Adeline had contacted Sarah a few days earlier to let her know she had two rescue puppies in need of a good home. She was hoping that Sarah and Cayman might want to give one of the two puppies a new home. Adeline had helped them adopt Dakota 12 years earlier when she was just a puppy. Sarah and Cayman had talked it over a few days earlier. With Dakota getting older and slowing down, they thought it was a good time to take in a new puppy. Cayman thought it would be good for Dakota to have a friend and Sarah thought it would be good for Emma to take on the responsibility of raising a new puppy. They hoped having a new puppy to raise as her friend, that it might help relieve some of Emma's pain when Dakota's time finally came.

They went inside the clinic. Sarah told Emma that they were there for her to pick out a puppy to raise as her friend. Emma and Sadie were super excited about the news! They walked with Dakota back the hallway where the two puppies were caged. Dakota was wagging her tail as she peered at the two small puppies. Emma looked at both puppies for a moment and quickly pointed to the all-white puppy and said, "She's the one, and I'm going to call her Chenoa, for white dove." Dakota barked in excitement as she went over to the new puppy, wagging her tail and licking Chenoa's face. Adeline picked up Chenoa and handed her to Emma; there was an instant bond.

Adeline spent nearly an hour describing all of the things Emma needed to know about raising a new puppy. She told Emma that Chenoa has had her first set of shots, and that Emma would need to bring the puppy back two times to finish the series of vaccines. Adeline gave Emma some pointers on how to house train Chenoa. And she also described some tricks on training Chenoa to listen and respond to commands. Adeline told Emma to bring Chenoa back once a week, and she'd help her with obedience training. Emma thanked Adeline for her advice, as they all said their goodbyes and left the clinic.

Driving to Sadie's house, Emma and Sadie took turns holding and petting Chenoa. The two girls were so excited about the new little puppy. Cayman stopped outside Sadie's house and they all jumped out of the truck. Sadie thanked Emma for letting her stay over and she thanked Sarah and Cayman for a wonderful day. Emma and Sadie hugged as they said goodbye and that they would see each other in school the following week. Dakota gave Sadie a goodbye bark, as the others waved and drove off.

As they were driving west toward home and the sun was setting over the water in front of them, Emma said, "It was another perfect day." Emma thanked her mom and dad for a special day, and for adding another friend to their family.

A week later, during the fall of 1980, Emma began seventh grade at Cypress Cove middle school. She was eager to resume school and to see all of her old friends. It was her first year in middle school and she was looking forward to the new adventure. Her grandparents walked over to her house to help send her off on her first day of school. Vicki, Sarah's mom, took photographs of Emma with her mom and dad before she hopped on her bicycle, waved goodbye, and rode off to school.

Emma soon heard that the middle school was adding a boys' swim team. Her parents taught her how to swim before she could even walk, and all of her friends knew that she was one of the strongest swimmers in town. Emma asked the coach if she could try out for the boys' swim team. His response was quick and short. "The swim team is for boys, and you're a girl." Emma already knew she was a girl; he didn't need to tell her that. His response made her even more determined to prove herself, and she wasn't about to take no for an answer. She approached the coach a second time and asked again. "If I prove I can swim as fast as the boys, may I please try out for the team?" The coach's answer was pretty much the same. "It's a boys' swim team, and you'll never be able to keep up with them."

Most of the boys trying out for the swim team were friends of Emma's and they knew that she was as strong a swimmer as any of them. Emma and several of the boys trying out for the team got together and hatched a plan. The boys convinced the coach to leave the end swim lane open during the tryouts. They told the coach that lane was bad luck. And for tryouts, none of them wanted to swim in that lane. The coach reluctantly agreed to leave it open. The tryouts were set for Saturday morning, and open to the other kids in the school to come and watch.

When Saturday morning arrived, the stands were full of classmates and teachers, all there to watch the first Cypress Cove middle school swim tryouts. The boys were in the pool warming up by taking easy laps across the pool and back. The tryouts consisted of the swimmers waiting on starting platforms and diving in the water when they heard the whistle. They were to swim freestyle across the pool and back for a total of fifty yards. The swimming pool was an eight-lane competition pool, also used by the high school swim team.

The coach signaled the boys to take their places on the starting platforms. Seven boys climbed onto the starting platforms and took their positions, to await the sound of the whistle to start the race across the pool and back. The coach blew the whistle and the seven boys dove into the water, swimming for the opposite wall. The girls' locker room door was near the end swim lane starting platform, which the coach had left empty at the boys' request.

When the boys were out a few yards from the starting platforms, Emma came out of the girls' locker room and stepped up onto the starting platform. As the students in the stands started cheering, Emma dove into the water and swam as fast as she could. She reached the opposite wall before three of the seven boys, who had started before her. She turned to make her way back to the finishing wall, and all of the kids watching from the stands were jumping up and down, cheering for Emma. By the time she was half way back to the finish, she had passed two more of the boys. There were two boys left for Emma to catch. Emma finished a half of a stroke behind the second boy, to take an unofficial third place in the tryouts.

The coach was furious! Maybe it was because she snuck into the tryouts, or that she could swim as fast as the boys, or because he realized he should have let her officially try out. Whatever the reason, on Monday morning, Emma was in the principal's office with her parents and the coach. She apologized to the coach and the principal. Then she asked them both. "Now, may I please join the swim team?" Sarah and Cayman were having a hard time hiding their pride in Emma. They knew sneaking into the swim tryouts was wrong, but they were impressed with what Emma had accomplished. The principal said no, and that she was never to do anything like that again. Emma promised that she wouldn't sneak into swim tryouts, ever again.

That wasn't going to be the end of Emma's run in with the Cypress Cove boys' swim team. The Tutelar swim coach heard about what had happened, and he wanted to see if there was something he could do to help. Because Emma spent a portion of each school year attending the Poaceaehatchee school, she was eligible to swim on their team. The Poaceaehatchee did not have a middle-school-level swim team, but they had two levels of swim teams for older students – a first-level team that competed with Cypress Cove's junior varsity team of freshman and sophomore students, and a second-level team that competed with Cypress Cove's varsity team of junior and senior students.

Chapter Ten

The Poaceaehatchee coach discussed Emma's dilemma with the swim team's captain, 14-year-old Songaa. Songaa told the coach, "I've heard about Emma challenging tourists to race around the pier and back to the beach. They say she always wins, even against older boys. So, even though she's only 11, let's see what she can do against our swimmers." Emma was thrilled that the Poaceaehatchee swim team was willing to give her an opportunity to try out, and she wasn't about to let them down. The coach scheduled a tryout for Emma after school the following day. She arrived early and began warming up in the pool while she waited for the others.

The coach and three boys from the swim team arrived at the swim facility twenty minutes after Emma. After giving the other swimmers some time to warm up, the coach asked the four swimmers to take their starting platforms. He counted down from three and blew his whistle to start the two-lap, fifty-yard freestyle swim tryouts. The swimmers dove into the water and swam the first lap to the opposite wall.

When they made the turn, Emma was in third place, a half of stroke behind second place. By the time they reached the middle of the pool, she passed the second-place swimmer. She was only one swim stroke behind Songaa when they finished. He quickly jumped out the pool, and helped Emma out of the water. He congratulated her on a strong swim and welcomed her to the Poaceaehatchee swim team. That moment, the two of them became instant friends.

The Poaceaehatchee first-level swim team had one swim meet each school year with the Cypress Cove junior varsity swim team. The meet was scheduled to take place in Cypress Cove one Saturday morning in November, two days after Emma's twelfth birthday. She told all of her Cypress Cove middle school friends that she joined the Poaceaehatchee swim team. Emma let her friends know that she would be competing against the Cypress Cove junior varsity high school boys' swim team on Saturday. She hoped they would be there to support her. The coach for the Cypress Cove middle school swim team was also the coach for the high school team. He didn't know yet that Emma was going to be competing against his junior varsity team on Saturday.

Saturday arrived, and it was "standing room only" at the Cypress Cove swim facility. It seemed that everyone in Cypress Cove knew that Emma was going to be there, except the same swim coach who hadn't let her join the middle school team. The Cypress Cove and Poaceaehatchee boys, except Emma, warmed up in the pool before the meet. The coaches sent them back into the locker room, as they normally do before a swim meet began. The Cypress Cove coach announced his four swimmers, as each of them came out of the locker room and took his place on the starting platform.

He handed the microphone to the Poaceaehatchee swim coach to call his swimmers to the starting platform. He called his swimmers to the starting platform – one by one. When he got to the fourth swimmer, he announced "Emma Marie Taylor, please take lane eight starting platform." The crowd clapped their hands and roared as Emma stepped onto the platform.

The Cypress Cove coach quickly took the Poaceaehatchee coach aside and they talked for several minutes before taking their places for the meet to start. No one knows for sure what was said, but it couldn't have been good, because arms and hands were flying while the Cypress Cove coach seemed to be yelling his disapproval. The two coaches returned to their spots, and the starter counted down to the sound of a loud airhorn that started the race. Eight teenage junior varsity level swimmers, including 12-year-old Emma, dove into the water and swam as hard as they could to the first turn.

Emma and a Cypress Cove boy made it to the turn first, followed by her teammate Songaa in third place. As they made the turn, Emma began to pull ahead of the boys. The crowd was screaming so loud, some said they could hear it a mile away at the pier. By the time she reached the middle of the pool, she was one stroke ahead of the second-place Cypress Cove swimmer. Emma finished first, two strokes in front of the Cypress Cove swimmer, Songaa was third, only a half stroke behind the second-place finisher. Songaa and the other boys jumped out of the pool and congratulated Emma on her win. The Cypress Cove coach went straight to the locker room without acknowledging Emma's win. And that was the last swim meet he ever coached in Cypress Cove.

Emma's parents and both sets of grandparents – the Deeres and Coopers, were in the crowd, watching and cheering the whole time. Her grandfather, Henry, wrote a story for the cover of the Sunday newspaper, titled "Twelve-Year-Old Girl Wins Junior Varsity Boys' Swim Meet." The cover included a half-page photograph, taken by Emma's grandmother Vicki, of Emma holding the first-place swim trophy on the awards stage. It was a defining moment for school sports in Cypress Cove and Southwest Florida.

Now that the swim meet was over, Emma was focusing on her writing class. She immediately fell in love with the class and with writing. She was doing really well, consistently receiving top marks. Emma enjoyed helping with writing the descriptions for the conservancy exhibits. She would write and rewrite descriptions of the animals and stories about where and how they lived. She told her mom that she liked writing about the animals' lives and their habitats the most. Sarah knew that writing was in her blood, but Emma really started to blossom as a writer in the seventh grade. She did well in all of her subjects, yet all she talked about at home was writing.

Emma's teacher encouraged her and gave her confidence to write longer and more detailed stories. In the evenings, during dinner, Emma shared her stories with her mom and dad. She wrote about growing up at the conservancy, and about adventures she had with her mom and dad. She wrote about surf fishing, working in the botanical gardens, and going on a bicycle adventure in the Cypress Forest. She captured every detail of the events, as if they had just happened. Every time her mom told her stories about adventures she took with her dad, Emma would write them down in her journal. Emma filled her first journal quickly and she wasn't slowing down.

Over the holiday break, Emma's teacher gave the class their next writing assignment. They were instructed to write a 300-word story about why they liked having a pet, would like to have a pet, or wouldn't want a pet. Emma knew right away it was going to be an easy assignment. She couldn't imagine not having a dog as a friend in her life.

My story is about having a dog for a friend.

When my dad was five years old, his friend, Luna – meaning moon – helped him get through a tough time. Dad's parents died in a plane crash, and Luna comforted him through his grief. She stood by him, through two funerals, and stayed by his side while he grew up in a strange home. She asked for nothing in return.

When my parents were dating as teenagers, they went on a picnic in the Cypress Forest. A large Florida black bear stepped out of the woods and walked toward them. Their friend Boone took a stand between them and the bear. Boone stood his ground until the bear turned and walked back into the woods. Boone's name means miracle, and they said it felt like one, when he saved their lives that day. He asked for nothing in return.

I can't imagine life without my best friend, Dakota. Her name means friend, and she lives with me and my mom and dad. We consider her a member of our family, not a pet. She brings us joy, she's there when we're happy, when we're sad, and when we're sick. She has never asked for anything in return.

Just a few months ago, we added a new friend to our family. She is an all-white puppy, named Chenoa, meaning white dove. We know Chenoa will be a good friend to Dakota and comfort her as she is getting older. Chenoa will ask for nothing in return.

Having a dog, cat, or bird living with you and your family is a gift. It becomes your best friend and a member of your family. It asks for nothing in return.

Story by Emma Marie Taylor

Emma liked writing so much, she asked her mom if it would be okay to talk with Grandpa Henry about writing. She hoped her grandpa would give her pointers to help her improve her writing skills. Sarah and Cayman both thought that was a great idea. Henry had an impressive resume as a writer. He was a writer for the Chicago Tribune, he had written several novels, and he wrote for the Cypress Cove Chronicle. Sarah invited her parents to dinner so Emma could tell him about her passion for writing and ask his advice and tips about how to be a good writer.

Her grandparents were always delighted to see her, and gladly accepted the invitation to dinner. They arrived early so Emma could tell her grandpa about her writing class at school. While Emma and Henry talked about writing, Vicki helped Sarah and Cayman get dinner ready. Emma was so excited, she just started blurting out about her writing class – how she liked the teacher and loved writing. Grandpa Henry smiled and asked Emma to please slow down. By the time Sarah called them outside for dinner, Emma had described the class, some of her assignments, and how she would like him to help her with her writing skills.

The two of them decided that if it was okay with her mom and dad, she could spend a few hours each week with him at the Cypress Cove Chronicle. Working with her grandpa, she would learn more about writing types and styles. At dinner, Emma asked, "Mom, Dad, is it okay if I go to the Cypress Cove Chronicle for a few hours each week to spend with grandpa to learn more about writing?" With a big smile, they quickly said yes.

Once a week, Emma rode her bike straight from school to the Cypress Cove Chronicle to learn with her grandpa. He described how stories were chosen, how they were written and edited, how they made it to print, and finally, how they made it to the readers. After a few weeks of reviewing the mechanics of writing news stories, he assigned Emma to review short articles for her thoughts on editing revisions. She became good at editing very quickly. Henry gave her a homework assignment for her next visit. He asked her to write a 200-word column about what 12-year-old kids did for fun in Cypress Cove. Henry liked her sample column – so much so that he met with the editor and proposed that they would run her column in the next print as a test column.

The editor suggested that the column be printed under the heading "Kids Living Local," by Emma Marie Taylor. She was thrilled about the idea of having her own column in the Cypress Cove Chronicle! Henry told her not to get too carried away just yet, that it was only a test run. He said to Emma, "We need to wait and see how the reading community reacts to your column." Well, it did not take long. The feedback on the column was great. The editor asked Henry to work with Emma to write a new column every two weeks. Henry and Emma brainstormed some ideas for the next two columns. They decided she should write about kids' favorite swimming beaches and favorite parks.

Henry guided Emma to approach the columns as a journalist. She would need to interview kids her own age, gather their input and quotes in order to draft the next two columns. Emma had fun writing the columns. They were published in the Cypress Cove Chronicle at two-week intervals.

The columns got rave reviews. The newspaper editor asked Henry to work with Emma to write a weekly column. The Cypress Cove Chronicle editor paid Emma a small fee for each column. She was excited to get paid for something she loved doing. Emma asked her mom to help her open a savings account to deposit her paycheck. Sarah and Cayman couldn't be prouder of their daughter.

It was nearing the end of her seventh-grade school year. Emma, along with the other students, were given an assignment to read aloud something they wrote as part of their final grade in the class. The parents of the students were invited to attend the readings. Emma read a poem she had written on an early morning while sitting on the beach behind her parents' home.

Feeling at Peace

As the moon was setting in the western sky,
the water became still and the air became calm.
I could hear the world waking up.
Birds started to sing and the fish began to jump.
I could still see stars in the sky.
As I sat and pondered what the day would bring,
I could feel the warmth of the sun on my back,
as it started to rise behind me.
It was the most perfect moment in time.

It was as it should be.

A poem by Emma Marie Taylor

At that moment, it became clear to her family that Emma was masterful with words, and writing would be in her future.

Chapter Eleven

Sarah and Emma were almost home from their beach walk with Chenoa on that warm, sunny, summer morning in 1981. The two of them were walking up the sandy path through the palm trees to their backyard where Cayman and Dakota were sitting on the verandah. When Emma saw her dad, she ran up the path. "Dad, dad! Mom told me the story again!" Cayman smiled as he sat with Dakota, and watched his daughter running toward him.

Sarah and Emma took seats next to Cayman, while Chenoa laid down next to Dakota. As they all sat and watched the waves roll onto the beach, Emma asked, "Mom, dad. What happens next?" Sarah, replied, "Honey, you are still writing your story. I'm sure you will do amazing things with your life."

Present Day – 1991

It's been 10 years since those early mornings on the beach, when her mother would tell her the story about the boy who swam with alligators. Since that beach walk, 22-year-old Emma graduated from University of South Florida (USF) in Tampa, with a degree in literature and creative writing. She just returned home to Cypress Cove where she loved growing up and especially treasured spending time with her parents at the conservancy learning about animals and nature in Southwest Florida. She always knew that Cypress Cove and the conservancy would be her home.

Emma spent the first few days back at the conservancy, reconnecting with old friends and meeting new staff members. She was surprised when she went to the conservancy animal hospital to find that there was a new veterinarian on staff. It was her friend from the Poaceaehatchee swim team, Songaa. They were both startled when they first saw each other, then they gave each other a big hug.

Emma and Songaa wasted no time reconnecting. The two of them spent the entire afternoon catching up on the last several years. It was almost as if they were never apart. From her first day back, they spent as much time together as possible. They had lunch together in the conservancy picnic area almost every day. Emma loved being around the animals, and she offered to help out in the conservancy animal hospital to be closer to Songaa. They joined the volunteer turtle watch together, and walked the beach in the mornings before work. Her parents were delighted to see the two of them coming up with adventures of their own.

Working at the conservancy provided Emma with the fulfilment of caring for nature and the environment, and it afforded her time to focus on her passion for writing. After returning home from college, Emma spent every spare minute she could working on her first novel. She remembered when she was 12, telling her mom, "I want to be a writer like Grandpa Henry." Her mom told her, "Honey, follow your heart, follow your passion, do what you love to do. You can be whatever you want to be."

Living in beautiful Southwest Florida and remembering the stories her mom told her while she was growing up provided Emma with the inspiration to write and publish her first novel. During the fall of 1991, Emma Marie Taylor wrote and published "The Boy Who Swam with Alligators." It was a story her mom told her about growing up in Southwest Florida with her dad, Cayman.

Reference Guide

Map of Key Locations

This map is a fictional representation of Southwest Florida. It depicts the locations of Cypress Cove, the Poaceaehatchee Village, and key locations within the region.

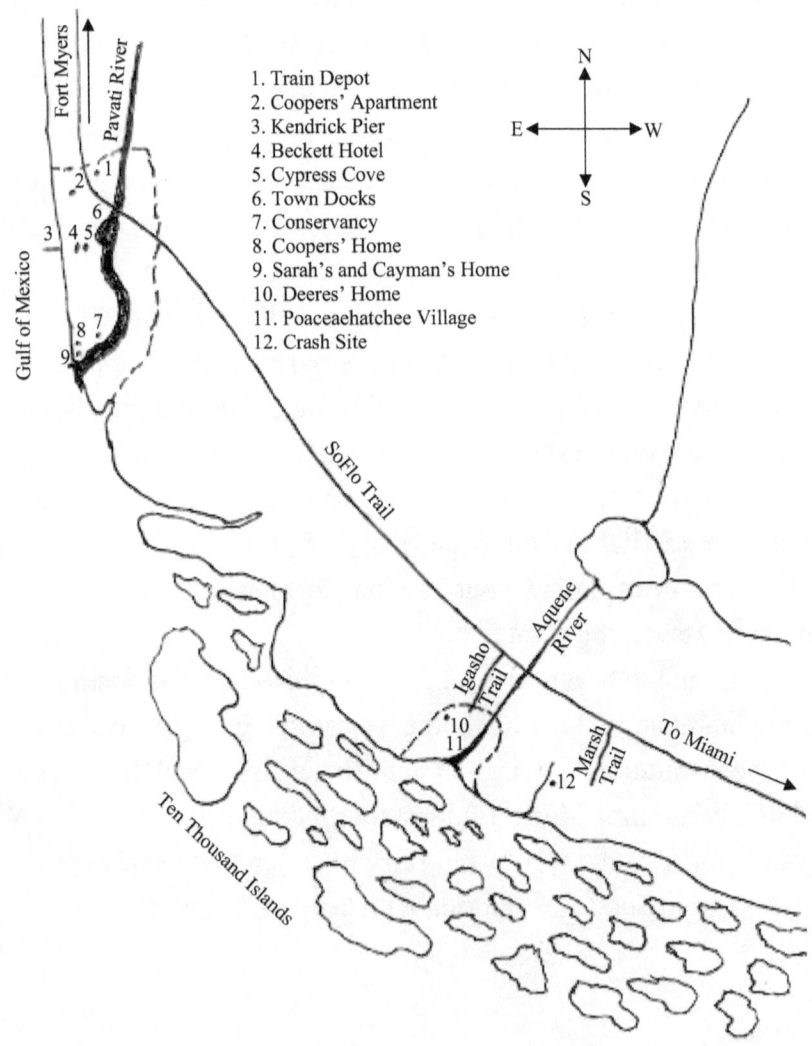

1. Train Depot
2. Coopers' Apartment
3. Kendrick Pier
4. Beckett Hotel
5. Cypress Cove
6. Town Docks
7. Conservancy
8. Coopers' Home
9. Sarah's and Cayman's Home
10. Deeres' Home
11. Poaceaehatchee Village
12. Crash Site

Glossary of Names, Words, and Meanings

Aiyana	Sacred Moments Gallery proprietor's name, meaning eternal blossom
Alo	Cayman's adopted father's first name, meaning spiritual guide
Aquene	Name of river in the Poaceaehatchee Village, meaning peace
Boone	Sarah's and Cayman's dog's name, meaning precious or miracle; he was black and brown
Catori	Emma's Tutelar friend's name, meaning spirit
Cayman	Tutelar name given to Grayson after rescuing Boone, meaning is from the lineage of alligator
Chenoa	Emma's dog's name, meaning white dove; she was all-white
Dahteste	Name of the horse Sarah rode, meaning warrior woman
Dakota	Sarah's and Cayman's dog's name, meaning friend; she was black and gray
Deere	Cayman's adopted family's last name, meaning precious
Elu	Sacred Moments Gallery proprietor's name, meaning beautiful
Etu	Cayman's adopted brother's name, meaning sun
Everglades	Name of national park, meaning river of grass
Fish-Hawk	Etu's boat's name, meaning osprey
Hatchee	Name of diner in the Poaceaehatchee Village, meaning river
Igasho	Name of the trail road from the SoFlo Trail to the Poaceaehatchee Village, meaning wanders
Langundo	Name of the park where the first annual seafood festival was held, meaning peaceful
Luna	Grayson's dog's name, meaning moon; she was black
Migisi	Name of the horse Cayman rode, meaning eagle
Nocona	Tutelar word for trot or run

Nodin	Airboat driver's name, meaning wind	
Pavati	Name of the Cypress Cove River and Bay, meaning clear water	
Poaceaehatchee	Tutelar's village name, meaning grass river	
Sakari	Cayman's adopted mother's first name, meaning sweet	
Seabright	Name of Etu's fishing charter business, meaning glory at sea	
SoFlo Trail	South Florida's connection highway between Fort Myers and Miami	
Songaa	Name of Poaceaehatchee swim team captain, meaning strong	
Tutelar	Native American tribe, meaning protector of the land	

Sketch and Photo Reference

Photographs by Sarah; sketches by Cayman

Page	Year	Sketch or Photo
7	N/A	Photo of the original SoFlo Trail
20	1956	Sketch of Luna, Grayson's dog friend
29	1957	Photo of entrance to the Poaceaehatchee Village
31	1957	Sketch of a pelican at the Marsh Trail
32	1958	Sketch of the moon setting over the gulf waters
37	1959	Photo of the airboat Sarah and Cayman rode in
39	1959	Photo of racoons during the airboat ride
42	1958	Sketch of sea turtle nest hatching
48	1959	Photo of sun setting behind a palm tree
49	1959	Photo of Milky Way from the Marsh Trail
55	1959	Photo during the beach cleanup campaign
57	1959	Photo of sunflowers near the Poaceaehatchee Village
61	1960	Photo of birds during shorebird nesting season
65	1960	Sketch of Sarah while horseback riding
69	1960	Photo of sea star on a sandbar
75	1960	Sketch of SOS signal made of rocks on the beach
78	1960	Sketch of momma loggerhead returning to the sea
92	1961	Sketch of Taylor Estate in Dimerling, Ohio

107	1961	Photo of snowy egret that caught a small fish
108	1961	Photo of white birds in the trees at the Marsh Trail
112	1962	Photo of Cypress Cove fireworks from the beach
113	1962	Sketch of rocket launch from Cape Canaveral beach
127	1963	Sketch of an old tire and a dead tree in Dimerling
130	1964	Photo of a water runoff pipe on Cypress Cove beach
133	1964	Photo of a pond in the Cypress Forest
137	1964	Sketch of Sarah's engagement necklace
138	1964	Photo of a seahorse Sarah placed back in the water
145	1964	Sketch of Cayman's dad's Dodge pickup truck
148	1965	Sketch of Sarah's and Cayman's house on the beach
150	1965	Photo of clouds, lightning, and the moon over the gulf
152	1965	Sketch of Sarah's and Cayman's wedding rings
155	1965	Photo of a heron standing near rocks on the beach
160	1965	Sketch of Etu's charter boat, the Fish-Hawk
164	1966	Photo of boardwalk over the conservancy wetlands
169	1967	Sketch of Sarah's parents' house on the beach
173	1968	Photo of a cockle shell on the beach
179	1968	Photo of a shell tree on the beach
182	1968	Photo of a pelican flying in front of sunset
199	1976	Photo of a food stand at the seafood festival
203	1976	Photo of the lobster claw flower Emma planted
205	1977	Photo of snowy egrets sparring over Emma's bait fish
207	1977	Photo of the shark Emma caught from the beach
210	1978	Photo of trail Emma rode during a bicycle adventure
214	1978	Photo of sea turtle at the conservancy animal hospital
215	1978	Photo of alligator at the conservancy lake
218	1979	Photo of an osprey diving for a fish
228	1979	Photo of Sarah's and Cayman's truck camper
237	1980	Sketch of Sarah's and Cayman's tent on the beach
239	1980	Sketch of the Taylors' plane crash site
241	1980	Photo of a lone mangrove tree
243	1980	Photo of sunrise and heron at the Marsh Trail

Timeline of Significant Events

1700s	• The Poaceaehatchee Village was established
1886	• Cypress Cove was founded
1880s	• The Pavati River and Bay were named
1890	• The Beckett Hotel was established
1914	• The Kendrick Pier was built
1926	• The Southern Railroad was extended to Cypress Cove
1928	• The Harriet Fuhrman Lake was named • The SoFlo Trail highway was officially opened
1938	• May: Mary Dennis graduated from college • May: Robert Taylor graduated from college • September: Mary and Robert Taylor were married; honeymooned and purchased 75 acres in Cypress Cove • Cypress Cove's population was 1,253 • Poaceaehatchee Village's population was 240 • The two-mile, single-lane Igasho Trail was built
1939	• Taylor Tire and Rubber Company was founded
1942	• May: Vicki Dawson graduated from college • May: Henry Cooper graduated from college • October: Vicki and Henry Cooper were married • Mary and Robert moved into the Taylor Estate
1943	• January 4: Grayson Taylor was born in Dimerling, Ohio • September 3: Sarah Cooper was born in Chicago, Illinois
1945	• Vicki Cooper established Special Moments Photography
1946	• Grayson got is first dog friend, Luna
1947	• December: The Everglades National Park was established
1948	• Cypress Cove's population was 1,465 • Taylor Tire and Rubber grew to 2,500 employees • July 4: 5-year-old Grayson's parents' plane crashed • July: Tutelar conducted funerals for Grayson's parents • July 4: Grayson was taken in by the Tutelar
1951	• Grayson and Etu attended Tutelar school together
1956	• Cypress Cove's population was 4,656 • January: Luna, Grayson's dog, died • March 13: 13-year-old Grayson became Cayman after

	saving Boone from alligators
	• The Coopers vacationed in Cypress Cove
	• Sarah and her mom visited the Poaceaehatchee Village
	• Sarah captured a single photograph of Cayman
1957	• Summer: The Clearwater Inn was built on the Pavati Bay
	• Fall: Cypress Cove Airport opened to commercial flights
	• Fall: 14-year-old Sarah was a freshman at Cypress Cove
	• Fall: Sarah met Cayman; they were both 14
1958	• Summer: Sarah and her parents moved to Cypress Cove
	• Summer: Cayman took Sarah on an airboat ride
	• Fall: 15-year-old Sarah was a sophomore at Cypress Cove
	• Fall: Cayman and Sarah witnessed a sea turtle nest hatch
1959	• Winter: Cayman, 16, received rite-of-passage assignment
	• Summer: Cayman and Sarah went fishing and snorkeling
	• Summer: Cayman and the Coopers saw the Milky Way
	• Summer: Tropical storm hit Southwest Florida
	• Fall: 16-year-old Sarah was a junior at Cypress Cove
	• Fall: Sarah initiated a beach cleanup campaign
	• Fall: Sarah and Cayman opened Sacred Moments gallery
1960	• Winter: 17-year-old Cayman completed rite of passage
	• Spring: Cayman and Sarah visited a bird nesting beach
	• Spring: Sarah invited Cayman to Junior Dance
	• Summer: Cayman and Sarah went horseback riding
	• Summer: Sarah and Cayman joined turtle watch
	• Summer: Sarah and Cayman were stranded at sea
	• Fall: 17-year-old Sarah was a senior at Cypress Cove
	• Fall: Sarah initiated effort to protect the mangroves
1961	• Spring: Sarah graduated from Cypress Cove high school
	• Summer: Cayman, 18, was discovered as Grayson Taylor
	• Summer: Grayson traveled to Dimerling, Ohio
	• Fall: Grayson began working at Taylor Tire
	• Fall: Sarah, 18, was a freshman at Glades University
1962	• Summer: Sarah and Cayman watched 4th of July fireworks
	• Summer: Sarah and Cayman witnessed a rocket launch
	• Fall: Sarah, 19, was a sophomore at Glades University
1963	• Summer: Sarah visited Cayman in Dimerling, Ohio

	• Fall: Sarah, 20, was a junior at Glades University
1964	• Summer: Boone protected Sarah and Cayman from a bear
	• July 4th: Sarah and Cayman were engaged
	• July 5th: Sarah and Cayman found a seahorse
	• Fall: Sarah, 21, was a senior at Glades University
1965	• Spring: Cayman, 22, left Taylor Tire and Rubber Company
	• Spring: Cayman gifted Taylor Estate to historical society
	• Spring: Sarah graduated from Glades University
	• Summer: Sarah and Cayman built their house
	• October 6th: Sarah and Cayman, both 22, were married
	• Fall: Etu launched his fishing charter business
	• Fall: Sarah and Cayman founded the Jumpstart Foundation
1966	• Winter: Sarah and Cayman, both 23, founded the conservancy
1967	• Spring: Sarah and Cayman built Sarah's parents' house
1968	• Spring: 24-year-old Sarah was pregnant
	• Summer: Boone died, Sarah and Cayman got Dakota
	• November 27th: Sarah, 25, gave birth to daughter, Emma
1972	• Fall: 4-year-old Emma attended Poaceaehatchee preschool
1973	• Summer: Emma spent time at the conservancy
	• Fall: 5-year-old Emma attended kindergarten
	• October: Big Cypress National Preserve was established
1974	• Fall: 6-year-old Emma attended 1st grade
1975	• Fall: 7-year-old Emma attended 2nd grade
	• Winter: Emma helped with animal feeding at conservancy
1976	• Spring: The Taylors volunteered at the seafood festival
	• Summer: Emma helped at the botanical gardens
	• Fall: 8-year-old Emma attended 3rd grade
1977	• Summer: Emma's parents took her surf fishing
	• Fall: 9-year-old Emma attended 4th grade
1978	• Summer: Emma's parents took her on a bicycle adventure
	• Fall: Emma's 5th grade class went to the conservancy
1979	• Summer: Emma and her parents went to the pyramid house
	• Summer: Emma's parents took her to Illinois and Ohio
	• Fall: Emma's 6th grade class visited the Poaceaehatchee Village

1980	• Summer: Emma's parents took her camping
	• Fall: Emma and her parents went to the Marsh Trail
	• Fall: Emma got a puppy; she named it Chenoa
	• Fall: Emma, 12, attended 7th grade
	• Fall: Emma met Songaa, 14, Poaceaehatchee swim captain
	• Winter: Emma swam in a boys' swim meet and won
	• December: Emma began writing stories and poems
1981	• Cypress Cove's population was 17,581
	• Summer: 37-year-old Sarah told Emma the story about the boy who swam with alligators while walking on the beach
1991	• Spring: Emma, 22, graduated college, returned to Cypress Cove, and reconnected with 24-year-old Songaa
	• Fall: Emma wrote "The Boy Who Swam with Alligators"

Book Club Discussion Guide

1. Is there symbolism of the Taylors' naming their Cessna 170, Osprey?
2. The Tutelar did not contact authorities when they found the plane crash. Why?
3. Is there symbolism represented by the feather in Cayman's hat?
4. Do you think Mila and Etu more than just friends?
5. Why does Cayman choose not to tell Sarah that he is Grayson Taylor?
6. Why do you think Sarah pursued a major in environmental science, rather than photography?
7. Cayman did not keep his given name Grayson. Why?
8. Cayman chose not to stay in Dimerling and take the helm of Taylor Tire and Rubber Company. Why is that?
9. Why did Cayman donate his family home in Dimerling to the historical society?
10. Why do you think Cayman chose to keep his dad's 1948 Dodge pickup truck?
11. Why do you think Cayman gave Sarah an engagement necklace, instead of an engagement ring?
12. Why didn't Sarah and Cayman build a house for his adopted parents, the Deeres, like they did for her parents, the Coopers?
13. Do you think the Cypress Cove swim coach quit or was he fired?
14. Do you think Emma and Songaa dated throughout their high school years?
15. Why do you think the author included four dogs woven throughout the story?
16. What do you believe happens next for Emma and Songaa?
17. Who is the key figure in the story? Is it Cayman? Is it Sarah? Is it Emma? Or is it someone else?
18. Who is the storyteller? And to whom is the story being told?

Acknowledgements

I want to thank my wife, Kelli. She has been an essential part of this journey from the very beginning. Through countless hours of reading, rereading, and thoughtful discussion, she helped shape not just the flow and continuity of the story, but the way it feels on the page. Her perspective, patience, and belief in this work made a lasting difference, and I am deeply grateful for everything she brought to these books.

About the Author

Rod Baxter writes stories about place, memory, and the quiet forces that shape people and communities over time.

After a long career in operational excellence and process improvement, he turned more fully toward storytelling. His fiction often explores the intersection of history, stewardship, and human connection—where landscapes carry memory and ordinary people uncover extraordinary truths.

He lives in Florida with his wife, Kelli. Together they enjoy walking, biking, volunteering in their community, and continuing their shared adventure side by side.

His stories—including the Wren Alder Mysteries—explore how the past leaves its marks on the present, and how patient observation can reveal truths long buried.

Other Books by Rod Baxter

Nonfiction
- Lean Six Sigma DMAIC Workbook
- Operational Excellence Handbook
- Strategy Deployment Handbook
- Discovering Your Inner Leader (co-written with Kelli Baxter)

Fiction & Narrative
- Lattes and Libraries – Book One
- Ashes in the Archive – Book Two
- Echoes in the Harbor – Book Three
- What the Land Endures
- Side by Side, A Life Built in Partnership

www.ingramcontent.com/pod-product-compliance
Lightning Source LLC
Chambersburg PA
CBHW020309200626
46814CB00006BA/2167